THE DUNGEON

THE HIDDEN ORDER OF MAGIC: SHAKEN BOOK 3

JUNE LEUNG

THE DUNGEON

Book 3 in *The Hidden Order of Magic: Shaken* series by June Leung

ISBN: 978-988-75426-4-3 (epub ebook)

ISBN: 978-988-75426-5-0 (paperback)

Get Bonus Prequel Story!

Join June's newsletter for exclusive bonus prequel story
juneleungbooks.com/prequel

CHAPTER 1

LIA

Lia and Helen were lying on the bed in the clan's guest room with Lia hugging her wolf plushie close. She'd told Helen about what happened a while ago, a silence lingered in the room.

"Finally, you decided to end your misery, huh?" Helen asked.

Lia had been staying with Helen in the clan since the day after defeating the gang. She'd blocked Adrian everywhere he could possibly reach her. She wasn't staying in her place nor Helen's. He would find his way in, she didn't need that happening. The clan was probably the only place he wouldn't dare go.

"I don't know. It felt good at that moment to spit it out, but it hurts… a lot…" Lia rubbed her swollen eyes, which kind of hurt given how much she had been crying. "I don't even know whether I can move on…"

"Really? What do you see in him? Even after the hell he put you through?"

"He saved you. He broke his own rules for me and he took care of me… At least before he pushed me away." *And those blue eyes and his handsome face aren't that bad.* Lia sighed, tucking a few loose strands of hair behind her ears. It didn't matter, though; she had been in bed almost all day. Her hair would be a mess regardless.

"If he wanted nothing with you, he could have said something."

"I wish. He kissed me again in the hospital." Lia stared at the blanket as a few drops of tears landed on it.

"Wait! What?" Helen's eyes widened in shock.

"Yeah, in the hospital. He was by my bed when I woke up. I don't know how he snuck in. He said we would talk later, but…" Lia sniffed, trailing off.

"But there wasn't a talk. You ended up walking away." Helen clenched her fist. Lia flicked her eyes to Helen's hand. If Adrian was here, Helen would have punched him, probably breaking a bone or two.

"When we were in The Orbit, he hugged me. I think he wanted to kiss me."

"No way!"

"I told him he could stop pretending to care about me, and he could stop the pained look and longing gazes. He said nothing. And when I told him in the drive-thru that he didn't need to come up with an excuse anymore, when I told him I would stop bugging him, he still said nothing other than offering me his car."

"What did that mean? His car?"

"Well, it was late and he wanted me to be able to drive home. He said he would send Ben to take back the car the next day. I didn't let that happen, though."

"So he drove you back home?"

"Yes… There wasn't a single car on the street and I doubted I could catch a cab. He said nothing on the way either."

Helen hugged her tightly. Lia hugged back, leaning

onto Helen's shoulder. Helen asked, "But with your power, you really think it is a good idea to shut him out completely? What if you need training?"

"I don't know… But I can't see him again. If only I didn't have this power… Maybe I just need a few days of break." Lia sighed, rolling back into her bed.

Why does this hurt even more than the wait for his petty little talk? Why must I have this stupid power? Why must I still think about him?

CHAPTER 2

ADRIAN

Adrian stared at his glass. His penthouse looked lonely and empty, especially under the bleak white light. He closed his eyes briefly—almost everything he could see reminded him of Lia. The window she liked, the couch they ate ice cream on, the office she trained in… He let out a heavy sigh. Still, there were no messages or calls. She seemed to have no interest in staying in touch with him.

Well, she shouldn't, given how he kept pushing her away. What Lia told him that night in the drive-thru still stabbed into him. He gulped down the whisky, the liquid burning a trail of fire down his throat.

She would go elsewhere, and it was to respect my choice.

This wasn't what he wanted, but the world wasn't there to satisfy him. Or maybe he should've tried with her. With Evelyn and her threat going around, the chance of him beating her without the Elements knowing seemed low, if not zero.

He'd only thought of himself. He only wanted to try with Lia when things were easy, when he didn't need to fight against anything. Benjamin warned him about that.

He also knew it himself: if he didn't fight for what he wanted, he wouldn't get it. But Lia wasn't an item—would she care if he tried? Or would she even want him to try?

If she didn't want to see him, she knew to stay in the clan, somewhere he didn't dare go. The risk of being spotted was too much. Even if he did make it, what if Lia called the Elders on him? That wouldn't end well. He poured himself another glass, downing it.

No matter how much Lia hated him, she wouldn't let the Elders kill him, right? They did fight the monsters and the gang together.

He was reaching for the bottle again when there was the turn of a key at the door. Benjamin walked in and sniffed in the air with a scowl. "My King, what is happening? I thought after fighting the gang, you would finally tell Lia."

Adrian shook his head, gesturing to the seat beside him. Benjamin sat and took the bottle, putting it further away from Adrian. "Tell me, what's stopping you? The gang is now gone. Her power probably is almost settled."

"It wouldn't change the fact that she deserves someone better. You know I am a jerk to everyone—before I hurt her even more, maybe I should stop." Adrian sighed. A jabbing pain pecked at his heart. Nothing made sense with Lia, especially what he felt for her. He coughed to clear his throat and Benjamin patted his back.

"I didn't call you to talk about my relationship with Lia. When I was heading back that day, guess who I bumped into? Or rather, guess who found me?"

"Someone bad?"

"Bad is an understatement. The others don't know yet. I don't even know how to break it to them." Adrian stared blankly at the empty glass, his heart hammering in his chest. Was it a good choice to tell Benjamin now?

Benjamin wouldn't like it, but he could be the only one that would support him. At least Benjamin knew Lia.

"What?" Benjamin's brows knitted, his gaze too intense for Adrian to ignore.

"Evelyn found me. As you all have been warning me."

Benjamin gulped audibly as his face fell. "Seriously? Wow… I guess I shouldn't be too surprised, though. Nothing could stay under wraps forever. I guess the time has finally come."

"Ben… I need to keep Lia alive," Adrian said. When Benjamin didn't answer, Adrian grabbed his collar. "I said I need Lia to live!"

A mischievous glint flashed through Benjamin's eyes. "Do you think I am brave enough to say no? Do I not know what will happen if I insist for you to keep the pact instead?"

Adrian flinched and he let go of Benjamin, slumping back onto the couch. He wasn't going to forget all the terrible things he was capable of. "Fine. Please help me. Lia… after everything, I don't want her to…"

"But you made her leave you. What's stopping you from letting Lia die? It will save a lot of trouble if we keep the pact."

"Benjamin!" Adrian bit the inside of his mouth, resisting the urge to punch him. His blood burned. Maybe he didn't dare try to have a relationship with Lia, but it didn't mean he would be fine with her dying. She deserved someone better, not to be killed by Evelyn.

"Are you sure the others would be fine with it? After all these years, we have been living peacefully. We all warned you to just get rid of Lia."

"Do you really want her dead?" Adrian's heart skipped a beat. Benjamin at least wasn't that against her, right?

He'd gone against Adrian's orders and trained her. What was going on in Benjamin's mind?

Benjamin sat up straight, pinching the bridge of his nose. "I don't want to see her dead either. She is innocent in all this. None of this is her fault. But... Have you told her yet?"

Adrian let out a wry chuckle, shaking his head. He gestured to his phone on the coffee table. "She blocked me, so no."

Benjamin glared at him, the gaze chilling Adrian to the bone. "You know what Evelyn would do. You're the one who made the pact. How dare you not even try to warn her." His hand jerked, but he seemed to push down the urge to fight him. "If I didn't know better, I'd think you want her to die."

"No way! I'd rather I die than her! You know that."

"I also know you aren't even trying. Is a device really going to stop you from doing what is important? At least try harder! I wonder how we survived before phones were invented." Benjamin huffed, his body tense. "If you don't even want to try, I will. And not to boast, but I think Lia does have a soft spot for me."

"What the hell? I am going to tell her. You keep your hands to yourself." Adrian flexed, glaring at Benjamin. He told Adrian he wasn't interested in her a while ago—that was still the case, right? This better be a joke, if Benjamin dared... His throat tightened. Benjamin did seem to be a more decent guy than he was. Well, the bar was low when it got to being better than him. "You feel something for her?"

Benjamin stared at him like he was a unicorn or had grown another head. "Excuse me? I was just messing with you. No, I don't feel that way for Lia. Are you seriously going to give up on her?"

Adrian shook his head. "This is not giving up. There's never been anything between us." Crap, saying that hurt.

"I've told you that day on the balcony. No one could stop you if you wanted to be with her. I don't know what the others would think, but at least you should try to let Lia understand what is happening with her, OK? Even if you are too much of a jerk to fight for someone you know you love, let her fight for herself."

"I will."

Benjamin was right. The clan probably wouldn't be too helpful against Evelyn, but he should at least warn them. He flicked his eyes to his phone. Right. Just a device wasn't going to stop him.

Benjamin chuckled and said, "I am proud of you, my King. I know it is hard for you after all that happened. Don't make yourself regret it."

"I don't know anymore. Lia already told me she wanted nothing to do with me and she isn't waiting for an answer from me."

"You won't know if you don't try. Should I let the others know? We need all hands against Evelyn."

There was no telling whether the rest of his magicians would agree to fight Evelyn instead of killing Lia. Especially that one… Should he risk pissing them off or should he let Lia die? That wasn't too hard of a question; Lia was not dying anytime soon.

"Do tell them. Leave out Evelyn for now please, I will tell them in person. Whatever they think, I need Lia to live."

"I see. All the best, my King." Benjamin nodded with a smile on his face. "If you don't mind me asking, what are you going to do?"

"Why are you asking me? You know I don't need to tell

you everything." Adrian's heart skipped a beat. He didn't have a plan yet.

"You can find a way, right? You are the King, after all. And you are softer than a marshmallow for her."

Adrian huffed. Benjamin sure loved to mess with him. "I will try to wait until she leaves the clan. I don't want the risk."

"You'll figure it out." Benjamin patted Adrian's shoulder. "I suppose you called me here for me to help convince the others to let Lia live, right?"

"Yes. Ben, I really need you to help. Among them, you are the only one that will be on my side. You know those two are not going to be on board. While we don't do voting, I don't want to force them into it. I doubt I stand a chance fighting Evelyn on my own. She is not going to come on her own."

Benjamin tilted his head to the side with a mischievous smirk. "We shall see. I better go check on them. To be frank, I don't even know whether I could reach them or not."

"I hope it works." Adrian's gaze followed Benjamin as he left. He picked up the bottle Benjamin intentionally put away, pouring himself another drink. His hand shook as he thought of the rest of his team. They had never wanted Lia alive since the beginning. She was a bit too close with the Elements. Evelyn showing herself wouldn't help his case either. As he took a sip, the bitterness of the liquid burned his throat.

They would understand him, right? They had been fighting as a team alongside each other for a long time. He'd given them their power. They would support him, wouldn't they?

CHAPTER 3

LIA

A few days later, Lia and Helen were snuggled together on the couch in the lounge with a bowl of caramel popcorn on the coffee table in front of them. Lia reached out for a sip of her soft drink as the video game loaded.

Helen leaned back on the couch with her arms folded behind her head. "I don't know, Lia. Although I love playing video games with you, fourteen hours straight for days is not good for you. Not to mention you've unlocked everything in all my game files, there's now nothing new for me to play."

Lia smiled wryly, rubbing her eyes. "I know, but I can't risk my brain having free time to think. Even sleeping takes effort."

"Is there something else you can do?"

"I don't want to think about it. Video games are easy and a time waster. But it serves as a lifesaver at times." Lia shrugged, holding the controller tightly as the new round began.

After another few hours of gameplay, Lia finally set

down the controller on the coffee table. The bowl was empty.

"How about we go grab tacos tonight? At least go out a bit?" Helen nudged her side. Lia shook her head. Helen asked, "I thought you love tacos."

"I do, but I don't want to go out. Let's call for delivery instead?"

"You know the Elders don't like random people hanging near the clan." Helen rolled her eyes. "And I thought you might want to take a stroll in the park."

"I said I don't want to go out!" Lia turned away.

"Why? What's so bad outside?" Helen scowled. "Wait! Does this have anything to do with that man?"

"Why must you mention him? Yes. I don't want to risk bumping into him. Who knows if he'll be waiting for me right outside? I tried hard to forget about him. This is just difficult… I guess trying to forget is harder than trying to remember. If only my studying back in college worked this way."

"And you are letting him strip you from everything you enjoy?"

"Please, at least for a short while. I really need a change of scenery. I'll be fine, I promise."

"OK… I guess. But I really think too much screen time is not good for you. At least we can walk around the clan? I can grab tacos for both of us later so we don't have to cook."

The two of them tidied up, then walked down the corridors of the clan. It was quiet with everyone else busy doing their own things. It had been that way since Lia stayed in the clan. Everyone seemed to be on edge after the meteorite monsters appeared. Patrick was probably in training, Eric should be trying to look for new cases, and

William was likely hunting for evidence about dark magicians.

Lia gulped at the thought. It wasn't that she cared about Adrian; she was simply worried about herself. William wouldn't be very happy if he found out she had dark magic.

"Where're we going?" Lia asked. Helen was looking at the floor, as if deep in thought.

"Um… I don't know. Maybe we can go to the library?"

"Of course, I am going to be interested in books, right? Who would have guessed?" Lia chuckled, playfully smacking Helen's side.

"Hey! It is not my fault the clan has nothing fun."

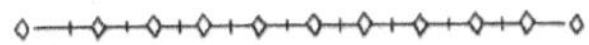

IN THE LIBRARY, they split up to look for something interesting. The library was comforting, and the smell of antique books and wood never got old. Lia's eyes relaxed in the warm yellow light. She walked past various tall bookshelves at random, hoping to bump into something fun.

At a corner, Lia walked into a woman with golden hair and glasses putting a few books from a cart up on the shelves. "Hello Sophia. Hard working here, huh?"

"Oh, Lia! Glad to see you here. Fancy reading a book today?"

Lia took a step closer to the cart, peeking over the books. "I don't know, kind of hoping to stumble across an interesting title. Who returned these books here?"

Sophia picked up a few more, putting them back to the shelf. "William just sent them back earlier. He seemed to really be looking at the forbidden magic recently."

Lia seemed to catch a mischievous glint in Sophia's

eyes, she asked, "He took out new ones after returning these?"

"He did, but I don't know whether they'll be worth his time. If it is in the books, we should've found them much earlier."

"I've only heard of the other kinds of magic from rumors." Lia eyed the top book. *The Bloody Mystery—The Guide to Summoning the Devil.* It sent a chill down her spine, especially when she thought about how Adrian ripped the gang's men apart. If this was about him, the title wasn't that far off. "Do you think they exist?"

"Everyone would hope forbidden magic doesn't exist. If it is forbidden, there's probably a reason. Better not to poke the beast, though. William never actually talks about it, so I don't think he knows a lot." Sophia turned to the cart when Lia was holding the book. "You want to take a look at this?"

"Um… I guess I will give it a try," Lia said. Sophia nodded with a small smile on her face, but it seemed forced. Lia asked, "Something's on your mind?"

Sophia's eyes widened and she quickly schooled herself, pushing her glasses up the bridge of her nose. "Nothing. I'm just wondering why both you and William are suddenly that interested in finding out about dark magic."

If Sophia knew it was dark magic, why did she call it "the forbidden magic" a short while ago? Lia said, "Since the meteorite monsters, he's been talking about his suspicions. I haven't been around long enough to even know why, but he seems to be worried."

"You can't blame him. From what I heard, if they are real, it would be scary," Sophia hummed, putting the last book from the cart into its place.

"Do you know anything about dark magic?"

Sophia flinched, flicking her eyes to Lia. "Why do you ask?"

She looked suspicious. Lia wanted to ask more, but she wasn't supposed to know a lot either. If Sophia told William, Lia might get into trouble. Lia said, "I think there may be something in the books."

"Oh, you aren't wrong. But I think most of the books are just fiction; at least I don't have a way to prove any of them to be real." Sophia smiled, fixing her tied up hair. "Got to go. Enjoy your book." She pointed at the cart, bidding Lia goodbye. Lia waved back.

Lia headed to a corner in the library. Helen was already there with a book opened in front of her. She was staring at the ceiling. Lia gently knocked on the table. "Hey, you don't have to be here with me. I know you don't love books. I'm fine reading by myself."

Helen startled, shaking her head. "Nah, I'm fine reading with you. I'm just thinking about something."

"What are you thinking about?" Lia raised her brows and took a seat.

Helen stared blankly in front of her for a while longer, rubbing her temple. "I don't know. I think you should be safe now after we fought those that were after you. But I can't shake the feeling something is wrong."

"What kind of wrong are we talking about?"

"That William may find out something. And something's going to be wrong with you. I guess I'm anxious not knowing what will happen, like there's a large grey cloud above. Will it rain? Will it bring a storm? Will it just disperse and nothing will happen?"

"Other than it dispersing, none of them sound good," Lia said. Helen's hunches had been very accurate before—was it bad to hope she was wrong?

"Yeah…" Helen sighed, tucking her hair behind her shoulder.

They stared at each other for a while longer before they each buried themselves into their book of choice.

Lia ran her hand along the fabric cover of *The Bloody Mystery—The Guide to Summoning the Devil*. Was it really about Adrian and his magic? If so, would it have something relating to her?

She flipped to the index page, going down the entries. While she was sure she knew every word, she wasn't sure she understood the phrases. It read a bit awkwardly. She flipped to a random chapter, hoping the passages would be easier to understand.

It read, "Rejecting the offer from a devil seldom means death, but rejecting them down the road could be dangerous." Adrian did offer her to take his trade for more power, but since her dark magic showed up, he didn't talk about that. She sighed; even with their relationship now, she couldn't even forget him. Despite what she told him, part of her still wished the banter they had would come back some day.

"The devil seldom asks for more than one could give, but what he wants will always matter. What they could give is beyond the imagination of the mortal mind." She'd be happy enough if he would let her know what he felt. He was quiet when that topic came up.

She jumped over to the last chapter of the book. It read, "Regarding the death of the devil: nobody has tried to kill the devil. The devil is believed to be able to read the minds of mortals. With every attempt to kill the devil, he has never been summoned successfully, thus no one knows what is needed or how one can kill the devil. It is also not known of the number of devil(s). It is believed that the devil is invincible until the last of his bonded mortals is killed."

Lia carefully traced her finger along the old, yellowed page as she reread the sentences. Was the information accurate? Or was it even about Adrian? He didn't seem that invincible when he was slashed by the gang's men nor shot by the crossbows, but he did heal quickly.

Wait, I should be here to forget about him. Why am I choosing to read a book that may have a link with his magic? Dammit… Now I want to ask him about his magic. My magic.

Lia shut the book in a whim, pushing it away.

"Hey, something wrong?" Helen asked.

"Nothing… I wonder why I have to think about him all the time…"

Helen glanced at the book and chuckled wryly. "I guess we should try to do something else. Maybe the library isn't the best place to be." Lia nodded.

The two of them picked up their books and handed them back to Sophia at the counter. She smiled at them as she thanked them and set the books aside. Lia swore she saw a mischievous glint in Sophia's eyes when she looked at her, but she couldn't point her finger at the reason. No way Sophia would know about her dark magic, right? No one in the clan other than Helen should know.

CHAPTER 4

LIA

Lia and Helen went to the arena, hoping Patrick had already finished his session so the two of them could have some fun together. When Lia pushed open the door, there was a loud bang inside. They hurried in.

"What's happening?" Lia asked.

Patrick was on the floor, supporting himself with both arms. William stood by the control panel up on the balcony, looking down.

"Oh, nothing's wrong, I just asked William how strong the glass shield is, and he told me to try it out. Let's say it didn't go well." Patrick chuckled, standing back up.

"I told you the shield is strong." William walked down the stairs from the balcony as the glass shield slowly retreated to the side of the rectangular field area. Lia and Helen met Patrick in the center of the field.

"So that was the bang? I thought something exploded," Helen said, looking between William and Patrick.

"I shot at the shield. And had fun evading my own blast." Patrick shrugged, fixing his messed up curly brown hair with a soft smile.

William said, "I thought the two of you would be outside. The weather is great today."

"I wanted to, but Lia didn't." Helen rolled her eyes.

"Yeah, not today." Lia shrugged.

"Even training seems fun to you?" Patrick asked with amusement.

"I wanted to play video games, but she banned me from it." Lia smacked Helen's shoulder playfully.

"Hey, you've been playing for hours straight every day. Can't blame me for trying to stop you." Helen deadpanned, shoving Lia gently.

"I will start the game mode for you two then. Have some fun," William chuckled, shaking his head, he turned to walk up to the panel.

"You two have fun. I'll go grab a late lunch. See ya tonight." Patrick stifled a yawn as he waved them a goodbye.

Lia and Helen remained in the field. Helen nudged Lia's side. "Ready to be beaten in real life?"

"Right back at you!" Lia rolled her eyes, tickling Helen. The glass shield slowly emerged from the sides, closing above them. With a beep, the competition mode started.

Different types of virtual monsters began appearing in the field. Helen and Lia wielded their magic, getting ready to fight.

Remember, do it slowly, don't make William more suspicious than he already is…

Lia focused her thought and her power, taking out just the needed amount. She hauled an ice ball at a werewolf, hitting it in the shoulder and knocking it off its course. It rolled on the ground, trying to free his frozen arm. She shot ice shards at it, putting an end to it.

"Sorry, I already shot down a zombie, so the first kill is mine!" Helen shouted while she aimed at a small beast the size no larger than a cat, sending leaf blades flying at it.

A beast with extra sharp fangs dashed towards Lia on all fours. She raised her hand in front of her, willing an ice blast. She managed to freeze the beast split seconds before Helen's leaf blade hit.

"Sorry, am faster!" Lia laughed as she turned to a dinosaur-like monster which was snarling at them with sharp fangs.

"Grrr!" Helen huffed, looking for another target while moving to the side from the jaw of a dino.

The two of them were shooting at monsters and occasionally stealing each other's target. Lia often glanced at the scoreboard, making sure the two of them were close. If she were to win, the score still needed to be close.

As she shot at the monsters, something felt off. It wasn't as exciting as she remembered. Maybe the virtual monsters weren't that challenging, or there was something lacking in them that made hunting them down boring.

The virtual monsters actually aren't living before I 'kill' them—is that the reason?

Her mind went back to the gang's base, when Adrian and Benjamin tore through their enemies. It was much more tense than now. Maybe the stakes were high enough to make it interesting.

After the last monsters fell, Lia and Helen stared at the scoreboard, Lia won by two points. She patted Helen in the back with a smug smile. "Sorry, you aren't beating me this time."

Helen crossed her arms in front of her chest. "You got lucky this time. This time only."

"You two seemed to really like this mode, huh?" William asked as he approached.

"Only trying to beat the overall high score is getting boring," Helen said.

Lia nodded, her mind still wandering. Slowly nausea spread in her stomach. She blinked, she better get out before William could find out anything. "Helen, the restroom together? I may have drunk too much soda earlier."

"Oh sure!" Helen raised her brows but followed without question. William rolled his eyes, muttering something about women going to restrooms in a group. The two of them waved him a goodbye, agreeing to show up for training the next day.

Outside of the arena, Helen grabbed Lia's arm. "Hey, you don't look good."

"To my room instead," Lia barely managed to utter the words. She was focusing on the power rush, trying her best to calm it down. It would help if she could sit down or lay down as soon as humanly possible.

They dashed down the corridors. Helen opened the door to the guest room, helping Lia rest on the bed. The nausea was gone, but the dizziness was overwhelming. Her body was on fire, burning hot when she rubbed her own arms. Helen frowned deeply. "What should I do to help?"

"It… will be OK. Maybe you should get out of the room."

"But you look pale. I…"

"Then get close to the door. Get out as quick as possible if something happens." Lia winced, holding her head.

You don't need Adrian to help. Slowly, from the head to the arms.

Lia struggled to push the urge of attacking something down, collecting the pieces of her power that seemed to turn her body into a fireball, threatening to burn everything nearby.

You have to do it right, Lia. Helen is here. Adrian won't be here. You can't hurt Helen. Slowly, slowly, from arms down to stomach.

The power seemed to be under her control again. She directed it into her stomach, feeling the warmth pooling there. It was still strong, urging her to do something. She rubbed her temple, trying to come up with something harmless to busy her power.

She spread out her palm in front of her, willing an ice ball. It slowly formed, glowing white. She held the ice ball, focusing on keeping it existing. As the ice ball kept emitting light, it slowly used up some of the power. She kept the ice magic trick going until she felt fully in control of herself.

"Phew!" Lia let out a sigh of relief. She rested the ice ball she created on her forehead, cooling herself down. This ice magic was sometimes handy.

"So…" Helen raised her brows at Lia, standing next to the door.

"Oh, I'm fine now. Sorry for scaring you." Lia gave her a rueful smile, patting the spot next to her on the bed.

"I'm not very scared. I've seen scarier things." Helen smacked Lia's arm, snuggling close to her. "How long do you think you can keep your power in check?"

Lia's smile faltered. "I don't know. Just trying to buy time… Maybe if I don't use that much magic, it will get better."

Helen nodded with a crease on her forehead, lying down beside Lia. "Maybe it will be better after we have dinner and you get some rest. I will ask Patrick to pick up takeaway for us instead. I think he's going out anyway. So I can stay with you if you don't want to go out. You have me worried."

"Sounds good. I hope I can stall for as long as possible. Hopefully, my power will be under control soon." Lia winced, tracing her fingers along the fold of the blankets.

She felt like a scary monster looming around Helen and she might hurt her like she did before.

"Did he tell you how long your training would last?"

"He had no idea either, or he didn't want to tell me. Who knows? He said it depends on how much power I actually have, which he has no way to find out."

"Oh… I guess we can only wish it'll get better."

"Yeah… And I'd prefer you to stop talking about him." Lia rolled her eyes, sighing heavily. She walked to the window, looking at the sunset.

The orange glow of the fading fireball painted the sky with beautiful colors, and she soon lost herself in the view. One of the only good things about being magicians was that they seemed to be rich, and somehow had the best view of Zitannas. Not only the guest room, but William's office also faced the sunset. Adrian's place had a full sea view.

CHAPTER 5

LIA

During breakfast the next day, Lia bumped into William in the lounge. He was chewing on his toast. "Morning, William." Lia smiled warmly to him. He nodded.

Lia poured herself a bowl of cereal with warm milk before sitting next to him. He took a sip of his coffee and said, "It seems like you are always here suddenly. Before, you avoided us like the plague." He eyed her with a glint of amusement.

"No way I see here as the plague. Here will always be my home. It's just…" *Come up with something, Lia!* "I kind of want some more peace after being attacked. It feels safe here."

He nodded, forking up his fried egg. "I doubt any unsolicited creatures dare to come in. I am not going to make things easy for them." He bit down on his food and set the fork down. "But one thing. I tried to track whoever attacked you, but every string seemed to break, and nothing was left for me to track."

I'm not surprised…

"Hm… Is there a chance they gave up after failing? Maybe sending killers after me is getting expensive?"

"I doubt it. Or whoever commissioned for your life gave up. I think it is a group of bounty hunters, which makes them hard to trace. They are a smart bunch."

Lia nodded, chewing her cereal. It felt wrong to let William find something that didn't exist anymore, but he wasn't going to believe that she could fight them by herself. It would be difficult to keep Adrian and Benjamin out of the story.

"I am still looking into the dark magicians." William said. Lia almost choked on the milk, she barely held up from coughing her lungs out.

"Found anything?"

"Not really. I have a hunch they have to be somewhere though. I don't know which is more pressing: the people after your life, or the possibility of dark magicians still alive." His face was unreadable, looking at Lia for her response.

"Um… so you think they are different people?"

"The dark magicians wouldn't fail twice. Not that I wish this would happen, but if the dark magicians are doing this for your blood, they would also attack Patrick and Helen, but nothing happened to them.

"I am thinking about the collector earlier, seeing you stole the meteorite. Maybe he found out and wants you dead. He sure is rich enough to get some bounty hunter behind you." He tilted his head to the side as he stirred his coffee.

"Oh… None of that sounds good," Lia said. But Adrian said he had wiped the collector's memory. That being said, they still didn't know who was paying the gang to kill her.

"I will try my best to keep you safe anyway. There are

few I can't beat," he said, his eyes narrowed in determination.

"For example?"

He cleared his throat awkwardly. "I mean… there's always the unknown out there. Better not to be too confident."

"Ah, sure. I see."

After they cleaned up, they headed to the arena. Helen was already sitting on the bench, scrolling through her phone.

"Patrick and Eric are out doing things, so it's just us today. Helen, you go first," William said as he pushed some buttons to adjust the settings on the panel.

Lia walked up beside him. "Can I skip today? I got tired playing with Helen yesterday." Her heartbeat quickened, hoping he wouldn't find her suspicious. There was no telling whether she would be OK today after what happened yesterday.

"Sure. You shouldn't rush it after the operation." He pressed the start button and targets started to appear. "Healing up well?"

Lia's hand instinctively ran up her side, touching the scar that was slowly fading. It sent a tingle down her body, she could faintly remember the feeling of Adrian's warm hands on her, and the rush of magic that healed her. There was a small flame inside her. Was it wrong to want Adrian around? It had been a while since she had seen him. She bit the inside of her mouth, thankful William couldn't read minds. "Yes, I don't feel pain anymore. Although I'm still a bit tired at times. I guess I need some time to fully recover."

"Good. You had me worried."

Down in the field, Helen was blasting and strangling

monsters with her magic. Lia took deep breaths, trying to keep her mind from wandering to things she didn't want to remember. It would be great if she could tell William everything, but she was still worried about what Adrian told her; she couldn't forget how William burned that woman alive.

"It seems Helen's been stressed recently. Any idea why?" William asked with a frown on his face. Lia shuddered, breaking away from her thoughts.

"I don't find her stressed. Maybe she was trying to cheer me up. But she mentioned having a hunch of something bad happening," she said, running her fingers through her hair.

"Really? Helen has hunches that are quite accurate."

"I'm also worried. Who knows what's on the horizon." Lia shrugged, keeping her eyes on Helen.

Probably has to do with me, anyways. I'm not even sure whether the gang is the one after me, or if there is someone else.

Finally, Helen shot down the last of the monsters. William and Lia walked down to join her. Helen was grinning, wiping the sweat off her forehead. Lia handed her a water bottle and she took a sip, letting out a relaxed sigh.

"Is it your turn now?" Helen asked Lia.

Lia shook her head. "I'm a bit too tired after playing with you yesterday. Maybe next time."

"Oh, do you want to go out for a walk with me then? We can go to our tree and spend the afternoon there."

"Um… I prefer staying in. My video game has a time sensitive event I have to beat." Lia said without hesitation. She already made it clear to Helen that she wasn't going out anytime soon. What was Helen doing asking when William was around?

Helen reluctantly nodded. "Fine, maybe next time then."

Lia let out a silent sigh of relief within her. Luckily, William knew nothing about video games and wouldn't care as long as it didn't interrupt training and cases. She also had been skipping things, so he probably wouldn't find it suspicious. He soon excused himself, leaving them in the arena.

As soon as the door of the arena clicked closed, Lia smacked Helen in the back. "Must you ask me to go out with William here?"

Helen winked. "You could've agreed to go with me. It would save you the trouble."

"C'mon… I really have no interest seeing him anytime soon." Lia frowned deeply. He had to be waiting somewhere, and she didn't know what to say if they met. Deep inside, she wanted to hug him and ask him what was on his mind. But she was the one telling him to stop pretending to care about her.

Helen's smile faltered. "Are you sure you aren't going outside anymore because of him? If I go with you, maybe he won't show up."

"No way. He's not afraid of you. Maybe only if I go out with Eric or William, he won't show up."

"Yeah… I guess. I was hoping to grab ice cream together."

"You know the shopkeeper there is his man." Lia glared at her.

"There is more than one ice cream shop in the world." Helen rolled her eyes.

"You may be right, but I really don't want to take the risk. You know I will be very happy to go out with you if…" Lia trailed off, giving Helen's shoulder a squeeze.

"That's fine. I know where you're coming from. I'm sorry. I just hope things will get better." Helen gave Lia a warm hug and a pat on the back.

"Before it gets worse, I am happy with where we are now." Lia sighed, hugging Helen back.

CHAPTER 6

HELEN

Helen walked down the stairs, stuffing her hands in her pocket. After failing to urge Lia to go for a walk with her, she gave in, deciding to get them ice cream from the grocery store instead. At least they could finish it cuddled together, watching a movie.

The sky was clear, despite the remaining heat from the morning sun. Helen walked out of the clan, heading to the parking lot a block down the street. She picked an alley as a shortcut. As she turned into it, she could hear someone else, their breathing sound faintly echoing the alley. In the shade, the smell of magical power tinkled her skin, sending a shiver down her spine. Helen snapped her head up, looking straight through the alley, but no one was there, probably hidden in one of the back doors to a building nearby.

"Come out, will you?" Helen shouted. It was the familiar magical tingle around. Adrian wasn't doing a good job concealing himself, or he intended for her to find him.

Adrian walked out of a back door. He was in a black

jacket, his hair dishevelled, and his head hanging low. Helen raised her brows. "This is why Lia refused to step out of the clan, knowing a creeper will always be watching."

He ran his fingers through his hair as if trying to tidy it. "I'm not looking for her. I'm looking for you."

Helen took a step back, summoning her magic. "What? Hold me hostage to make Lia show up for you?"

He snapped his head up with wide eyes. "Is this what you think of me?"

"Who knows what you devil will do. If you are not trying to capture me, why are you here?" Helen sneered at him, staring daggers. He averted her gaze, flicking his eyes to the ground.

"How's Lia?" he asked. Helen could barely hear him.

"Why don't you go ask her directly?"

He sighed heavily, leaning onto the wall in the alley. "You know she shut me off… There's no way I can reach her without pissing her off further."

"She finally did the smart thing, don't you think?" Helen snorted a humorless chuckle.

"Yes… She did. That was the smart thing to do."

Is he really pained by Lia ignoring him? Isn't he the one who always pushed her away?

"I don't understand. You keep pushing her away, but you look like you really care about her."

"I… it's more complicated than you think…" He trailed off, his gaze distant. Helen stared at him. Now that he was closer, she could faintly smell the alcohol on his clothes. "I hope Lia is alright…"

She gulped, a fire of rage simmering in her. *You break her heart and you are here wishing her well? Really?*

Before she could stop herself, she slapped him in the

face in a swift motion. He stumbled half a step to the side. Her eyes widened, poising her magic in case he fought back. He straightened and rubbed his cheek as he stared at the ground, his face blank.

"Stop pretending to be the victim here. I've been wanting to do that for a long time." Helen glared at him. He returned his hand to his side, nodding. "I can't believe Lia would care about someone like you and actually cry because of you." Adrian remained silent, leaning on the wall, his eyes glistening.

Really? He had nothing to say in response?

"C'mon Adrian. I've talked to you before about this. Do you want Lia or do you not? Be honest before I kick you in the pants." Helen scowled, marching a step closer to him. He backed up to the wall.

He smiled wryly. "Is this even a question? Of course I want… even keeping in contact with her would mean the world to me."

What is happening here? No wonder why Lia is frustrated. What is he doing?

"Why the heck don't you tell her? She thought you never cared. If you want to try something with her, you should have told her much earlier. Instead of her crying, thinking she has been imagining things." Helen poked his chest with her finger.

"I already told you, it has nothing to do with what I want. The world doesn't exist to fulfil my want," he sighed, rubbing his eyes.

Lia probably didn't know. Other than making Benjamin talk to Adrian, Helen also met him once, around the same day. Maybe she was stepping on lines, but she needed him to make up his mind. Nothing came out from the chat, he was a bit too stubborn.

"I don't have all the time in the world for you. If you are just here to bug me, I'm leaving."

Helen turned to leave and Adrian took a step to block her before reaching out a fist, gesturing for her hand. Helen glared at him, reluctantly reached out for what was in his palm. It was a small piece of amber the size of her thumb. Despite him holding it, it was cold. Something magical in it tickled her hand. She raised her brows at him.

"I doubt she wants to see me anytime soon. If her power runs over her again, stick it close to her skin. It'll drain some of it away so she'll be safe. You will take care of her, right?" His face twisted in pain, staring at Helen with pleading eyes. Helen faintly nodded, slipping the amber into her pocket before walking away.

Within steps, Adrian grabbed her shoulder, turning her to face him. She gulped, summoning her magic and slamming a leaf blade in his face. He ducked away. He held onto her and asked, "Please tell me how Lia is? I really need to know."

"I don't see why I should tell you about her personal life. You are just her mentor, right?"

He frowned, a sob escaping him. "I have my reasons…"

"What? For her to go back to her life later? C'mon! Even if this is really what you believe, I am sure you've never told her, huh? You are hurting over this, and you still don't want to let her know."

"Please… Just tell me how she is?" he growled, his chest rising and falling rapidly. Helen winced as his grip tightened. He flinched, letting go of her. "I'm sorry… I don't mean it."

"She's alright, except sometimes crying over you and never wanting to leave the clan. You haven't killed her yet."

"Thank you. Helen, one more thing. The gang is not

the only people after Lia's life. Please really take good care of her," he said with a serious face.

Helen froze, her mind blank. "Who else is after her?"

"Someone very strong. I don't know how she would feel if I told her this. I'm worried she'll think I am making things up to keep her by my side. I swear this is real and I am not lying. If something comes up, you have to tell me, please?"

"OK… I guess on the front of keeping Lia alive, we are still on the same page. If you want to know something, message me. As you said, I am not sure whether she wants to see you just yet."

"Thank you." He beamed, letting out a relieved sigh.

If only he wasn't mysterious and kind of a jerk, maybe we could actually be friends.

He stared at her for a moment too long, his smile faltering. A glint of sadness flashed through his eyes, she shivered at the intense gaze. "What's that look for?" she asked.

He shook his head, zipping up his jacket. His eyes glistened with tears. "I think I actually envy you. If only I were just an Elements' magician…" He rubbed his forehead. "It doesn't matter anyway. That would never happen."

"You mean, if you could give up the dark magic, you would?"

"Without a blink of the eyes, yes. Maybe in a world where Lia also didn't have it." He shrugged, looking up at the sky despite a tear rolling down his cheek. He wiped it off with the back of his hand.

"You love her?"

He looked briefly at her before returning his gaze to the sky. "She made her choice." He turned away from Helen, walking down the alley with his head low. "You take good care of her. My words still stand. If anything happens to her, I am not letting you live."

Helen stared at his retreating form down the alley and frowned deeply.

But you forced her hand…

CHAPTER 7

LIA

While Helen was out buying ice cream, Lia retreated to her room, locking the door. She rolled on the bed, hugging her wolf plushie tight. After she caught herself dozing off, she sat up straight, shaking her head to clear her mind.

Maybe she could try working on her power. If she kept working on it, maybe it would be better than letting it bottle up.

Rubbing the comforting fur on the plushie, she closed her eyes, slowly calling up the dark power within her. Breathing in and out rhythmically, the warmth of the power surged up in her. Lia willed ice magic instead, focusing her mind to create an ice wall by the door, giving her power something to do.

It did make her stronger than before. When she learned more, maybe she could finally keep people around her safe.

Busying herself with holding up the ice wall, the warmth of the new power slowly faded. Lia opened her eyes, releasing a relaxed sigh. It wasn't as strong as yesterday; she'd probably used up quite a bit and it needed time to recover. She wiped the sweat off her forehead with the towel on her bedside table.

She remembered how she moved the man with her mind in the gang's base. She set her plushie in front of her, locking eyes with it and ramping up the power inside her, but it didn't move a single bit. She shook her head, rubbing her chin. She tried to focus on it again, but her mind seemed to wander too much for her to stay focused. She pointed at the plushie with her finger, frowning deeply. The plushie seemed to shake when a loud knock came from the door. She jumped, pulling the blanket up, knocking the plushie face down on the bed.

Helen was grinning at her. "I got us tacos and ice cream for dessert." She tugged Lia's arm, pulling her to the lounge.

"Thanks."

"You'll get them much more frequently if you would actually step out… I mean if you would tell me." Helen didn't sound as happy as she looked.

"Did something happen?"

"Nah, I still don't think you'll go out with me despite me asking. Just don't want to spoil the fun."

"Oh, that's OK. William sure is happy I am here, though." Lia gave her a reassuring smile.

Pushing open the door to the lounge, Eric was on the couch, watching a movie. The paper bag of tacos was on the coffee table in front of him.

"Oh, didn't expect you here." Helen rolled her eyes.

"I was guessing these are yours. I was about to dig in if no one came for them." Eric chuckled, patting his midsection. He moved to the side so they could take a seat, turning off the movie.

Lia took her taco, opening the wrap. She turned to him as she found his gaze on her.

He said, "I'm happy. It feels great to be like the old times when we hung out together."

"Well, you Elders don't really hang out with us." Helen dipped her nachos in the spicy sauce.

"I always think you don't enjoy an old soul like me." Eric let out a hearty laugh, chewing on his chocolate bar. "But still, seeing you playing together is great. You don't know what you're missing until you actually lose it."

Lia almost choked on her soda. It felt wrong that her mind pulled up Adrian's face at once. *I think of him more when he is not around. Don't think of him, will you…?*

Lia quickly busied herself with her taco, the cabbage crunchy in her mouth and the spicy beef was always the best. Luckily, the others were oblivious to her thoughts.

"How's William doing recently? Is everything good for him?" Helen asked.

Eric let out a sigh, tidying his dark brown hair. "He seems to be very keen on finding out whether dark magicians are out there. And trying to find out who is after Lia's life. While I agree we should find the murderer, I don't know about the dark magicians."

"What do you mean by 'don't know'? What will happen if they exist?" Helen asked.

"I'm reluctant to find out. Out of sight, out of mind? I kind of worry what the dark magicians will do when they know we know about them. Of course, I will try to destroy them, but there's no telling what they are up to if they have been hiding all these years. Maybe I'm just avoiding the fact.

"But William is not wrong. If they are somewhere, we have to know. They will always plan to eliminate us, at least both William and I, just as we do." Eric frowned deeply, gripping the edge of the couch.

"They sound dangerous," Lia said.

"Indeed, we can't let the devil walk the earth. They will try to kill everyone." Eric gritted his teeth. The tension in his body was visible.

"Then you really should help William and let us help if needed," Helen said.

"I am more focused on finding the one behind Lia's attacks after William takes on the other part. But all the traces of evidence are gone..." Eric shook his head, his shoulders slumped.

So, William and Eric are really on the same page and both are no wiser. Great. Lia sighed silently to herself. *All this hiding behind each other's backs...*

CHAPTER 8

ADRIAN

Adrian stumbled into the bar in the late evening, reaching for the rooms upstairs, a glass and a bottle of scotch in his hands. At least it would be quiet up there and no one would see him drunk. He pushed a random door, sitting down on the bed and setting the bottle and glass on the bedside table. He let out a heavy sigh, glancing at his watch. There were still five minutes before Benjamin could hand over his shift and come up. He'd told him countless times to just hire a few more staff, but he refused.

His heart hammered as he stared at the wood-textured wall. At least he tried. He told Helen to be careful. It seemed Lia wouldn't talk with him any time soon. Maybe the existence of the clan would deter Evelyn.

Someone knocked and pushed in just as Adrian downed the first glass of his alcohol. Benjamin huffed. "King, don't drink too much. How can I help you?"

"Have you… been able to get in touch with them?" Adrian asked, his heart racing. He did too many terrible things that it could be hard to mend. What if his own team didn't even want to see him again?

Benjamin nodded, but his face was blank. "I managed to leave a voice message and they've listened. Well, at least the sent receipt said so. I think that's already a breakthrough. They will come back anyways. With how our magic works, it would be to their benefit."

Adrian sighed, setting down the now-empty glass. "Still, only because they have no choice not to. Anyways, I managed to tell Helen."

Benjamin chuckled. "Could've guessed."

Adrian's eyes widened in shock. "Excuse me?"

"Well, the bruise on your face gives you away." Benjamin's smirk lingered, a bit too annoying.

"I guess so…"

Benjamin took a seat by his side, glancing at the bottle on the bedside table. "I doubt Lia would have done that."

"Right… She's too kind. I would rather she punch me. I guess it would feel better than getting slapped by Helen."

"Good gracious! Try harder with Lia, would you?"

"I haven't been feeling that well recently. I don't mean with Lia. There's something on my mind I couldn't get off. How's The Orbit?"

"Other than the hotel seeming to be a lot quieter from the outside, I've not seen a lot of changes. What's wrong?"

"I seemed to smell more magic in the air. Though Zitannas' power makes it hard to feel other magical things amidst the large city."

"You think it is The Orbit's magicians? Should it be Evelyn instead?"

"No idea. I don't know those in the gang very well. Just like us, there could be more around. News of them getting beat would spread in no time. Evelyn did say she would give me a month. I don't know whether she'll keep that up, but I could use the time. If only Lia would at least talk to me in a month." Adrian rubbed his temple. With Lia's power getting more stable, he didn't know when she would be back. Gosh, he hated himself. It was so unfair to Lia.

"Sadly, our spy master is not here, huh? I suppose I can ask around. Maybe some others will have some idea."

"Don't make it obvious. I don't want Evelyn catching any more attention than she has. You know we barely made it here."

Zitannas had a lot more to it than the average human knew. If Evelyn tried, she may get some of them on her side, and he didn't need that. With his track record, there was no telling what could happen. Maybe he could fight some of them, but he couldn't fight all at once.

"Of course, I do think our recent deal earned us a bit more room," Benjamin said.

"That deal is a bit too new to be stable. I won't count on it. Only the cash and the supply matters. There's no trust with them."

"Well, I can't say I disagree. I will look into it."

"Good… Do you really think the two would come back? After what I did…?" Adrian flicked his eyes to Benjamin, his gut twitched. Lia better not know what he did to his people.

Benjamin let out a heavy sigh. "I can't speak for them. But I think they understand. If you tell them how you feel for Lia, maybe it would be easier. They only know you want them to be back for an emergency. As you wanted, I haven't told them exactly what's going on. You can't expect them to know how you feel for Lia. Heck, even Lia doesn't know how you feel."

Adrian groaned. "I told you I don't feel anything for her."

"Liar."

Adrian glared at him. Benjamin huffed, shaking his head. "C'mon. It is one thing to not tell her, and another whether you really love her. You aren't thinking you can fight Evelyn without the Elements knowing, right? There's no way life would be the same anymore. May as well let Lia know and let her decide for herself."

"I can't even talk to her right now." Adrian downed the rest of his drink, reaching for the bottle, but Benjamin took it and set it further away. Adrian scowled, returning his hand to his side, staring at the glass. "I have my reasons. I know what's for the best."

"Wait." Benjamin sat up straight, his gaze intense, as if searching Adrian's face. Adrian raised his brows. Benjamin cleared his throat. "What if the Elements team up with Evelyn?"

Adrian's eyes widened. Dammit! He never thought of that. His blood chilled. If he insisted on not killing Lia, Evelyn would go for her. He had absolutely no idea what William would think. If Evelyn just wanted Lia to be dead, she could let William know about Lia's power, and he would probably kill her himself. Who Lia was and what she had done for the team, William wouldn't care. For him, the only good dark magicians were the dead ones.

If Evelyn didn't tell William about Lia's power and decided to barge into the clan, there was no telling what would happen. William probably was no match for the dark magic, but Lia would still die for sure. If William was going to die, he better die under Adrian's hand for what he did to Ariel. Adrian grunted, shaking his head.

"My King. If we are thinking of the same thing, then there's only one way to keep Lia alive with the highest chance and getting rid of Evelyn's threat. We don't need the Elements to be there to stab us in the back. But Lia wouldn't like it."

The Elements had to go down for things to work.

"Yes… she probably would hate me for the rest of her life. And hell, for a dark magician, that's a long time."

Benjamin chuckled wryly. "You would rather do that, right? You only want Lia to be safe."

"Is that even a question? Check to see if those two are really coming back. Please help me convince them. And still, don't tell them the details about Lia and Evelyn. I will do that myself." Adrian gently squeezed Benjamin's shoulder. William and Eric wouldn't worry him, but he would need every one of his team members to be around to even dare to dream of winning against Evelyn. After all these years, who knew how strong she had gotten.

"Sure. I will keep trying, as I've said. We all have a soft spot for you, just don't keep screwing up."

Adrian examined Benjamin's face, his smirk a bit too smug. He let out a heavy sigh. He hated how Benjamin was right. "I will try. Don't forget The Orbit."

"Of course. When did I ever fail you?"

CHAPTER 9

HELEN

I nside the clan, Helen wiped off her sweat with a towel as her training came to an end. It wasn't as hard as she expected; hopefully that meant she was getting better.

William was talking to Patrick as his session just ended before hers. She stretched her arms, rubbing them. Other than getting stronger, there was one thing she liked about training sessions—usually hers were in the morning, so it was time for lunch when they wrapped up.

"I guess this is everything for today. Get some rest. It's been a while since anything happened. I am not feeling the best about it. So the two of you better be on your toes." William nodded to them and left.

Patrick rolled his eyes, leaning back on the wall near Helen. "He always says that. I think it is a trick to get us to stay in training."

"You wanted to get stronger anyway. Even if he didn't say that, you are still going to stick with training."

There was a buzz, and they both checked their phones. Helen's heart skipped a beat when she saw a message from Benjamin. "It seems I have to go. See you next time?"

"Sure." Patrick nodded, heading to the bench to gather his stuff while Helen headed to the door.

Helen went to the lounge, hoping there was no one inside. It had been a while since she heard anything from Benjamin. Speaking of which, what Adrian told her a few days ago surfaced. He said there was someone very strong after Lia—was Benjamin asking her about that? But shouldn't he ask Lia directly? Lia probably hadn't blocked him like she did with Adrian.

No one was in the lounge. She sat on the couch and checked the message.

> *Hey, you have some time today?*

She rubbed her chin. This was a bit random and broad from him. Or did something happen with Adrian? That man was a stubborn nut to crack.

> *Yes. And what's this about?*

> *Well, I am heading to The Orbit later today. Would you want to tag along?*

> *A very strong magician like you is scared of that hotel?*

> *I am not, come on... There is also something I want to ask you about.*

Helen frowned, though she knew it was safer to talk face-to-face in case someone in the clan got hold of her phone.

> *I think I can, tonight?*

> *I am thinking now. Up for it?*

> *I need my lunch.*

> *Count it on me.*

She stared at her phone, not sure whether he meant it. But if he wanted to pay for food, why not? Benjamin gave her a location for them to meet up, and she headed out of the clan to the bus stop soon after.

◇—┼◇┼◇┼◇┼◇┼◇┼◇┼◇┼◇—◇

WHEN HELEN GOT off the bus, Benjamin was leaning on a lamp post near the parking lot of The Landmark. The Orbit was a block away. He seemed to be oblivious about her walking up to him. "Hey." She poked his shoulder.

He almost jumped, straightening so much that he hit the lamp post. He rubbed the back of his head and chuckled. "Well, didn't see you. Let's get going."

"Come on. You're not that oblivious. What's on your mind?" she asked as they headed to the entrance of the mall.

"A lot…" he sighed, sinking his hands into his pocket.

The Landmark was a high-end mall, not somewhere she would go a lot. Not to mention after the meteorite monsters, driving past Central Park brought back too many memories. Inside the mall, there were name-brand shops she didn't even know how to pronounce. Not a lot of people were around, probably because it was an afternoon in a normal workday.

"Tell me what could make you worried? Or would Adrian be mad about it?"

"Well, do you happen to have a trick or two to help people in conflict to be OK with each other?" His frown deepened as they stopped by the directory board of the mall.

"Who are they? You pissed off Adrian again?" Her heart skipped a beat. She made him talk to Adrian about Lia a while ago. In their attack on The Orbit, he seemed to be fine with Benjamin. Had that backfired now that Adrian and Lia weren't talking to each other?

He smiled wryly, shaking his head. "Not really. Adrian and I are fine. Just someone else is not fine. He needs me to talk to them, but I don't even know how to talk about it."

"You up for sushi?" She pointed at the directory. He nodded and they turned that way. She continued, "Well, without more context, it would be better to just let them talk about it. If I had an idea, I would've used it on Adrian and Lia yesterday."

He laughed, shaking his head. "I know, right? I don't even understand why."

"You know him a lot better than I do and you still have no idea?" She lifted her brows as she gestured to the waiter for them to get seated. While Benjamin poured the green tea, she took a dish of tuna sushi from the conveyor belt.

"I mean… His reason is not that bad. If it was a century or more earlier, I'd let that slide. But I can't imagine how he was still clenching on it."

"How old are you guys really?" she asked.

He smirked as he took a California roll for himself. "Asking about age is not very polite."

"When did you get the idea that I am polite?" She narrowed her eyes on him.

"Longer than you can imagine. Back to the topic. It seems an outsider like me could do nothing, right?"

"I think it is the case. It is not our problem after all. Though no wonder both of us are affected by it." She shrugged. Before the swordfish went too far away, she snatched the dish to the table, taking another bite. There were few benefits of eating out in an expensive place; other than the food seemed to be tastier, maybe the price tag helped.

"Is Lia alright?" Benjamin took a sip of his tea.

"You mean her power? I… think so? I met with Adrian a few days ago. I think you know about it. He gave me a piece of amber." It probably wouldn't be for the best if she told him how she slapped Adrian.

"I see." He let out a heavy sigh. "Why must we get stuck between them?"

"I wonder. I guess we are a bit too keen on helping them a bit. Anyways, why are you going to The Orbit?"

"The King wanted to know whether there are still some of them around and whether they are still going after Lia."

"He told me there is someone very strong that is doing that." She frowned. Maybe it would also be safer for Lia to stay in the clan.

"Indeed." He rubbed his temple. "We don't even know how it will end."

"The oh-so-mighty Adrian also didn't know?" There was no sign of a smile on his face. Even when they were barging into The Orbit, he wasn't at all tense. But now…

"I think he is nervous but doesn't want to show. For him, I could understand. He can't quite talk about his own struggles. That's an old enemy. Another dark magician like him."

"You?" She lifted an eyebrow. Benjamin was also a dark magician?

"Not the same. She is an origin. I am just a little dark magician with the King as my origin. Adrian leant his power to me. The origin is much stronger."

Whoever that was, this didn't sound like good news. "Why Lia? No way Lia knows her?"

"Those with power think differently. When they have power, they want to stop others with the same power. Lia is also an origin. Though she is still in the learning phase, that woman won't risk letting her gain power." He took another sip of his tea, but his hand was shaking slightly.

"Lia wouldn't pose harm to anyone. She just wants to help more people."

He stared at her for a moment longer than comfortable

until he cleared his throat. "I know. Lia is almost the most harmless woman I've ever met. But for me, the King, and that woman, our world doesn't work like that. Somehow Lia expressed her power under the King's wing didn't help. If Lia had never known she had the dark magic, or no magician was with her, maybe that woman wouldn't care. She and the King fought very hard back in the day."

Helen swallowed with her throat dry. "So she thinks that Adrian will join hands with Lia and become a threat to her."

Benjamin nodded with a solemn face. "Yes. That woman and the King have a grudge that goes way back. Probably no better than the one… Never mind. Let's say it was no fun."

Helen squinted. Maybe it was about Adrian and William? That she already knew, but Benjamin should know that she knew. Why was he hiding it?

As the meal wrapped up, Benjamin called over the waiter. Helen blinked. "Are you sure you are paying for me?"

He chuckled. "Funny you didn't ask till now. Yes, I said it in the message. I don't want to see you survive on ramen for the rest of the month."

She rolled her eyes. "While William doesn't pay a lot, it is not that bad."

"It's the King's money anyway." He winked as he signed the bill and handed over his card.

"After he paid you, it is your money."

"Except he doesn't pay me."

She stared at him. "What?"

Benjamin peeked as the waiter walked off to swipe the card, he said, "We use his card. So it is his money."

She laughed. "Feel like living in your mom's basement? No wonder you don't dare piss him off."

He huffed, rolling his eyes. "Well, I contributed in earning the sum, so no, I am not living in a basement."

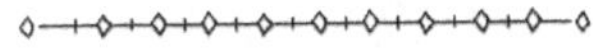

IT DIDN'T TAKE LONG for them to arrive at The Orbit from the mall. It was a good sunny day, not too hot for Helen yet. The Orbit looked to be quiet. Compared with the last time they were there, the parking lot seemed to have a lot fewer cars. Maybe there were less people in the afternoon than at night.

They walked inside. Most of the decorations looked the same as the last time. Helen's eyes went to the small lounge area at once. She and Benjamin were there last time, had the fun of finishing a cheesecake there and the fun of messing around, breaking a wine glass on purpose. She smiled at the memory, right at the time when Benjamin looked to her and winked. It seemed he was of the same mind.

By the lift area, he tugged on her elbow. "Hey, I think it is a good idea we use the way we communicated last time we were here."

"Right, it seems to be better," she said. He took her hand and a warm stream of power trickled inside her. It scared her last time that happened, reminding her a bit too much of the way Adrian attempted to kill her when she found out about Lia's dark magic. Slowly, the warm flame lit by Benjamin's power settled inside her, giving a gentle sense of him being around. She willed, *testing?*

He flashed a smile and pressed the button for the elevator. *Come on… you know it's going to work. Testing, really?*

Does Adrian know about this? I think when he asked you to look into The Orbit, he didn't mean you should bring me along.

If he is going to be mad, then let him.

The elevator arrived and they walked inside. He took out the key card they stole from a waiter last time, swiping it on the panel. Benjamin's voice came up in Helen's mind. *I already did a basic check. There's no smell of dark magic around. It should be fine. Just have to check whether the gang is still strong.*

You think it is a good idea to walk right in? Her heart skipped a beat. Was he ready to fight if there was someone inside?

There's no better way to check. The woman posed a threat to the King; she should expect this. I remember you can do something to their system, right?

She nodded. *Yes, suppose nothing changed, I can mess with their surveillance cameras.* The door opened and she shivered at the bleakness of the basement. It was cold and lifeless. Last time, it didn't take long before they were 'captured' and brought directly to their boss. Maybe this time they had to walk around themselves.

It wasn't hard to locate the control room again. Helen kicked the door open and prepared her magic, but there was no one inside. They exchanged a glance and walked inside. Last time, there were two inside, though finished off by Benjamin before she could even blink. The screens were turned off, she checked whether the cameras were recording, Benjamin leaned against the wall and stared at the door.

Benjamin frowned. *It seems like nothing's here.*

We shall see. It looked like they hadn't repaired their system yet. Maybe that woman wouldn't spend the money on the gang. Without their leader, no one else wanted to pay either. *Nothing needs to be done. It is not working anyways.*

Are you sure?

Very much so. I doubt anyone cares.

OK. Benjamin nodded, and they headed out of the room.

Back on the path, they took random turns. It was dead

quiet. Last time, at least there were some low humming sounds of machines. *Ben, I don't feel safe here. It's too quiet.*

You have a guess on why that is?

No. Maybe they moved out?

I wonder. If I were them, I'd stay here. It is unlikely for people to re-search the same place.

Do you mean we are no people? She smirked as he rolled his eyes. The deeper they went through the halls, the more the unsettling that stir in her stomach was.

Soon, they arrived at a larger empty space in the basement that looked like a common room for everyone to gather, the walls were the same blank white. There were at least two other entrances to the space.

She squinted at the side that she figured should be the front of the room. On it was a space that looked cleaner and brighter white than the paint around it. Could there have been something hanging there before? She pointed her discovery to Benjamin. He followed her gaze and soon frowned.

His answer came, *I don't think we were here last time.*

You are right. I wonder what that could be.

That spot looks clean though.

I don't know whether it's of any significance.

She nodded; he was right. It was probably some Christmas decoration, if a gang would even be interested in that. They moved on, finally arriving by the door of the room they'd been held hostages.

Her heart skipped a beat, the place had been tidied up. She blinked, making sure she wasn't imagining things. When they left a while ago, there had been blood everywhere from what Adrian and Benjamin did. But now, the carpet seemed to be new, it had the fresh smell of cloth and the lighter shade of red. *Someone had to be here after we left. I remember some of them escaping when we were fighting.*

She was walking in when Benjamin grabbed her elbow, pulling her back. He shook his head. *I doubt it would be a good idea to stay. Clearly, some of them are still around. Maybe we should leave.*

You know some of them have to be here. She was going to say something more when Benjamin tensed. Now that she paid more attention, something seemed different in the air, but she couldn't point a finger on it. He nudged her to leave. She shrugged and followed.

When they finally arrived in the parking lot, she was panting. Benjamin was almost running when they left the basement. After the door of the hotel closed behind them and they were back in the bright daylight, she asked, "What did you see? Why such a hurry?"

"I figure I should trust your instinct a bit more. Inside the room, somewhere, there is a faint scent of dark magic." He frowned deeply, his hands clenched into a fist.

"From someone after Lia?" Her heart skipped a beat— no wonder he wanted to leave.

"I think so. I am not sure whether it was traces left by her or her people or if it was a trap."

If Adrian wasn't confident fighting that woman, it would be smart before they got themselves into trouble. She let out a sigh of relief regardless. The sun and the fresh air outside always calmed her.

"You think they know we were there?"

"Probably not. Holding back my power is the default. The magic inside the room is too weak for any magician to be there. Someone was there before, but not at that moment."

They took a turn, heading back to Benjamin's car. There was a low thud, Benjamin spun around. Helen quickly moved to the side as two men dashed at them from an alley. She summoned her vine, catching one of them around the waist. Benjamin had an ice shard in his hand, dashing for the other one.

There was a flame from the hand of the one Helen caught. The fireball soon burned through her vine. She grimaced from the sharp pain in her arm as the vine burned. She blinked, retreating the vine. As that man dropped, there was a glint in the corner of her eyes. She ducked when Benjamin's ice wall also spawned, something stuck on the wall.

When she blinked and turned back to the fight, the two men were nowhere to be found. "They escaped? Or did you burn them into ashes?"

His face was solemn. He walked to the ice wall and pulled something from it. "They aren't here to fight. It's a warning."

He showed her a white thin metallic card. It was thin enough it could stab into something, maybe her neck. On it was a carving of a dragon.

"What does this mean?" She had seen the tattoo on the gang's men, but that was a snake and a sword, not a dragon.

"I think this is meant for me, not you." He turned the card over, but it was empty on the other side. "The dragon's the sign of the woman after Lia."

"Oh, is this an origin thing? Does Adrian have a sign?"

"No. It's just a gimmick for her to feel good." He shrugged, looking closer at the card.

"Why doesn't he use one? A gimmick could be fun." The card seemed normal; at least she didn't feel any magic on it. Benjamin pulled out his phone and took a photo, then dumped the card into a bin beside the road. She lifted her brows at him.

"It already served its purpose. That woman has a very different goal from the King. She is ready to take on the world, while the King only wants his revenge." There was a flash of a mischievous glint in his eyes. "A sign, right? Talking about the devil in Zitannas is enough for them to know. There's no need for a sign."

"I think he didn't like to be called a devil?"

"Well…" Benjamin pinched the bridge of his nose. "It depends on who is calling him that. If it was from someone else, outside of his people and his team, he would be fine with it and sometimes even insists for them to call him that. But it wouldn't end well if we, or in this case, I use it on him. He would be very mad about it." Benjamin shrugged.

"I guess he doesn't really see himself as a devil, then. Back to the card. Should I be worried?" she asked.

He leaned against the wall of the building, next to the entrance of a shop. His eyes narrowed as he considered. She could almost hear the gears in his head turning. He shook his head. "Probably not. That woman only cares about the King and his team, which is me. If they were after you, they wouldn't use the card. It meant nothing for you. It won't take long for them to realise that the Elements aren't a threat to her. Not to mention they regard Lia to be with the King and probably think he is hiding her somewhere."

"They would've chosen to attack you when I wasn't around?"

"I guess so. They were tasked to deliver the message anyways. While Lia didn't want to see the King and decided to stay inside the clan, it is better for her. Have you told her about those that were after her?"

She shook her head. "Not yet. Somehow I promised Adrian to keep that a secret as long as Lia wouldn't step out of the clan. He said he didn't want to make it looks like he was making up something to force Lia to him."

"He told me the same. You think that's a good idea?"

She smirked, tilting her head to the side. "What do you think?"

"I… I admit I'm not the best person when it comes to relationships. But I see why the King prefers that. I don't know how bad that night was after we cracked The Orbit, he didn't quite tell. I think you are much better than me with this."

She tucked her hair behind her ear as a breeze blew. "I am on the same boat. I'm also not sure whether that was a good idea. He had a point though. I've been pretending I never met up with him, which for Lia, it should be the case. Given my history with Adrian, Lia would believe that we won't meet each other."

"I am worried about the attackers. Would they attack you and Adrian?"

"Some time in the future, obviously. Zitannas is complex, though. If they are new, they may still be finding a footing around here. When they are both strong and are fighting each other, you don't launch unless you are very confident."

"They won't attack the clan?"

"I don't think it is high on their list. She knows the grudges between William and the King. The least she needs to do to kill the King, the better it will be for her. No point forcing William to work with the King.

"OK…" She nodded faintly. Maybe she would still be careful, just in case. She stared at the road ahead as they walked back to his car. Did the trip with Benjamin paint a target on her back?

CHAPTER 10

HELEN

The next day, Helen stood outside the closed door of the lounge, her heart racing. She resisted the urge to put her ear against it. William had gone in to talk with Lia. It had been only a minute or two, but it was already a bit too quiet to be comfortable.

Everything had been going fine until William called for the team. She and Patrick arrived on time, but there was no sign of Lia, nor did she say anything in the group.

When the door squeaked open, Helen almost jumped. William came out with a blank face. He nodded at her and gestured for them to get going. She hurried to follow, glancing at the lounge. Lia was facing the wall, away from Helen.

Helen and William went to the parking lot, where Patrick was waiting by William's car. Under the streetlamp, his shadow was long. It was already dark now, not her favorite time of day. Patrick greeted them and the team got into the car.

Helen and Patrick were in the back seat, as always. It made the empty seat by William's side glaring. If Eric wasn't with them, Lia would sit there. William was still solemn. She probably wouldn't like what was on his mind. William started the car and they set off.

Patrick asked, "I thought Lia was coming with us?"

William shook his head. "It would take too long for her to get ready. She said she didn't feel well."

"Oh… I guess the three of us can do it then."

Helen nodded faintly; it felt like a lifetime since they had been called for something strange in the city since the meteorite monsters. Maybe the power of Zitannas was at work once again. When they arrived, as soon as the car door opened, she shivered. It was a February night, but it was colder than she expected. It seemed like someone was watching her.

She got out and squinted into the darkness of Sunrise Bay. The sharp sound of a bird chilled her bones. She squinted just in time to catch the glint of a crow's feather. The crow had been standing on a very disgusting body.

William said, "It was reported a few hours ago. Some creature was spotted on the beach. There was an evacuation, but I guess this man didn't make it."

The clothes on the man were torn and there were bite marks on his body. Half of his arm was chewed off. She quickly looked away before it further upset her. The sand around the body had soaked up some of the blood.

Patrick stretched as William stared into the sea. She asked, "No clues to find what we need?"

William pulled out his phone, the bright light shining on his face as he scrolled the screen. The breeze from the sea made Helen shiver again. The bite mark on the body looked to be from a beast. She put her hand closer to the mark for a brief measurement; it had to be a large dog or some type.

She almost jumped at a shuffling sound getting closer

and closer. William and Patrick also turned that side to see. William switched off the screen, there was a pair of glowing green eyes staring at them. She gathered her magic, getting ready to strike.

Whatever that was leapt at them. Helen shot her vine, but it ducked away. She rolled to the side, away from its supposed head. It seemed to be a mess of branches and mud taking the form of a wolf. She frowned at the strange creature. It had everything resembling a wolf, just not the fur. It was huge, the level of the sand where it had been shielded its real height. It almost reached her chest on all fours.

Patrick launched a fire ball at it. It jumped to the side when William slashed down with an ice shard in his hand. The monster squealed in pain, spinning around to William when Helen's vine caught its waist. She squeezed the vine when the sand under her leg moved. She managed to snap the monster into two when something jumped up from the sand under her; it was another wolf-like creature. Helen jumped to the side a split second before its jaw would take her legs.

She shivered as she turned to face it. The new one was a bit smaller, it also had the mud and branches on its body; maybe this time, Zitannas' power affected some swamp. She rolled her eyes as she got ready to fight it when there was Patrick's shout. "What the hell is this thing?"

"Helen, fight yours. Focus." William's voice came from behind.

The two of them should be able to handle the first one, so she shot leaf blades against the smaller monster. It jumped towards her, unaffected by the blades.

It took a few tries before she captured its limbs in her vine. She was going to smash it when William shouted, "Helen, stop and just hold it."

She added another vine to hold the monster's waist when she finally turned around. There were two monsters on the sand, burning in Patrick's flame while trapped by William's ice.

She frowned. "Wasn't there one large monster?"

William nodded. "It was, until you snapped it into two. Then there were two."

The monster in her vine growled, its voice hoarse and deep. It was still fighting her vine. William quickly froze it with an ice beam. Helen retreated her vine as the monster froze and dropped on the sand as a large ice block. When she looked back to the two monsters, there were only two piles of ash left.

Now the beach was quiet as before, with only the sound of the waves and wind. Looking around the empty beach, there was nothing else. Helen asked, "So we are done with this?"

William scanned the beach. "I guess so. There doesn't seem to be anything else around."

Patrick leaned over to the ash of the monsters. "Agreed, this city really is special."

"Good for us to be able to use magic in the open without major drawback." William nodded as he typed on his phone, probably reporting back to whoever commissioned them to get rid of the monsters. Afterwards, he gestured for them to leave.

Before they headed back to the car, Helen looked back at the dead body a few more times. Before William and Patrick could see her, she picked up a branch and lifted the ragged sleeve from the body. On the half-chewed off arm, there was a tattoo: the head of a snake and the butt of a sword, the rest bitten off. Her blood almost froze, she dropped the branch and hurried back to William's side before he found out. He may have seen that and it didn't ring a bell for him.

She followed William with her head down. If she remembered right, that tattoo seemed to be the same one the gang in The Orbit had. But then why was he dead? Did it have anything with him being part of the gang? Or was it just a coincidence that he went to the beach when the monsters were around? She almost bumped onto Patrick when they arrived back at the car. She leaned on it as she emptied the sand from her shoes. Fighting on the beach brought some of them inside. Much better after they were gone.

Inside the car, it was quiet. William played soft instrumental music as they drove back to the clan. Helen leaned on the window, trying to put the pieces together. Why would the gang's man go to a beach? Or was she thinking a bit too much of it?

CHAPTER 11

BENJAMIN

Benjamin rubbed his chin as he stared at the whiteboard in his apartment. On it were some notes and his thoughts on what was happening in the city, especially when it came to The Orbit and Evelyn. From what he found with Helen, someone was using the basement, probably Evelyn herself had been there. It would match up with how the gang went after Lia. Evelyn also admitted sending them after her.

When his phone buzzed, he took it from the desk and glanced at the notification. It was just a useless one about the game he was playing recently, which Helen had forced him to download. He shrugged and checked the messaging app instead. It had been a few days since he reached out to the two in the team, but they still hadn't said a word. He stared at the sent receipt, they already played the voice message. His finger hovered the call button, his heart hammering in his chest.

He didn't need to worry. It wasn't his problem; it was between them and King, but he somehow had to be the middleman. The worst they could do was hang up on him.

He put the phone on speaker and dialled, the wait was dreadful.

It sounded like someone had answered, but there was no voice on the other end. "Hello?"

"What?"

"You heard my last message?"

"I said don't find me."

"I swear it is an emergency." He scowled, clenching a tight fist. The King hadn't left him with an easy task. On the other end of the call, there was a very faint noise of chatting. As expected, the two were together.

"What? You also pissed him off?" she asked.

"No. But please come back. We need the two of you back."

"Of course you won't, you are his pet after all. And is that a command?"

He pinched the bridge of his nose, holding back a heavy sigh. "He would tell you what's happening. Trust me, it is not made up."

"I don't care."

"Hey! Give it some thought, please. You know we would at least lose our magic if the King died."

"Then let him. He doesn't want me around."

"That's not the case. Think about it."

"Poor you had to beg both sides. You stay happy being his pet." The call cut before Benjamin could squeeze in another word. He sighed as he stared at the screen, it now lit up after the call ended. It flashed their number again. He leaned back on the desk with his brows knitted. Maybe Helen was right. If they were mad at the King, why was he the one making the call?

Well, he knew the reason. There was no way they wanted to talk to the King after what happened. Being called the King's pet was never easy either. He wanted too much to bite back, but it wouldn't help. He was just trying to keep everyone together on the team, no matter how he really didn't see every one of them eye-to-eye.

It seemed the Elements had a much easier time. Helen was Lia's best friend, and the other boy didn't seem to be one that would cause trouble. William and Eric had been friends for a long time. Maybe they had a much easier time with everyone not in a constant fight.

At least he tried. He would leave another message later if they didn't say anything. He couldn't blame them for leaving the city, though, after what the King did to them was… a bit too much even for him. He touched his neck, where the King grabbed him when he thought he felt something for Lia. He shivered and stared back to the whiteboard; better prepare for the worst.

The flapping of wings startled him. He straightened and headed to the window. The crow was here. It stood on the windowsill, flapping its wings at the window as if it was knocking on a door. He opened the window for it and it jumped on his wrist.

"Little guy, what did you find?" He walked to the kitchen and opened a jar of fresh chicken breast, giving the crow a piece. It gobbled down the meat. "What's that smell on you? I told you to have a look around the city, not to search the trash."

The crow cawed, flapping its wings as if it was telling him something. "It's OK, I will have a look." Its words he didn't understand, but its memory, he could see. He let the crow jump off his hand onto the kitchen counter, resting his hand on its head.

As he focused, the surroundings slowly faded, revealing the darkness of the night in his mind, and soon became what the crow saw.

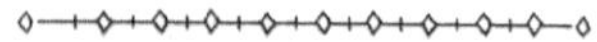

IT WAS LATE AFTERNOON, he was in the middle of the air. He took the crow's eyes and saw what it had seen. Luckily, he didn't fear the height. The city and the buildings looked flat from high above. The late afternoon sun on his feathers felt good, warm and cozy enough for a nap. Nearing Sunrise Bay, people were running. The crow was curious. He stopped on a beach umbrella, looking down at people running away from the sea.

There were two strange wolf-like creatures, both piles of mud and branches. The branches seemed to be stuck there when the mud solidified, there were still leaves on some of the branches. Despite the thing having four legs and running like a wolf, the mud wouldn't break and fall. They chased people away from the beach. When a few police arrived, the monsters buried themselves into the sand and disappeared.

The crow stared as the policemen evacuated every other human. A crow wasn't on their list. He waited until it was dark. There was no light on the beach. He shivered at the cooler wind from the sea, flapping his wings at times.

He was about to leave when a man on the phone showed up, his voice muffled by the waves. He flew closer, but still couldn't hear clearly. The man seemed to be searching for something on the beach with his head low.

Two other men trespassed the band the police had put up and made their way to the man. The two men got closer, and the one on the phone spun around and screamed.

The crow gasped, holding his wings tight, in the night, they wouldn't see him.

The man sent a few sloppy fire bolts, but none landed. There was something in the two men's hands that gave a glint in the darkness. They stabbed the man and he fell dead on the sand. After they made sure no one saw them and one of the men kicked the body to make sure he was dead, they left.

The crow shivered, it seemed humans were a lot meaner to their own kind than other creatures. After the two left, the crow was ready to leave and report back to Benjamin when the sand near the man moved. The two monsters emerged, sniffing at the dead body. They soon bit on the man, leaving his clothes ragged and blood seeping from a chewed-off arm. The monsters looked around and left.

The crow waited until the monsters were far away, before flying to the man's body. There was a weak scent of magic on him that was already fading. He hopped around, trying to spot the phone the man dropped, but there was nothing. Either the sand buried it or the other men took it.

From a distance, there was the sound of a car and bright white headlights. Three people got out of the car, heading his way, one woman and two men. The crow left, but the woman saw him.

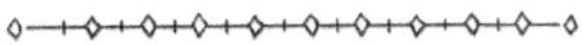

BENJAMIN BLINKED as the memory of the crow faded from his eyes. It made sense for the Elements to be there, but there were only three, which was concerning. "Hey, was there another woman with brown hair instead of blonde?"

The crow shook its head. Benjamin lifted his brows and nodded. "Wait… you step on my kitchen counter after you stepped on a dead body? Come on!"

It flapped its wings to escape, but Benjamin caught it, reaching for the tap. "You better clean up, chill!" The crow struggled for a while longer until it was certain he was only going to wet its legs. Benjamin took a sponge, adding some soap, and rubbed its feet. "I know you little bird doesn't care where you stepped, but when you are here, pay some attention." It cawed, hopefully in understanding.

After he dried the legs with a paper towel, he set the crow to the side of the sink. It jumped over the sink with a towel in its beak. Benjamin stared at it as it set the towel on the counter on the other side. "You mean I should wipe where you stood, huh? I would be, but thanks." He cleaned up the place and also his hands before he headed for the window. "Thanks a lot for letting me know. Is it time for you to go home or have fun elsewhere?"

There was no sound of its wings, he turned around. The crow stood on the jar of chicken breast, pecking at the cap. Benjamin smirked as he headed back. "Fine. You are hungry, huh?" He opened the jar and gave the crow another piece before it happily stood on his shoulder.

After he walked closer to the opened window in the living room, it flew away, doing a few turns in the air before disappearing into the darkness of the night. Benjamin let out a breath and closed the window.

Back inside his room, he stared at the whiteboard and added in the dead man. Who were the two men that killed him? Or rather, did this even have anything to do with Evelyn? The man could be just a random person.

The crow had good eyes, but he didn't know all the people in the scene. Maybe it was worth it to find out who the three were. He was about to mark on the white board when his phone rang.

It was Helen. She rarely called him, hopefully, it wasn't something urgent.

"Hello, Helen?"

"Hi. Have you heard anything about a monster just now?"

He knew, but he couldn't tell her how, so may as well pretend to not know. It was his luck that his friend saw it at all. "You expect me to be a spy master? What's that about? Zitannas always has monsters."

"Well, you aren't wrong. But I think this is different. The monster killed a man."

"So? Monsters always do that." He frowned, this wasn't the first day Helen was with the team, not even her first year, why the shock?

"If you stop interrupting, you will know quicker. Anyways, the victim had the same tattoo as those in The Orbit." Helen's voice was shaky, she seemed to be scared.

"You said what? The same tattoo? Are you sure?" Ben asked. The crow hadn't noticed it. If it didn't pay attention, there was a chance it wouldn't show in the memory.

"Well, it was on the half-bitten arm, so I only saw part of it. But I swear it was the same head of a snake and the butt of the sword. What do you think about it? Or am I thinking too much?" Helen swallowed audibly.

For Helen, the man was killed by the monsters, which he couldn't blame her. Who would kill someone in the gang? He and the King hadn't arranged that; it seemed Evelyn would want more people to kill Lia, not less. Was it for a conflict between Evelyn and the gang? Or was that just a coincidence and a third party did it? If that man was in the gang, there was a chance he had some enemies somewhere. "Tell me more?"

"When we were there, the monsters attacked us. Hm… I guess it was just the thing monsters did. I was that close to it chewing my legs off."

His heart skipped a beat. Her voice was shaky, a bit too much to his liking. He didn't need to see to know she was scared. "You are OK, right?"

"Yes, I ran away quick enough. Now that I think of it, maybe it is safer to be around you dark magicians," she chuckled.

"Come on. Don't you think our power is really endless. I don't think the King could help you grow another leg even if he was there." He let out a sigh of relief. While William was no match for the King, at least he could be helpful enough against monsters Zitannas generated.

"I will secure my leg for him to put back," she laughed.

"For now, I think it is just a coincidence that the monsters killed him. That man was unlucky to be there."

"I see. Hopefully I'm just overthinking it." She let out a soft sigh.

"You are back in your apartment?"

"Of course. No way I would call you if I was in the clan. It wouldn't end well."

"You are now scared of monsters?" he asked.

"Not really. I don't think they are that smart to take a lift."

"Was Lia there too?"

There was a long silence on the other end of the call. He was going to ask if Helen was still there when she answered. "No. William asked her to, but she refused to come. William let it slide as the time was running low."

"Because of the King?"

"I had no idea. She didn't even tell me." She let out a heavy sigh. "Somehow I think I should kick Adrian. Lia is… a bit too miserable in her state."

"I'm sorry."

"None of us can do a thing, I guess. Best of luck with working under him." Helen let out a wry chuckle.

"You stay safe. Don't get caught by William."

"Will do. Bye."

He bid her a goodbye and ended the call. His eyes

narrowed as he considered what was happening. The man's death better have nothing to do with him being one of the gang , otherwise, it would fall to the wayside even quicker than he could imagine. There were still guesses, but none of them were pleasant to even think about. With the two of the team out of the city, the cards would be stacked against them.

CHAPTER 12

HELEN

A few days later, inside the arena, Helen shot another leaf blade toward a virtual werewolf. She gasped, turning around against another monster. The strange mud and branches monster seemed to ring a bell for everyone. They had been training harder for a while after the meteorite monsters, but without some external push, sometimes it was easier to slide back to how things used to be.

She smashed through a few more monsters and her session finally ended. Part of her mind was still on the dead man they found on the beach. While it seemed to be random that one of the gang's men was killed there, she still didn't feel very comfortable about it. Maybe the body looked a bit too scary for her to shake it out of her memory. Despite Benjamin assuring her it should be fine, she didn't feel like that was the case. Yet she didn't have a reason to convince him, nor herself, other than it being a hunch.

The glass shield lowered and there came Patrick's voice. He seemed to be arguing with William. Helen headed up to the spectators' stand to get her water bottle and eavesdrop at the same time.

"Lia is skipping her training again?" Patrick scowled with his eyes narrowed.

William rubbed his temple and sighed. "I told you she finished her training early."

"You know that's not the case. Don't think I am that dumb, OK? Our training has been back-to-back since the first day I got here."

"Well, you know the meteorite monster kind of shook things up a little, especially when it comes to Lia."

"How long ago was that? She is just looking for an excuse to do nothing. She didn't even come with us the other night."

William rolled his eyes and folded his arms, his frown deepening. "I told you she wasn't feeling well."

"Maybe that's just another excuse." Patrick huffed, plunging down on the seat.

Helen took a sip of water, flicking her eyes between the two of them. "But if she really wasn't feeling well, it would be risky not only for her, but also for us. We took care of the monsters with no problem anyway."

Patrick grunted, shaking his head. "I am expecting everyone to at least carry their own weight. Lia wasn't like that before the meteorite monsters. It wasn't the first time she saw someone die. I just don't understand how big of a deal that was. It is time to move on from whatever that is stopping her."

William sighed. "I told you she's been training. Not to the extent she was before, I admit, but it seems to be the right training volume for her. You know her—when we need her to help, she'll be there."

"Whatever. You are the boss anyway." Patrick shrugged and stood, taking his phone and his bottle from the bench. "If there's nothing left to be done, I am leaving."

William nodded and Patrick walked away without bidding them a goodbye. Helen swallowed as Patrick left, let out a breath when he was out of the arena and the door was closed behind him. "Did Lia actually have her training earlier than us?"

"She did. A light one, though. She still didn't seem to be her best self. But she refused to tell me what's happening."

"Where is she now?"

"I don't know. Maybe back in her room. Maybe you should talk to her. There has to be a reason for her feeling down."

"Any guesses?" she asked, not knowing how much William knew about the dark magic. He had been looking into it, but said nothing about any findings.

"There has to be something other than the meteorite monsters and all the events happening around it. Not to mention we still haven't cracked the code of who went after her and stabbed her. Maybe that's what she's worried about."

Helen blinked. If he hadn't mentioned it, she would have almost forgotten. Since beating the gang in The Orbit, for her, it seemed the only problem on hand was to stop William from finding out Lia's power. William probably still didn't know about the gang and how Adrian already smashed it. "I think so. If they could send three against her, maybe there could be more people waiting to hunt her."

"I just wasn't expecting she would refuse to tag along with cases," he sighed, rubbing his knitted brows.

"What did you talk about that night? If you can tell me, of course."

William stared at her for a moment longer before he said, "Nothing much. I asked whether she wanted to go with us, but she refused. When I asked for the reason, she said she didn't feel right. I brought up how she was fine earlier in training. And… well, maybe you already know, she broke out crying."

"What?" Helen's heart skipped a beat; she had absolutely no idea about that. That night, she had checked that Lia was fine staying in the clan for another night before she headed back to her apartment. Lia didn't look like she'd been crying, nor did she tell Helen anything.

"She didn't tell you? Well, like I just said, she cried. I didn't have time to comfort her for long when there were monsters out there. I hope she is feeling better now." William frowned and sank his hands into his pocket.

"I guess I'll check in with her."

"Yes, please. I think she'll tell you more than she will tell me."

"Are you implying she is hiding things from you?"

"No. The two of you are friends. She probably wouldn't regard me as one." There was a wry smile on his face, but he wasn't wrong. William was more of a mentor and even their boss. She bid him a goodbye and left, messaging Lia.

Turned out Lia was in the guest room. Helen pushed the door in to find her sitting on the bed with the lights off and the blinds lowered. "Hey, Lia. Is everything OK?"

She combed her hair with her hand, patting the empty space on her side. "OK or not is relative."

Helen took a seat, giving Lia's shoulder a squeeze. "Then how is it currently?"

"Not the best. Not that bad, either." Lia shrugged, her lips pursed into a thin line. There was a tension inside her that Helen couldn't put a finger on.

"William told me you cried that night when he asked you to join us for the fight."

"He told you, huh? I don't even know why I was crying. It was a bit too scary to think about another monster. Somehow… it feels like something A would do to force me out of the clan."

Helen's heart skipped a beat; it seemed Adrian's plan on not telling Lia about the other dark magician going after her life was a smart move. That man actually knew what would be on Lia's mind. "You think he created the monsters?"

"I don't think he would, even though he pretty much despises every other living creature. But I can't stop myself from thinking that could happen. When William asked, I also worried about my power. It is… not going that well." Lia grabbed on the blanket as her gaze dropped.

"It is getting closer for you to go back."

"I think so. And I hate it," she sobbed.

"You still haven't talked to him since then?"

Lia sniffed, rubbing her eyes. "No. What's wrong with me? I… sometimes still think about him, about something more than my power."

"What's so bad about talking to him? Like, at least send a message?" Helen ached for Lia. It seemed she was really upset.

"I don't know how to feel about that. I am the one who blocked him, and now I am the one begging him to take me back to fix my power…"

"I can't say for sure, but I think he understands. That's better than if something bad really happened." Helen frowned, gently shaking Lia.

"I know. I will talk to him when I am ready. I can feel how my power is going."

CHAPTER 13

LIA

Lia walked into the arena, her eyes half open as she struggled to stifle a yawn. "Hey, Lia. How are you? You look tired," Helen asked with furrowed brows.

"I know… I can't help feeling a bit tired recently." Lia shrugged, sitting next to Helen on the bench, waiting for William and Patrick. She stared blankly into the void in front of her.

"Did you play video games overnight again?" Helen asked.

"Nah, I actually got into bed early. Around eleven if I remember correctly. I don't even know why I am still tired." Lia tore her eyes back to Helen.

It was another week of messing around in the clan, uneventful days since there was that monster, well, she didn't even join that. She was just dragging the fate of eventually having to face Adrian yet again. There was a small tingle on her side, where he touched her and healed the wound.

Helen rested the back of her hand on Lia's forehead. "Hm, you aren't sick."

"Maybe I have been playing video games too much regardless." Lia covered her mouth as she yawned. Part of her knew it probably had to do with her power, but she didn't want Helen to worry about that.

Helen didn't seem to be convinced. She leaned closer, whispering, "Think it has something to do with your power?"

She had been trying to calm her power almost daily, but there was no telling how long she could help herself. There was once she almost gave in, and since then, for the past few days, she didn't dare call it up again.

"I don't know. It could be, but hopefully not." Lia shrugged.

Helen opened her mouth to talk but was interrupted by a click of the door. Patrick and William walked in together, discussing something with smiles on their faces. Lia raised her brows; the two seemed to get along well.

"Finally, all of us are here, huh?" Patrick waved to them as they met up. He looked to be a bit too cheerful for the early morning.

"Something good happening? Look at you," Helen said, patting his shoulder.

"I learned a new skill yesterday. I'll show you soon." He crossed his arms in front of his chest with a smug smile on his face.

"Super confident, huh?" Lia chuckled. It was great he and William seemed to be on good terms.

"If any monsters dared to appear, I'm kicking them real hard." Patrick winked.

William cleared his throat. "Enough chatting. Just get things done, will you?"

As Patrick prepared for his session, Lia and Helen went up to the spectators' stand on the side. Lia yawned again, leaning into Helen.

"Are you sure you're OK?" Helen asked with a frown.

"I guess?"

"Think you need more rest?"

"I don't know. Maybe I didn't sleep well." Lia shook her head, taking a sip of water from her bottle.

Down in the field, Patrick was flinging fire balls at the virtual monsters, occasionally sending fire blasts that burned a few in one go. The session looked easy for him.

"Is my memory wrong? I don't remember Patrick being this strong," Lia nudged Helen and asked. She pressed her voice low, though the glass walls were quite good at insulating noise.

"That's because you always hide in your room. He has been much stronger since last week. He seems to be really happy about it."

"Of course he would be." Lia nodded. He had been trying to get stronger since the meteorite monsters, to an extent that he'd decided to find out the secret to Lia's power. Under Adrian's very close watch on her, Patrick didn't succeed. However, if he was getting stronger, it was for the best.

After Patrick's session, it was Lia's. Lia and Helen managed to convince William to let them handle their own sessions. William reluctantly agreed, leaving the three of them in the arena. Maybe he also wanted more time to find the dark magicians. Otherwise, there would be no way he would agree to it.

"We can pretend you got your training if you really are too tired," Helen said with concern in her eyes.

Lia shook her head, walking down to the field. "It's OK. It will be done soon."

She stood in the center of the field as Patrick and Helen went up to the balcony. The field felt bigger and more spacious than before, or maybe she was feeling smaller. She took a deep breath, bracing herself.

At least William wasn't there. Whatever happened, Helen would be on her side. Patrick probably couldn't sniff out the dark magic. She touched the kyanite necklace, its chill surface grounding her.

A few monsters began spawning from the corners of the field. Lia focused, wielding her ice razors to throw at werewolves that ran towards her. A few bat-like creatures flew in the sky, shooting fireballs from their mouths. She pulled up an ice wall, blocking off a wave of fire. As the monsters got ready for their next attack, she sent ice blasts towards them, hitting a few. One of them landed on the running werewolf, and it stumbled. At this chance, Lia shot at the werewolf, freezing it into a large block of ice.

She turned to another werewolf, sending an ice beam at it, but it leaped away. Lia growled, ducking away from its claws. It wasn't that she would actually be killed by the virtual monsters, but getting clawed would still sting, as if being shocked. She moved behind the monster, grabbing its neck.

Lia willed an ice blast in her free hand, she could already picture the large block of ice. She almost dropped the virtual monster when her hand on it felt cold. She snapped her attention from her free hand to the monster. It was already a block of ice before she took her shot.

There wasn't enough time for her confusion; the other werewolves were closing in. Lia dropped the iced monster, turning to fight the rest of them. After shooting and firing shots, finally the last of them was beaten.

Lia could barely stand as the glass shield retreated, her heart hammering in her chest. Even her vision started to blur in the corners. She barely managed to reach the bench and took a seat. She almost fell to the floor on her back. Luckily, Helen wrapped her arm behind her back quick enough. Patrick seemed to be oblivious.

Something cold and smooth touched Lia's arm. She snapped her eyes open at Helen. Whatever it was made her feel better as the dark power that was creeping up seemed to calm itself. Slowly, Lia's breath levelled and her heart stopped racing.

"Feeling better?" Helen whispered. Lia nodded. Both Helen and Patrick were looking at her with concern on their faces.

"I'm fine." Lia twisted open her bottle, gulping down the water. "Maybe I should have eaten breakfast before training."

Helen shot her a knowing look, retreating her hand back to her pocket. The coolness on Lia's arm disappeared. "I told you to get up earlier, you sleepyhead. You had me worried."

"Maybe you should grab a big lunch then. Can't work with an empty stomach." Patrick gave her a reassuring smile.

"Sure, I will take a rest. Let me know when you are done." Lia nodded to Helen and waved a goodbye to Patrick before leaving the arena.

She barely managed to get on her bed, and as soon as her head touched the pillow, she fell asleep.

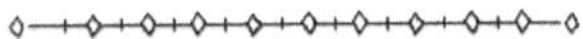

LATER, Lia stirred, her stomach rumbling. The pillow and blanket were a bit too comfy for her to get up. She squinted; from the gap of the curtains, it seemed to already be evening. How long had she been asleep? She didn't remember Helen calling her for lunch. Maybe she'd taken a nap that was too long.

As she pushed herself up, a jabbing headache hit her. She winced, rubbing her temple. Her every heartbeat sent another surge of pain into her head. She swore under her breath. Her limbs were numb and tired. Maybe she had fought a few virtual monsters in the arena, but it felt more taxing than it should be. She curled her body into a ball. The darkness in the room was strangely comforting.

Maybe it is finally the time to head back to misery?

Lia glanced at her phone. Would Adrian be mad at her? She swallowed. Maybe she'd told him off and blocked him, but they had never been together. It would be awkward. She closed her eyes, but a warmth surged through her body as she thought of him. She didn't want to, but she recalled being in his arms, feeling his warmth. It felt great to be around him. Maybe she shouldn't block him on every app and phone call.

Maybe Adrian didn't want to be friends with her, but he said he would be her mentor. He'd always kept his words and fought for her. If she went back for training, he'd still help her, right? She reached for her phone, grimaced at the bright light from the screen.

She'd already caused enough trouble by running away from her training, so maybe it was about time for her to learn. She didn't like every part of the process, but she shouldn't let people around her take the risk. She already attacked Helen and Benjamin; she didn't need another episode of that. If she killed another innocent, she would live in guilt for the rest of her life. If she attacked any of the Elders... Lia's blood froze. If Adrian was right, she would get herself killed.

It was already one in the morning. It wasn't a good

idea to call Adrian or send him a message this late. She would be asking for a favor with the training already. Maybe she shouldn't try her luck with waking him from his sleep. She would talk to him tomorrow. She could live another day.

CHAPTER 14

LIA

The next day, it was almost noon, but Lia was too tired to get up despite sleeping through the night. She kept rolling from side to side. It seemed lifting a finger was too tiring. She didn't have training scheduled, so William wouldn't know. If he didn't know, he wouldn't get suspicious.

As she slowly drifted back to her dreams, a ring from her phone cut through the tranquillity. She jumped from her sleep. Before she could see the message, Helen rushed in. "Lia, come! A new case for us!"

"I really have to go?" Lia asked. She picked herself out of the bed, despite the nausea in her stomach and her body aching. She should have at least grabbed dinner last night.

"William insisted. Patrick and Eric are out on another case. We need you. It seems to be a big deal that needs everyone, but only the three of us could make it in time. That's if you get out now!" At Lia's reluctance, Helen added, "William is one of the three of us. It should be fine."

"Isn't that what makes it not fine?"

"I don't think it would help to hide things if you don't go."

Lia took a deep breath and nodded. Maybe it was just a bad day for her; she may as well try to help to the best of her ability.

They got into William's car, speeding off and arrived at a building that was on fire. She barely stomached a protein bar in William's car before they arrived at the scene. She had never seen a fire that severe in her life. It could have been a movie scene. Flames swallowed the building's lower levels, still growing upwards. One of the sides was charred black. Thick smoke was coming out of the windows, or what was left of them. The heat radiating from the fire was warm on Lia's skin even from a distance. A few fire engines were already there, with firefighters busy gearing up.

"I'm not sure whether we should go in…" Helen said.

William said, "Come on, of course we aren't going in. I need the two of you to help from outside. Put your power to use." He pointed to a few people waving their arms frantically from the windows. All the aerial ladders were already busy, but there were more in need. Lia and Helen hurried to help while William went to talk with the firefighters.

Helen carefully hoisted herself up with her vine wrapping around her waist, getting close to the victims. Luckily, magical vines wouldn't catch the non-magical fire easily. Lia was on the lookout, shooting at burnt stuff that fell from upper floors while shielding Helen and a few firefighters on the ladders. The fire made the weather hotter than it should be, she soon drenched in sweat.

The firefighters were working quickly, running into the building and pulling out whoever they could reach, sending them to the paramedics. All fire hoses were on full force, with a helicopter overwatching the situation.

William seemed to have connections everywhere, making it possible to help in random police cases or… maybe fire cases. Lia sighed; it looked to be a tough day ahead. Whatever magic people saw, the strange force of Zitannas would push it out of their memory soon.

She wiped the sweat off her forehead while receiving a young child from a firefighter, bringing her to seek help. She was panting, looking at the firefighters in their heavy gear under the sun and the heat of the fire. She wondered whether they were human or some kind of mythical creatures. She handed the kid to the paramedics, then turned back to Helen's vine.

She created an ice wall just in time to block something that remotely resembled an air-conditioner from hitting Helen's head as she was getting hold of a woman. There was something on the woman's face that was shiny under the sun.

As Helen slowly lowered the woman with her vine, Lia grabbed her and gasped; a sharp piece of glass dug into the woman's face, reflecting the sun. She hurried to bring the woman to the ambulance so that Helen could focus on the next one. The rusty smell of blood slowly occupied Lia's senses, taking over her attention. She fought to focus on heading to the paramedics nearby, who were getting the woman settled on a stretcher. She panted as the woman was moved into an ambulance. Her heart beating a bit too strong.

Feeling lightheaded, Lia found a safe spot where she could keep an eye on Helen. William gave her a bottle of water that she downed in seconds.

"Lia, how are you doing?" he asked. Feeling Lia's forehead with the back of his hand, he frowned.

"I… I should be fine after taking a rest. Maybe it's heat stroke."

As Helen came back to the ground after helping everyone she could reach, Lia closed her eyes briefly, still breathing rapidly.

A migraine started, and she winced. The rush of her dark power crept up, going wild. She tried to stabilize herself, but she wasn't feeling in control. She squirmed, fighting her own battle.

I should have called Adrian yesterday…

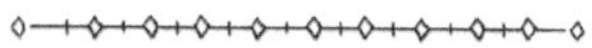

Helen

HELEN'S EYES widened at Lia's state. She would never forget how Lia jumped to attack her before; it looked a bit too close to how Lia was now. It would be at most minutes before she attacked people around her. Helen gulped audibly, reaching into her pocket and touching the cool amber there. But William was too close to Lia; there was no way he wouldn't notice.

Lia was holding her head in both of her hands, her face twisted in pain, grunting. William frowned, getting closer to her, when a loud bang came from the building. A few people screamed.

Both William and Helen jumped, looking towards the building to catch a glimpse of flame shooting out of a window, carrying a few machinery parts. Helen's breath caught, hoping no one was near the explosion. She took a few steps closer to the building and blocked the falling parts from hitting someone.

"What the hell!" William's shout jerked Helen's eyes to him.

Lia was missing.

Eyes wide and mouth agape, Helen rushed towards William. They looked around, but there was no sign of Lia. He turned and grabbed Helen's shoulder. "You saw what happened?" he was almost screaming. Helen shook her head.

"Dammit!" William released her and rushed to people nearby.

Helen froze, her mind blank. Her eyes followed William. She couldn't hear what he was saying, but everyone he spoke to shook their heads. Her stomach sank. Tears welled up in her eyes, she walked across the street and leaned on a lamp post, blinking back her tears.

Where is Lia?

CHAPTER 15

HELEN

Helen had no idea how long she had been leaning on the lamp post, but it felt like ages. All her strength seemed to have left. She mindlessly toyed with the piece of amber in her pocket. Adrian would be very mad.

I'm sorry… Don't haunt me at night, please?

She let out a heavy sigh, staring at the firefighters still busy running in and out the burning building. The fire was still going on but there was no one seeking help by the window, hopefully all of them already safe. If there's no one she could reach from the outside, then there wasn't anything else she could do.

She thought about searching for Lia, but it felt futile. Lia was too weak to be hanging around on her own; if someone took her, they would've left already.

A while later, William ran to her with a deep frown on his face. "We've got to go. We will search the surrounding area; maybe there are traces of Lia's disappearance. Whoever dared touch her will soon be very dead."

Helen nodded, gathering her strength to follow William. They ran through the streets around the building, looking at every inch of the area, trying to find a hint of what happened.

When they stopped briefly for a rest and to take a few sips of water, Helen's mind turned at full speed, trying to figure out what happened.

Did Adrian not say someone other than the gang is after Lia? Dammit… They will kill her in no time…

Helen's heart hammered in her chest. Although she really wanted to find Lia in one of the alleys, her hunch was now even stronger, suggesting otherwise. Their search would end up with nothing.

William was very tense, tapping his feet on the ground. His arms crossed. She could almost hear the gears turning in his head.

"What do you think happened to Lia? Where could she be?" Helen asked.

"I wonder… I have different guesses, but none seems to best fit what happened. I used to think whoever is after Lia wanted her to die, seeing both times, the killers were sent for her life. They seemed to show no attempt in capturing her. But there's no saying they must keep doing what they have done.

"I am leaning towards the dark magicians. I am pretty certain they are lurking somewhere. But I don't know whether it means there are two different groups of people after Lia's life or not. They may be connected to those who tried to kill her. From what I know, they will go to whatever length necessary to see their evil goal fulfilled.

"Maybe we can stop searching. If Lia is captured, and if it was them, they probably won't leave any traces. I have my fair share of experience with them. Whoever did it is very skilled." He sighed, running his fingers along his hair.

Helen gulped, William seemed to already know a lot. "Why would they want to catch Lia?"

"If it is the dark magicians, probably for her power. They seem to have an obsession to capture or to control magicians for their power. Lia would be a good target for them. She has the power and the potential, but she has yet trained up her combat magic, making her an easy target."

"What would they do to her?"

William shook his head, wincing. "Nothing good. They had their ways of torturing their prey. Back in the day, some of us that were captured by them... Either they failed to treat a dead body well or they wanted us to see it. The bodies were... something you will never want to see for yourself. I hope Lia isn't in their hands..."

But I hope Lia is in Adrian's hands. If she wasn't, it could only be worse. Adrian wouldn't hurt her. What happened between William, the Elements, and the dark magicians?

Maybe it was another gangster from The Orbit looking for revenge. They had been going after Lia. The thought sent a chill down her spine.

Please be safe, Lia...

CHAPTER 16

BENJAMIN

Hours ago, Benjamin had stopped in the closest alley he could use to hide himself from William's eyes. The crow told him that Lia was out there with her team. Maybe it was his little dream, but he wanted to tell Lia how Adrian had been recently. It wasn't fair to her for him to push her to talk to Adrian, but for his King, he would try.

The fire on the building was crazy. Even at a distance, the heat made the spring feel like summer, and even the extra moisture in the air didn't seem to help.

As he watched Lia and Helen protecting victims, he raised his brows with his arms crossed. The fire seemed to be nothing special. There could only be two reasons for William to take this case: either the fire was indeed special, or he was running low on cash. After the meteorite monsters, there seemed to be few ways for the Elements to make money.

He leaned against the wall, watching the team and the firefighters in action. Lia looked to be fine as she shot at debris. That woman looked strong and very capable despite some time away from her training. Benjamin sighed. He saw why Adrian would like her, but still there's no telling why he wouldn't let her know. When he knew Lia was out of the clan, he called Adrian, but no one picked up.

Lia received a woman from Helen's vine, shouting for the paramedics and settling her on a stretcher. Then Lia was walking away from the scene. The fire was still burning —where was she going? She stumbled to sit. William walked to her side, handing her a bottle of water. She downed it, panting.

There was the smell of dark magic in the air. Crap! Lia…

William was right there by her side. Benjamin's heart skipped a beat. Lia was shaking, holding her head. The chance of the power overwhelming her was too high for him to bet his luck. He didn't come to just look at her. If he didn't get her out safely, the King would tear him into pieces. Hell, where even was Adrian?

Helen was walking towards Lia as she reached for her pocket. William tensed, almost lifting his hand towards Lia. Benjamin flicked his eyes to the burning building. He mouthed a *sorry* to whoever that may still be inside the fire. He narrowed his eyes, focusing his magic into the building. He clenched a fist, cracking the nearest window. At least he was still in range with the psychic force. There was a loud bang of things breaking.

As Helen and William spun around, Benjamin jumped out of the alley with only a split second in his hands. He focused, connecting himself to the power field of Zitannas. *Please work!* he chanted, warping the memories around him as he dashed towards Lia. He grabbed her on the waist with one arm and lifted her under the knees with the other. She was hot like melting iron in his hands. His heart raced as he made his way back to the alley. He was drenched in sweat, the power inside him draining as he fought to delay William and Helen's senses.

It didn't help that Lia seemed to be immune from the memory warp trick. She seemed to know half of what was happening. She struggled as her hands wrapped around his throat. The choking and nausea hit him. He grunted, quickly draining Lia's power. Dammit, she was strong. He barely ducked into the alley before he heard William's shout.

"What the hell?"

Benjamin's heart almost jumped out of his chest. There didn't seem to be footsteps coming his way though. Hopefully, his magic was enough to deter them. He kept running back to his car by the other side of the alley. Lia was limp, her face buried in his chest as he held her tight.

He looked around, slowing his steps as he left the alley. There were people around, he better not look like a kidnapper. The fire seemed a world away, but William and Helen would be searching around soon. He opened the door of his car, putting Lia to the back seat. He hurried to get behind the wheel and started the car. He was drenched in sweat, panting from the rescue. At least when he pulled into the street, no one seemed to be paying attention.

Now that he was a bit at ease, a monster-like headache almost caused him to run the red light. He rubbed his temple, wincing as he hunched over the steering wheel. It was crazy how strong Lia had become. His throat tightened as her power seemed to be tearing at his organs and blurring his vision. No way he could drive. Where was Adrian? Benjamin slammed at his phone, the dialling seemed to go on for an eternity.

The cars behind him were honking. He took in a shaky breath. He had to get as far away as he could. He forced himself to sit up straight. Lia was in the backseat, unmoving. *You better keep the King happy, or else... Well, Adrian should be the one I am blaming...*

He steeled himself, starting the car again. His phone finally clicked and Adrian's sleepy voice answered. "Ben...?"

"What the hell are you doing! Before I crash the car with your precious girl inside, do something!" Benjamin shouted. It was absolutely not a good idea to drive when the pain was threatening to swallow him and his arms were a bit too numb to lift, not helpful to add in the shout.

"Lia? Gosh!" There was scrambling from the other end of the phone and Adrian finally sounded awake.

The pain in Benjamin's body slowly eased as if the boots that stomped on his chest lifted. He gasped, his lungs finally seeming to work. His vision cleared and driving became easy again. If he had failed to wake Adrian, Lia's power could have already killed him. He shivered at the thought.

"Ben... What's happening? You are with Lia?" Adrian asked, his voice trembling.

Benjamin nodded, despite Adrian wouldn't see him. He flicked his eyes to the back seat. Lia was still lying motionless. He wanted to stop and check on her, but they were on a highway. There was nothing he could do to help until the King was around. Benjamin cursed himself under his breath. Why didn't he try to make Adrian tell him more about the dark magic? "Well, when you are still a pile of drunk mess, the Elements were out fighting a fire. Lia could've died with William finding out her power."

"Dammit... is she still alive now?" Adrian swallowed audibly.

"Alive, yes, but unconscious. I am heading to the den. I think she needs more help than your office could give." Benjamin pinched the bridge of his nose. Lia didn't even stir from the two of them chatting hand-free on the call.

"I will be there as soon as I can." There was a low thud from that side of the phone, accompanied by Adrian's yelp.

Benjamin chuckled, shaking his head. "Turn on the light before you stub your poor toes again."

Adrian muttered under his breath before cutting the call.

Poor Lia had to suffer all these without any help. If only Adrian wasn't that avoidant of his feelings, and would actually care more about her. Or if only he knew how to help her more, just so she wouldn't be in such a misery.

There was now no turning back. William saw Lia struggling. Maybe he had felt dark magic there. William wasn't smart, but he wasn't that dumb either. She could no longer go back as if nothing happened. Benjamin swallowed, his throat burning. Would this push Adrian to finally make a decision?

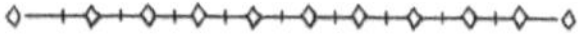

BENJAMIN GRABBED Lia as he arrived near the den. It was in a remote countryside, safely away from the rest of the busy city, with a five-minute walk to the entrance. He peeked at the road through the thicker forest to make sure no one was following them. He lifted Lia, she didn't move a bit. She better still be living, otherwise, he may as well die in a car crash than to be facing a mad Adrian. There's no sign of Adrian's car, he probably was still on the road. Anyways, he knew where to bring Lia.

Kicking open the hidden door to the den, he carefully made his way in with Lia in his arms. He squinted as his eyes grew to accommodate the dim corridor of the den. He was walking down the stairs into the den when Lia came out of her slump. Her eyes snapped open, glowing bright red. Benjamin's breath caught, and before he could drop her, she screamed like a fierce beast, snatching for his throat. He jerked back—his throat was spared, but she'd gotten his shoulder.

With deadly force, she twisted his arm off its socket, her nails digging deep into him and leaving his arm numb. Benjamin gritted his teeth, biting down a scream. He shoved Lia away with his other arm. He winced, she probably tore a few tendons. He willed his arm to move, but it didn't move an inch but shouting pain. It dangled at his side, the air knocked out of him.

Lia got up from the floor, her eyes still red as ice began to form in her hands when a shadow from his back pushed him to the side, pinning Lia to the wall behind her. He bumped into the wall and slipped down to the floor. Lia's eyes soon dimmed as she slumped onto the floor as well.

"Sorry I'm late." Adrian turned around. Benjamin never expected to feel such relief. Adrian hurried to his side, checking on his poor arm. Benajmin didn't feel a thing under Adrian's hand.

"Will it still work?" Benjamin grimaced. He had no idea how he'd stay alive with one arm.

Adrian chuckled as he rubbed Benjamin's arm, reaching towards his shoulder, but none of the touch registered in Benjamin's mind, probably still drowned by the immense pain. Adrian pinched the socket of Benjamin's shoulder. It shot another surge of pain, he barely held back a sob.

"You think I am out of tricks, huh?" Adrian rested both of his hands on Benjamin's shoulder. The pain made it hard to know where the hands were if he wasn't watching with his eyes wide with fear.

A strong and hot stream channelled through Benjamin's body, spreading to every part of him. Another pain lit inside him, he gritted his teeth, willing it to end. Eventually, the pain slowly left with a few popping sounds from his shoulder, a scratching noise, and jolts of electricity near the joint. It was still a bit too intense to keep his face straight. Hopefully, Adrian knew what he was doing.

He flicked his eyes to Lia as Adrian was busy healing his injury. She was lying by the wall with her eyes closed. His instinct shouted at him to get further away from her in case she launched at him again, but he shook his head. It wasn't Lia; it was her power.

After a minute, Adrian straightened, gently patting Benjamin's shoulder. "Feeling good?"

He wriggled his fingers and lifted his arm. Happy tears escaped him as he could finally move it. Stupid for him to take that as granted before. He let out a heavy sigh of relief, letting himself slump on to the wall behind. "Gosh! I thought I lost my poor arm."

Adrian winced, rubbing his temple, but he chuckled. "I'm not letting that happen anytime soon. She is fierce, right?" He glanced at Lia with a glint of sadness in his eyes.

Benjamin sat up, following Adrian's gaze. "I'm blaming that on you. You're the one leaving your girl unattended."

Adrian huffed. "I… She is not my girl."

"How about before she tears off my other arm, we get her settled first?" He carefully stood, holding on to the wall. His injured arm felt fine from Adrian's magic, but he didn't want the risk of hurting it that soon with his own weight.

"Sure." Adrian stood and reached for Lia. He leaned

down to her, wrapping his arm around her. He grimaced, a sob escaped him before he lifted her. His brows knitted.

Benjamin asked, "Is it bad?"

Adrian's voice was trembling. "Yes. I don't even know whether she'll wake up or not…"

CHAPTER 17

HELEN

"Is this really necessary?" Helen asked, shifting slightly in her seat. It was the day after Lia disappeared. Helen had just finished training and she and Patrick were in the arena with Eric sitting opposite to them. A deafening silence and a sense of emptiness lingered in the large space.

"It is William and my decision. We have no idea what happened to Lia. She's been attacked twice, and now she vanished before William's eyes. We worry whoever kidnapped her is after magicians and will probably target you down the road." Eric scratched the back of his neck, sighing heavily.

"But we aren't children. You don't have to follow us everywhere," Patrick said.

Helen struggled to resist a smile as she pictured William and Patrick walking on the street side by side when Patrick was on his way to shop for rock music albums. Neither of them was going to like this idea at all.

Eric said, "Do you think we have too much time on our hands? Before we know what is happening, we have to be careful. It would be better for you to stay here and stop going out. We cast a magic here, so that if someone tries to get in, it will alarm us. Especially anything magical."

"Shouldn't there have been something like that before?" Helen asked.

"Basic surveillance, yes; instant notification, no. We don't have the time to dig through footage when there haven't been any threats."

Helen said, "Would we trigger the magic?"

"No, but please don't sneak out because of that. Just stay here until we figure things out, OK?" Eric fumbled with his hair. "If even William couldn't sense anything, whoever captured Lia is very strong, or at least very fast. Don't take that risk."

Helen stared at the ground, rubbing her feet together. She had been trying to reach Lia through text to no avail. Although if she was captured by someone, she probably wouldn't have access to her phone anyway. They hadn't even been delivered.

Yesterday was extremely tough for Helen. She had been walking with her heart elsewhere since Lia disappeared. As she and William headed back to his car, she almost bumped into a lamp post and people a few times. She could hardly buckle the seat belt; her hands were shaking too much.

Back in the clan, William dismissed her from the rest of her training and cases that day, telling her to get some rest. She could barely register what was said. After she made it back to another guest room, she collapsed onto the bed, crying. She clenched the cover tightly, gritting her teeth. She should've been looking at Lia, not checking out the stupid explosion, then at least she would have seen who kidnapped her.

Maybe Lia felt the same when she was in the hospital

after getting chewed on by the meteorite monsters. Helen sighed; there seemed to be no way to stop bad things from happening.

She woke up to Patrick knocking on the door, letting her know dinner was ready but she had no appetite at all. She refused dinner and curled back up into a ball on the bed. What would happen if whoever was in charge of the gang got Lia? What were they doing to her? Was she already dead?

Her breath caught at the thought. Adrian would be very mad at her. Maybe it wasn't that bad an idea to stay in the clan. Glad she didn't reach out to him yet. He may not already know. If she found Lia before him, maybe it would work out. But that was Adrian after all…

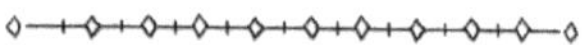

"…Are you listening? Helen?"

Helen snapped her head up at Eric's voice. Both Patrick and Eric were looking at her with concerned looks. "Sorry, I was thinking about other things…"

Eric sighed, patting her shoulder. "That's OK, I know it's hard. We are digging through surveillance cameras from buildings and cars nearby, hoping one of them caught what happened. Hopefully, we will find her soon."

Helen sank her hands into the pocket of her tracksuit pants. She flinched at the touch of the piece of amber Adrian gave her. The coolness of it sent a shiver down her spine.

Right. I have an angry devil waiting somewhere to chop my head off…

Patrick and Eric were still talking about something, but she stopped listening.

"So that's it, I guess. You stay here until we know what happened. Let us know if you really have to go outside." Eric nodded to both of them. Helen stood at once and excused herself.

CHAPTER 18

ADRIAN

It was cold inside the dungeon. Adrian sat on the floor, staring at Lia. Her wrists and ankles were clasped in metal chains, though she couldn't do much. She still hadn't opened her eyes. She was pale, and her hair lost its shimmer. The faint rise and fall of her chest was the only sign she was not dead. There was a glint on the chain from the light. He swallowed, shivering from the cold.

His vision blurred as a new surge of tears welled up in his eyes. What was he thinking to leave her alone? Why the hell did he let the walls of the clan stop him? He should've reached out to her earlier. It was his fault again. He knew Lia wouldn't last with her power for long. He knew it would only get worse when she got stronger. He did nothing. Why must he be such a jerk to her? If only she would fight the chains and chew him alive, that would be better than her tied up, lifeless. Gosh, he missed those brown eyes so much.

There was a click at the door, he didn't turn to look. He curled into a ball, wishing to disappear from the world. If only it was him tied up there, taking Lia's place. The footsteps became louder as they approached him. The numb pain tugged at him, every heartbeat was a torture in itself.

"King, at least eat something?" Benjamin sat beside him, his voice gentle yet filled with worry.

Adrian shook his head. He wasn't hungry; he couldn't think of anything other than Lia. What if she didn't wake up? Benjamin drained her power once that day and he needed to do it again to save Benjamin. No way her power was that strong.

He couldn't even figure out why she could go rampant in that short of a time frame. Dammit… Why didn't he try to know more about his magic? Why was he satisfied with not dying from it and only knowing a trick or two? He shouldn't expect to never meet another origin like himself. He gasped, the pain inside him hard to bear.

Benjamin nudged him. Adrian wanted to shove him away, but he was too tired to lift his arms. Why was he not dead? He'd gladly take Lia's place, if only…

"King… I know it's hard, but going without food for days is not good for you."

I'm still alive and that's not good for anyone. Adrian flicked his eyes to the paper bag in Benjamin's hand, carrying the faint scent of tacos through the air. *Lia likes tacos so much…* He shook his head. *Crap… This isn't at all helping.* Benjamin reached for his shoulder, but he slapped his hand away. "Can you back the hell off? I don't have time for you!" His voice cracked as tears bubbled inside him again. He sure was like a pile of mess.

Benjamin stared at him, his eyes filled with concern. Adrian growled. "Get out of here!" He wasn't a weak kitty face down in a gully on a rainy day with its coat soaked.

"Difficult days, huh?" Benjamin set down the paper bag, but he wasn't leaving.

Is this a joke?

"King. I know it is the case when you're not even drinking." Benjamin turned the can of beer in his hand, the can Adrian brought the first night Lia went down. He should've finished it that night, but he was in no mood to drink when he saw her there. It remained untouched in the past whatever days.

"Whether I've touched it or not has nothing to do with you," Adrian snapped, launching at Benjamin and aiming for his throat.

Benjamin made no attempt to duck away, just setting the can down as Adrian tackled him onto the floor, straddling him and wrapping his hands around Benjamin's throat.

What was he doing? He said he would do better than hurting his people again.

Benjamin was almost the only one left that would still bear with him. No... he was the only one. Lia already decided to cut ties with him. When she woke up, she would run for her life. Hopefully, far enough that even Evelyn wouldn't find her. The other two on his team... He couldn't even contact them. The remaining one on his team wouldn't pick his side.

Maybe he couldn't afford to lose Benjamin. He let go of him, collapsing back to his place by the wall. He let out a wry chuckle as a few tears fell down his cheek. Still, just because he had no choice... Just like his team had no choice but to bear with him. This was messed up.

"Adrian... What's on your mind? Will it help if you talk about it?" Benjamin sat up.

Would there be anything that could help? Hell, he didn't even know how long he had been sitting in the same place, nor did he have any idea how long Lia had been out.

Everything blurred in his mind. He remained in silence for who knew how long.

Adrian ran his hand over his face, wiping away the stray tear. "When she was suffering, where the heck was I? I said I would help her and that I would protect her, but where on earth was I? I was just a pile of drunk trash while you were risking your life to save her." He slapped his palm over his eyes, lacking the strength to sit up straight. Benjamin said nothing, so Adrian went on.

"It was so stupid. When Ariel was killed, I, for the love of whatever was standing far far away like a useless jerk. And I had the guts to say I would get revenge for her. When Lia was on the brink of death, I wasn't even in the damn scene… What the hell was I even thinking!" He gasped, shaking his head. The pain in his chest swallowed him as a sob escaped his throat. "It… It seems I am just here crying all the time. It is tiring. How useless can a jerk like me be?"

Benjamin pulled him into a tight embrace, helping him to sit back up.

Adrian flinched. He just tried to strangle Benjamin, what was he doing? He let out a heavy sigh, letting Benjamin hold him. What had he done to deserve someone that was still by his side? All he did was bring everyone misery.

After Adrian seemed to be able to hold his tears, Benjamin patted him and pulled away. "If you know it, I know you will try to help her." Benjamin seemed a bit too calm. He should be angry instead.

"Whether I will or not is not important. The thing is that I did nothing."

"Well, you didn't know what was happening."

"And that is the problem. I could've put in more effort. I did nothing." It was painful to even say it out loud, why was he such a useless pile of mess when it came to people he cared about?

Benjamin let out a heavy sigh and looked towards Lia. Adrian followed his gaze, though it shattered him into pieces every time he saw her in that state. It didn't help to know it was because of him.

"She is a kind woman," Benjamin said.

"Yeah… I don't even know what she sees in me. If she didn't make it this hard, it would be easier for both of us."

"What the heck are you talking about?" Benjamin glared at him, the intensity chilling Adrian's blood to ice. "You keep pushing her away and it is her problem?"

"Is it not? If she didn't try to make something happen, she wouldn't end up here." Adrian pointed towards Lia, his throat tight. His hand soon dropped. "I mean… it is impossible. Things I've done. As soon as she knows, she'll leave."

"If you really want her to leave, why don't you just tell her?" Benjamin stared daggers at him.

Adrian shivered. *But I… I am so sorry, Lia…*

Benjamin shoved him in the chest. "Let me tell you what you're doing. You're waiting for Lia to die so that you can go cry about her, like you cried for Ariel. I think I already told you this. You are just pretending to be the victim all the time. I don't care what you think. This is what you are doing. Hell, maybe you are the one setting Ariel up to die and for you to mourn. You sure love to torture yourself and make everyone feel sorry for you, huh? It sure is easier to just lie around and cry than to actually fight for her and help her, huh?"

Adrian's heart skipped a beat. He wanted to argue, but nothing came out of his mouth. Was Benjamin accusing him of killing Ariel? Well, Ariel did die because of him, so that probably counted? It felt like a hand grabbed his throat, while something stomped onto his chest until he broke into pieces. He shook his head frantically, burying himself between his arms. "No… I'm not doing that. No!"

Benjamin stood, towering over him. He pointed to Lia. "You go and say that to her face. You said you would take care of her, but when things got hard, all you did was run away. And you have the audacity to push her to fight the monster as if you are the Almighty. I have had enough with you torturing her and trying to get her killed at every corner. It's OK if you're still in denial, if you never admit your feelings for her and you keep waiting for her to die. I don't care what you think. I am taking her under my wing instead. I know I can't help her with her power like you can, but I would rather die trying. At least I'll know I tried my best. Not like you."

Adrian remained frozen. His gut twitched. Did Benjamin also feel something for her? He sure wanted to love Lia, to be with her, but he was a devil. What would happen to her if she knew…? Well, she was already in this state because of him, maybe it couldn't get worse. "Ben… Do you feel something for her?"

Benjamin snorted a humorless laugh. "No. I've told you this countless times. Not romantically. But I sure want her as a friend. And I for sure am bored and annoyed with how you are treating her. Who knows whether or not I will fall for her later."

Adrian turned back to stare at the cold hard floor. "I have my reasons."

"Spill. They better be good enough to warrant Lia almost dying," Benjamin growled, grabbing Adrian's collar.

Ariel's face flashed in Adrian's mind and a surge of sadness swarmed him yet again. "I… what kind of man would I be if I just walked away from Ariel to love someone else? I already betrayed her, letting her get burned by the Elements. Hell, am I now wanting to go for someone else? If it wasn't for you all, I don't even want to be here, breathing and causing all the mess."

Benjamin's gaze softened. He let out a heavy sigh, letting go of Adrian. "I thought after all these years, you would have allowed yourself to move on. I thought we talked about it a while ago."

"Don't pretend you understand! I can never move on. How do people even move on? It was my fault she's dead. Do you even know how much she sacrificed for me before she was killed? There's no way I could let her go. There's no way I can just go and fall for another girl like Ariel was never in my life." A sob escaped him. Adrian bit the inside of his mouth, willing the tears to stop. He flinched when Benjamin laid hand on his back.

"I am sorry we haven't invented a time machine."

Adrian snapped his head up, glaring. Was Benjamin mocking him? He meant it when he said he was upset - how could Benjamin say this to him? Ariel was his everything, how could Benjamin—He almost jumped for his throat when he gestured to Lia.

"My King, it is always your choice. Are you going to live in a past you can't change and risk Lia dying, too? Or are you going to let the past go and try to not also lose your future. I'm grateful you haven't killed yourself because of us. But look, maybe you pissed Lia off, but she deserves to know how you feel. No random guy fights a blood thirsty gang for someone he doesn't care about. And no one would break the pact for someone he doesn't care about. Before Lia slips out of your life, do something."

"I told you I was just trying to make a deal, not fall in love with her. Everything is just for the deal."

"You've barely mentioned it once with her. I don't even think you were still even trying. Stop fooling yourself."

"It sure sounds easy, huh?" Adrian let out a wry chuckle, shaking his head.

Benjamin patted his shoulder again. "I'm not saying you should act like Ariel never existed. I've told you before: you can feel sad and grateful for Ariel at the same time. Maybe I am evil to say this, but Ariel's long gone. She would want you to be happy, and you know it."

Adrian let out a heavy sigh. Ariel was the most joyful and caring person he'd ever met. She would brighten everyone's day. Without her, his world had already crumbled into chaos and dust. "You don't know that. What if Ariel didn't think that?"

"Then she is mean to you. If you died instead of her, would you want her to cry about you for the coming centuries, or would you want her to find someone she loves and live happily? She would be happy with someone who truly cares about her and would accept her past, like it is the thing none of us could change." Benjamin scowled, gently shaking Adrian's shoulder as if he was trying to shake some sense into him.

Adrian stared at him. He hated that Benjamin was right. He wouldn't even have a problem if Ariel forgot about him, as long as she was happy. He swallowed. "Still… what if Lia wouldn't accept it? What if she hates that I still think of another woman at times?"

Benjamin groaned. "Gosh, how are you this dumb when it comes to relationships? Can you figure out what's your problem and what's someone else's problem? If she doesn't even allow you to think about Ariel at times, that's her problem. And you don't know what she thinks. You go ask her."

Would it be that easy? What if Lia was still mad at

him? Before he could say something, Benjamin glared at him. "Lia is already in a coma. I think it's a good time for you to think about it. Would you prefer a world without her instead? Look at you. You've eaten nothing and you've drunk nothing for days. I doubt you could live with the fact that you killed her. If you think Ariel dying is your fault, Lia's death would be ten times your fault."

Adrian looked to Lia. Her eyes were still closed, the vital power from her almost undetectable. Even him shouting at Benjamin and their fight didn't wake her. Since Lia showed up in his life, things did seem to be better. At least that was the case before he remembered how much a devil he was and how he owed Ariel.

He closed his eyes, letting quiet tears fall. He could still recall how it felt with Lia in his arms and how her lips felt. He would give everything if it meant she would come out of the coma. Maybe he should at least try, right? At least he should tell her, even if she would just push him away. At least he could face himself.

If he had the guts to push Lia to keep fighting the monster, he probably should kick himself in the pants to try to fight himself. It was just asking Lia a question or two, no way he couldn't do it. He flicked his eyes to Benjamin, who was staring at her. "Hey, Ben…?"

Benjamin turned to him, raising his brows. Despite his hammering heart, Adrian asked, "Do you think I can really ask her about Ariel? Would she be angry?"

"I thought we've established that Lia had a kind heart, and she is the one that can manage your temper. You are softer than a barbecued marshmallow when she is around. Look at you. You've never even dropped a tear in front of me nor anyone else before she appeared in your life." Benjamin smirked, strangely Adrian didn't feel bad looking at that.

"Is that a good thing?" He was supposed to be a devil —always cowering in the corner wasn't the right thing to do.

"Well, you have to let yourself feel and process things. Crying isn't bad," Benjamin said, rubbing Adrian's back.

"I hope you're right." Adrian let out a heavy sigh. It ached to see Lia still tied up. The den was located where Zitannas' power was the strongest, which was very tasty for a dark magician like him. They could only hope that Lia would also benefit from it. There was a warm stir in his stomach that felt great, but it wasn't from any magic.

"You know I'm always right. And King, thank you. I am so honored to be the one you decided to talk to." Benjamin grinned like the smug little jerk he was.

Adrian chuckled, shaking his head. "Don't let it get to your head. And don't you dare tell others." Maybe it was better than keeping it buried inside him.

Benjamin gestured to zip his mouth. "No soul will know, not even from my dead body. Rest assured." He picked up the paper bag, handing it to Adrian. "Well, before it gets cold, eat something. When Lia wakes up, I don't want her to see you a mess."

The mention of Lia tugged at Adrian's heart, but he smiled back regardless. He took the paper bag. "Thanks, Ben. I owe you again for Lia's life. You should also know I truly appreciate you, despite how I always lash out at you. I really need to control my temper." He unwrapped the still-warm beef taco.

"Right, otherwise you would be like the other royal snobs." Benjamin chuckled, throwing a chip into his mouth.

Adrian rolled his eyes, swallowing the spicy taco. His stomach rumbled, reminding him how long he had gone without any food in his system. The food soon disappeared, with Benjamin stealing some nacho for himself.

"Are you going to a bed or are you still sleeping here?" Benjamin asked after they sat for another while.

Adrian rubbed his temple. He had no idea how much time had passed; the dungeon without a clock nor the sun didn't help with the sense of time. "Maybe later. I still want to…" His eyes flicked to Lia, although she probably wouldn't wake up even if he would stay for another day.

"OK, you take good care of yourself." Benjamin smacked him in the shoulder, waving a goodbye and left with the trash in his hand.

After the door clicked closed, Adrian stood and walked up to Lia. She was pale, her face still, as if time had stopped on her. His breath rugged, it pained him to see her unconscious. His hand shook as he stopped himself from caressing her cheek, it felt wrong. He took in a deep breath, taking in her scent. His heart skipped a beat. He wanted to hug her, but maybe she didn't want it, especially when she was fast asleep.

Her power was weak. It may have gotten better, or maybe it was just his deceptive wish. He leaned back on the wall and closed his eyes.

Lia… Would you grant me the chance to tell you how I feel?

CHAPTER 19

HELEN

A few days after Helen was instructed to stay in the clan, William called her to his office. Helen walked inside, hoping there was good news about Lia, but he looked even more stressed than before. His t-shirt was wrinkled, his hair was messed up, and the smell of coffee in the room was suffocating. His office was still perfectly tidy, despite a large pile of documents on his desk. He looked up as she closed the door behind her and smiled wryly. "Good that you are here. Look at this." He turned the screen of his computer to Helen, gesturing for her to take a seat across him.

There was a video on the screen from a car parked near the burning building. Lia and William showed up in the frame. Helen resisted the urge to run away, not wanting to relive what happened.

The event of the day played before Helen's eyes again. Lia hunched down, holding her head. From the distance of the car camera, she could still feel Lia's struggle and pain.

In the video, Helen was walking towards Lia and William when there was an explosion. She ran off to block the burning objects and William briefly looked at the explosion. Then the video blurred, as if the camera was knocked off. When it finally cleared, William grabbed Helen's shoulder. Lia was already gone.

Helen's eyes widened in shock, she flicked her eyes toward William. He shook his head. "If this is a coincidence, I count myself unlucky. But every video I managed to get is… affected in the same way."

He proceeded to show a few more clips, some obtained from shops nearby and some from cars. Despite the different angles, in every video, shortly before Lia disappeared, every file was corrupted in almost identical ways.

She stared at William. "How come…?"

"I wish I knew. Now that I think about it, it can only be the dark magicians. I don't remember any of our magic being able to cause this kind of effect. Hell, I don't even know what that was." He rubbed his temple as if torn in thoughts.

"So what are we going to do? Do you know where Lia is?"

"Sadly, no… While I believe the dark magicians are around, I have no idea where they are hiding. They are very good at that: both hiding their physical location and their magical power."

"Oh…" *I don't even know if this means good news or not. If Lia was with Adrian, he probably won't come after my head.*

"But I think if we get close enough, we can certainly find out something. I guess there's no choice but to cruise around the city in depth." His eyes narrowed in determination, clenching his fist.

"You mean going through every spot in the city? That would take a long time we likely don't have." Helen frowned. While she wanted to keep Lia safe, this didn't sound like a good plan.

"I have a list of places that are possible for them to hide. Places I don't have an eye on yet."

"What do you mean 'have an eye on'?"

"We aren't the only magicians. Maybe I've never told you explicitly, but I think you already know. Not all magicians work here. Actually, most of them work in different places, just like the non-magic people. Their power isn't as strong as ours. They didn't report anything strange. So we are going other places."

I knew it. Mike can't be the only magician not working in the clan with us. Being a police officer must be handy with William's cases. Adrian now seemed to be even better at hiding than I expected.

"Good to know. When should we start?" she asked.

"Now. Let's go." William stood and turned off his computer, tidying up the documents on his desk. He handed her a piece of paper with a few locations on it, none of which looked familiar to her.

"Can I get into the right clothes first? See you in the parking lot in ten minutes?" Helen asked, looking down at her slippers. When William insisted she and Patrick stay inside the clan, it was a bit easier to be in slippers when there was no training planned.

"Sure, I will wait for you there."

She quickly went back to her room, needing some space to process what was happening. She still had no idea where Lia was. If she really was with the dark magicians, why hadn't Adrian let her know? But rather than asking him now, it seemed the priority was to help him stay under William's radar. She didn't know how much William already knew. From the length of the list of places, he didn't know much. But he could find out more in any minute. With her hands shaking, she pulled her phone, but then she remembered her messages to Lia weren't even delivering. She thought of letting Adrian know, but she wasn't sure whether he knew Lia had gone missing. If Lia wasn't with him, she would be telling him to hunt her down. She stuffed her phone back into her pocket.

After Helen changed, she headed to the parking lot. She took in the fresh air. Feeling the warm sun after a few days getting stuck in the clan felt great. She didn't realise how much she enjoyed being outside before.

William was standing beside his car, staring at the ground with his arms folded over his chest as if deep in thought. When Helen walked up to him, he snapped his head up. He pulled open the car door and the two of them settled. The car hummed to life, bringing them to the first location on the list.

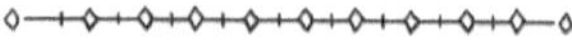

THEY ARRIVED at a luxurious looking restaurant. Helen stared at the well-embellished entrance from the car, then at herself. *Em… William should have told me what type of places we were going to.*

William looked to be comfortable in his jeans and a random shirt. He got out of the car, looking over the restaurant. Helen stood beside him. "It seems they aren't open yet. We are too early."

William nodded faintly. "It is fine. Can you try to feel the magical power here? It doesn't fade easily. If they've been here in the last few days, we'll know. The dark magic feels different. It lacks the kind of tranquillity our magic has, there's always something in it that feels dangerous. And maybe your hunch could help."

She stared at the building in front of her, her mind moving back to her time with Adrian. Their first encounter was nothing tranquil; he was menacing and almost killed her. The magical power from him was frightening. But once Lia stepped in, being around him was bearable. It seemed he could contain his power very well.

Helen frowned - he didn't give off the kind of feeling that was different from Lia in terms of magical power.

"Feel anything?" William asked. She shook her head.

"Nothing special. This place doesn't feel important." She sighed to herself. Her body felt numb since Lia had disappeared. The amber was still in her pocket, reminding her of how Adrian would be on her back and how she failed to help Lia. Hopefully her hunch was still working.

"Let's head elsewhere, then," William sighed, getting back into the car.

"You really think we can find Lia by going to all these places? Zitannas is a large city." Helen raised her brows as she fastened her seatbelt.

"I don't know... Maybe I am just trying to do something instead of sitting around." He shook his head, wincing as they waited at a red light. Helen reached for his shoulder and gave it a squeeze.

"We can do it. Lia is tougher than we expected."

"Very confident there, huh?"

Helen gulped; she hoped she was confident. She had no idea what was happening with Lia either. Though she wasn't sure whether Adrian even knew about what happened, she didn't dare contact him. "I don't know. It's just a feeling, but I think Lia is OK. She will wait for us to find her."

William eyed her for a moment too long, and the cars behind them started honking. He stepped on the pedal, turning to the road. "I hope your hunch is right. It usually is, so fingers crossed it is also right this time."

The next location was a cafe. The bell rang gently as

the two of them walked in. Helen took in the scent of coffee, the pleasant smell cleared her thoughts and her lips curled up on their own.

William picked a spot beside a bookshelf and Helen sat opposite to him. She said, "This seems to be just a comfy cafe."

"Yeah… You don't expect them to have a big sign somewhere, do you?" He sat back on the sofa, his face solemn. Helen faintly nodded as she surveyed the scene.

A half-bald old man was sitting next to a cupboard with a middle-aged woman next to another bookshelf across the cafe, and a nerdy-looking guy with messy hair and a pair of square glasses was burying his head into his laptop. It looked to be just a normal cafe, at least the patrons looked and felt to be normal people.

The barista approached them with a menu in her hand. "What will it be?"

William glanced at the menu, ordering for both of them. After the barista walked off, William flicked his eyes back to Helen. "Feel anything here?"

Helen looked around the cafe, closing her eyes briefly. She could feel a low hum of something magical. "Something magical is around, but it is very, very weak."

William rubbed his chin, looking around. The patrons were busy with their own business. The barista served them coffee and left quietly, as if not wanting to interrupt their conversation.

Helen couldn't peel her eyes away from the barista. She was around twenty, probably working in the cafe part-time in between university courses, something Helen also did herself. She swore she saw a mischievous glint in the barista's eyes when she set down their coffee. Now she wasn't sure whether she wanted it or not.

The barista was tidying the counter, piling up the

menus for the next patron, oblivious to Helen staring. Helen narrowed her eyes, focusing all her senses on the barista. It was her. The weak tingle of magic came from her, but at this intensity, she likely didn't know magic, but simply had the potential to develop it.

Helen looked back just in time to avoid getting caught staring. William was eyeing her with raised brows. Helen traced her fingers along the rim of her cup, wondering whether she should take a sip. William was waiting for her observation, she didn't know whether she should tell him or not. Who knew whether that girl had some correlation with Adrian? But if she pretended to not know something that obvious, would William find her suspicious? "The barista feels like someone with potential, but she doesn't actually know magic."

"I see… That's also my thought." William nodded, flicking his eyes to the barista briefly. There wasn't any new patron, the barista was now busying herself on her phone.

During their stay in the cafe, Helen often took a peek at her. "Will you go dig her potential like you did for Lia and me? Maybe she would join the team."

"Maybe. If she can learn about her magic, we'll go from there, but not before I figure out the dark magicians, otherwise, it will be even more dangerous to her than now." William took a sip of his coffee. Helen's eyes widened momentarily, but he gave away nothing. Maybe the mischievous glint in the girl's came from how the two of them stared too much at others in the cafe.

Helen flicked her eyes to the barista again. Her breath caught when she was also looking her way. Helen gulped, wondering what the barista was thinking. She smiled warmly at Helen with a nod, but had no intention of walking over to them.

Helen frowned deeply, not sure what to think. She took

a sip of her coffee. *If something really is wrong with the coffee… magicians heal quickly, I guess.* She set down the cup with a soft sigh. William looked at her with raised brows.

"I'm just missing Lia. Any information from Mike?"

William ran his hand over his face, shaking his head. "The videos you saw earlier are from him. I already asked him to pay extra attention, but there isn't anything noteworthy yet. Oh… unless you count the unusually slow business in the hotel in the city center. The Orbit, I think. Those luxurious places aren't for me anyway."

"What kind of slow business are we talking about? It is the largest in the city, right?"

"I think so. There are fewer cars than usual going in and out. But that happened before Lia disappeared. Also, I have not been looking at a hotel. What if it isn't the best use of our time?"

"But then when did the business of a hotel become interesting to the police?"

"I have no idea. While Mike is pretty high up there in the force, there are still people over him."

"You think there's more to it?"

"It could be."

After they finished their coffee, they proceeded to a few more places, but nothing was noteworthy. It took almost the whole day before William finally called an end to it. Helen got back to her room, took a shower, then collapsed on her bed. Focusing on spotting magic with the intention of not finding anything related to Adrian and with the intention of not letting William know what she knew was mentally exhausting.

Helen took out the piece of amber from her pocket. She toyed with it in her hand, tracing its cool surface with her fingers. Now that Lia had disappeared and William was dead set on finding the dark magicians, there was no way things would revert to their old ways. She let out a sigh.

At the buzz of her phone, her heartbeat quickened, hammering in her chest. Something with the message felt different without her reading it. She hurried to lock the door to her room. She laughed at herself. It was just a message. Why was she getting nervous about the text?

She took a seat on her bed, pulling out her phone. Her fingers shook as she turned on the screen.

It was Adrian.

CHAPTER 20

LIA

Slowly, the darkness and the numbness faded into the background. Lia fought to open her eyes. Her eyelids heavier than she remembered. It was dim around her. As her senses came back, the cold metal surface behind her sent a chill down her spine. She tried to move her arms, but they were chained out to her sides along with her legs. She struggled against the restraints, but all she got was the clinking of the chains. Faint footsteps approached her. She squinted, barely making out a silhouette in the dim lighting.

"Finally, you are awake! You got me worried."

The light turned on, she winced from the brightness. After she got accustomed to the light, she opened her eyes. "Ben?"

Benjamin stood in front of her with a cheerful grin, his eyes travelling from her head to toes. Lia froze. *Why am I tied up?*

"Lia, how are you feeling?"

"I feel constricted, and probably betrayed. What is happening?"

His eyes widened, he flinched. "Woah, woah, easy! Not betrayed, of course. If I dare to even think about it, I would be very dead before I could move a finger. I got lucky fishing you out under William's nose without him knowing what happened and finding out about your dark magic. We had to tie you up so you didn't hurt yourself…" His phone beeped. He pulled it out to check, winking playfully. "If you are feeling alright, Adrian is waiting to see you."

Lia raised her brows, she swallowed dry. The last thing she remembered was helping to save victims from the fire. It was the first time she had been outside of the clan since they fought at The Orbit. Then she blacked out. Did Adrian tie her up because of her power? Or did he tie her up because she pushed him away? Was she too mean for thinking he would do that?

She rolled her eyes at the thought, and decided to play along. If Adrian thought he could do whatever he wanted, he was dead wrong. She took a deep breath and nodded. He took a step closer, unlocking the chains. Soon, she was free again, she rubbed her arms, stretching them. He gestured for her to follow.

"Adrian wanted to stay until you woke, but I urged him to find some distraction for himself. He will fill you in with what happened," he said as they walked through corridors.

Lia looked around. She didn't recognize the surroundings. The walls of the poorly-lit corridors were made of grey bricks with wooden tiles. She could see her shadow when she walked past the light bulbs that pretended to be candles. The place looked old, but well-maintained.

Does Ben know what happened between Adrian and me?

They arrived at a heavy wooden door with no sign on it. Benjamin knocked, and they went in.

It was dark, without a pinch of light. Lia wanted to walk further inside, but Benjamin held her elbow, urging her to stop. She squinted and tried to look around. When he closed the door behind them, the room was completely dark. A suffocating magical power filled the room. She could faintly hear Benjamin breathing next to her, her heartbeat could interrupt the silence.

Slowly, as her eyes got used to the darkness, she could make out someone sitting on the floor in the center of the room. She wondered what was happening. She wanted to ask, but Benjamin seemed to read her mind. He tightened his grip on her arm before she opened her mouth. The figure in front of them stood as the lights came on.

"Adrian? Oof—" Before Lia could finish, he rushed forward, wrapping his arms around her and pulling her into a tight embrace, with a sob.

Wait! What is happening? He really thinks he can make me his by locking me up? I know he never follows rules, but really?

She wanted to push him away and perhaps slap him in the face, but despite her wish, she patted his back. Was it wrong to find comfort in his arms after what he did to her?

"What is happening?" Lia looked at Adrian for the first time in a while. His hair was dishevelled, there were bags under his half-opened eyes. Faintly, she could smell alcohol. Her heart ached as she furrowed her brows. All her anger seemed to disappear. "Are you drunk?"

He shook his head, pulling her into another hug. "Lia, are you feeling well?"

"Not until I know what's happening."

Adrian nodded, taking a few steps into the center of the room. Lia looked around at the wooden weapons hanging on the walls. The floor was covered with soft rubber mats. He was barefoot, so she took off her shoes and followed him. They sat, leaning on the wall. The brick wall was cold on her back.

"Ben fished you out. By the time you were here, your power was already overwhelming you. You almost broke his shoulder. You should go thank him later."

Lia struggled to remember what happened. She remembered helping a kid escape the fire and helping Helen blocking off burning objects, but then she drew a blank.

Adrian continued. "I tried my best… I… I was worried that you wouldn't make it. Hell, these have been the longest few days I've ever lived. I had to tie you down so you didn't hurt yourself and for us to keep an eye on you. Hope it was fine with you."

"It's not like I could complain." Lia rolled her eyes. Adrian swallowed, averting her gaze. She nudged him. "Thank you for saving me. I can't wait for the day when I can be the one saving others, not being saved."

Adrian's gaze was intense on her, the hesitation and passion apparent. Lia found herself immersed, if not hypnotised by his blue eyes. *What does he still want from me? Waiting to push me away again?*

"Go thank Ben. He's the one who saved your life. I was just a pile of useless junk when you were in danger." He reached out and held her hands, his face serious. "I know you made it clear you want nothing to do with me anymore. I know I hurt you. I have a lot to tell you, Lia, so hear me out till the end, please?"

She sucked in a deep breath, bracing herself for what was coming, she nodded.

"I know you are angry with me and want nothing to do with me. I know I am dumb and hurt you. You said you won't want an answer from me anymore, but I really want to give us a try. I realized… I can't live without you. The few days you were in the hospital freaked me out. And you being unconscious for the past few days made for some of the most painful days I've walked the earth." His voice cracked, eyes shimmering as tears welled up.

Her mind seemed to stop working. She hoped he meant his words. Maybe she was angry before, but she wasn't now.

He raised his brows at her silence. "It is OK if you don't want to see me anymore. Frankly, I also didn't want to see myself. Don't feel pressured to agree to anything. Everything can be temporary. I can wipe your memory after your power stabilizes so you don't have to remember a thing about dark magic or about me. These are probably painful memories for you anyways. No loss in losing them." He stared at the ground sheepishly, a few spots on the rubber mat darkened by his tears.

She wanted to agree, not every part had been painful. Despite her wish, her voice was shaky. "That's a big change in your attitude. What for?"

What was she doing? What if Adrian still pushed her away? He said he couldn't live without her, but did he really mean it? Or was he just enjoying playing with her feelings?

She winced, willing her thoughts to stop for a second, to give her a break. Despite her mind, her heart wanted him to mean his words, but he'd always pushed her away no matter what he said before.

He flicked his eyes to her. "You remember I mentioned there is someone who also has my kind of power?"

Lia nodded, faintly remembering what he told her when they discovered her power. She sighed. It felt like so long ago.

"She is here, demanding me to keep my pact with her and have you killed."

Lia's eyes opened wide. Adrian lifted her hand, kissing her knuckles. She jerked, yanking back her hand. His face twisted as she looked away . "I am sorry... I shouldn't... I was meaning to tell you, but I couldn't reach you. I am fighting her. I'm not going to let you die. Not after all we've gone through."

There is no 'we'! Stop it!

"Who is she?" She frowned. Although she was still ambivalent, if someone wanted her dead, maybe she should pay attention.

"Evelyn. An old enemy... We were friends until something came up. We fought until we were certain we couldn't take out each other. We made a pact, agreeing not to see each other again. We agreed on our territories, and... to kill whoever displayed our type of power."

If anything, that sounded like bad news. Adrian looked stressed. But what if this was something he made up just to keep her around him? "Benjamin? He also has dark magic."

"It is different. We are talking about the power of the origin. Benjamin is no match to that. His power comes from me. And no dark magicians can be stronger than their origin. You have the power of the origin; that's why your power showed up on its own. Other dark magicians learn from the origin that gives them the power."

"OK...? So Evelyn wants to get rid of other origins."

"Yes. She doesn't want someone out there that could build an army of dark magicians and fight her."

"You aren't scared of that?"

"You wouldn't do that to me," he chuckled.

"So confident?"

"Well... I'd rather die in your hands, then."

She swallowed—that wasn't what she meant. "How strong is Evelyn?"

"She is strong. Very strong. The gang was nothing compared to her. And I guess her people are tough, too. Years ago, we were on an even playing field, but I'm not sure anymore. It will probably take all I have to fend them off."

This does sound a bit more real.

"Are you sure when you said you couldn't live without me? Because it feels like I've never really mattered to you. You simply pity me for having your power. It seems like fighting Evelyn would be a dumb decision. You don't have to fight for me. There's never been an 'us' anyways. I'm just an Elements' magician. What am I to you?" Lia shook her head. Her heart raced, hammering in her chest. Before she had this sorted out, she didn't know what to think. It was hard enough to be in the same room with him.

He lifted Lia's chin and their eyes met, his shiny blue eyes stormy with emotions she couldn't point out. "Well... After what I have or haven't done, it is only fair for you not to believe me. Remember when I said nothing can happen between us? I admit I'm hiding the main reasons from you.

"It's special to me how you always give yourself to fight for people you don't even know. You don't only fight for them, you'd do the stupidest things for them. Almost getting squashed by a giant cobra, getting drowned by a pile of slime, asking for a devil's help to save Helen...

"I guess I just like that about you a bit too much, and you are the one trying to not call me a devil. I mean... you sometimes remind me of Ariel. At least how I feel about you. She is the one you saw William burned. The one I loved... love? I feel like a traitor every time I feel something for you. That's why I insisted there be nothing between us.

"I... I never intend to hurt you... I just... can't keep

myself away from you. It is fine if you don't want me anymore. I just think I have to tell you… I will still keep you alive regardless, so there's no pressure to even consider throwing me a bone. I can't even bear the thought of you dying, not having the chance to let you know. I've had enough of not saving the people I love. Maybe you should choose to wipe your memory after all this craziness. At least you will still live." He looked down, his voice cracked. Lia moved closer to his side, caressing his face and wrapping her arms across his back. He leaned into the touch.

If she was still in doubt when he said he couldn't live without her earlier, she wasn't anymore. He'd cried when he first let her know about Ariel, when he told her as a reason to not tell William about her dark power. He wouldn't joke with something he held that close to his heart.

"Thank you for telling me." She squeezed his hand. "You don't expect I would know that, right? I'm not like you, I can't read others' mind."

He smiled wryly, holding her tight as if his life depended on it. "I figured that out after Ben knocked some sense into my tiny brain," he choked. "I'm sorry, Lia. Maybe this still is not a good idea. I can't… I can never forget her… This will not be fair for you." He shook his head, pulling away from her with a pained look. She wrapped her arms around him, holding him still as he turned to face her with a confused look.

"It's OK. You don't have to forget her. Just… don't keep hurting yourself. I don't think I will ever understand how it feels. When I saw Helen lying on the floor, bleeding out, it scared the heck out of me. It was like… the whole world was falling apart. It must be much more painful to lose someone you love. We can walk through it together if you want to and when you are ready." Lia stroked his back, his body shaking from tears.

"After all these years, I don't always think about her, but when I do… How would you think if after your own death, the one you love went off loving someone else? Aren't they the biggest jerk and traitor in the world?" He looked at her with teary eyes, his voice shaking.

"I… I'm not dead enough to know the answer. I guess I would be happy to see the one I love happy. If they find someone that makes them happy, that's good… I guess? I won't be there anyway.

"You always think I should be with someone else, saying it will make me happier. Although that's not true, you did what you thought was best for me even if it meant making yourself suffer. I'd guess Ariel would feel the same way for you. Maybe she would suffer more if she knew you hurt yourself over her."

He stared at her with disbelief, his warm breath on her face in their closeness.

She continued. "You make it awkward asking me that. You know how much I want something to happen between us." She squeezed his shoulder, which he met with a weak smile. "As a matter of fact, thank you for always taking care of me, staying with me when I was upset and helping me through the monsters. And if you are too dumb to know, I'm very happy around you. At least when you don't push me away."

His eyes shimmered with tears, but his smile soon faltered. "Even so, I don't know whether you should accept me… Things I've done through these years… I'm a devil. Not to mention how I treated you, I…"

He shook his head, pulling away. "And what if something happens to you because of me? What if you are killed because of me? I don't even think I could live with it. Maybe it will be better if we aren't to——"

Lia held onto him, pressing her lips onto his, stopping him from talking. His eyes widened in shock. The kiss lingered until Lia pulled away just enough to look him in the eyes.

"You don't get to insult my choice," she smirked.

Realising she was paraphrasing him, he chuckled.

Lia stroked his cheek, swiping the tear away. "We will find a way if we try. You already failed in keeping yourself away, right?"

"You aren't angry with me? Don't you hate what I've done?" He frowned.

Her eyes narrowed, poking him in the chest. "I think I should be, but you make it very difficult. I wish you would have told me earlier. If you keep making both of us suffer, I will be very pissed."

"You never fail to impress. You have no idea what I've done. I am really a terrible devil and probably up to no——"

Lia pressed her lips against his. He frowned, then he kissed her back passionately until they both needed air.

"I'll take that as you still want to try something out with me?" He raised his brows eagerly.

"Actually, you are the only thing stopping the 'we'." She poked him in the chest. "Are we giving us a chance?"

He nodded, raising their hands to kiss her knuckles. "Yes, we are. I doubt I can live without you." She beamed, pulling him into a tight embrace.

"One more thing I want to ask: is seeing me almost dead the only reason you told me your feelings?"

He chuckled wryly. "Before Evelyn appeared, I thought I could fix things, that you can master your power and turn it into ice power. The Elders would be no wiser, I would wipe your memory so you could go back to your life as before. I'm sure Helen would keep your dark power and me a secret from you. If something really happened between us and I ended up having to wipe your memory, it would be…" A sob escaped him, he shook his head.

It would be like the one you fell in love with was dead… Worse, I would be walking around with no idea what happened and he would have to watch as a stranger to me. Living with the pain…

He rubbed his temple before he continued, "I don't think I could survive that kind of thing once more… I had to keep my mouth shut, before I said things I shouldn't.

"But with Evelyn here, there is no way I can keep you alive without fighting her; there is no way I can fight her without William finding out; there is no way you will be able to go back to your life as before. I can't wipe everyone's memory. In the end, I selfishly only wanted to try with you when it was easy and would benefit me…"

Lia rubbed his back and he pulled her over, sitting her on his lap. He buried his nose into her hair, his warm breath sending a tingle down her spine. She chuckled as his nose tickled her ear. "I guess I see why. Thank you for always thinking about me, although I would much rather you let me join your decision making, especially when it has to do with me."

"I'll try." He nibbled at her earlobe, his hands running up and down her body. She shifted to hug him again.

"Better not make Ben wait too long." He pulled away, helping both of them to stand back up and wrapping his arm around her waist as they walked to the door.

"He's outside?" Lia blushed, flicking her eyes to the door, no one was there.

"Of course. He wasn't going to stay and listen to what I have to tell you." He laughed.

Lia rolled her eyes, playfully pushing him away. "What? Is it so embarrassing to be with me?"

He turned her to face her, his face dead serious. Pushing her back up the door, he whispered to her ear. "Me with you is hardly embarrassing, but for the world, I doubt they could stop watching us. They would get too jealous."

"You must be the reason. Don't blame me."

His blue eyes darkened with desire. "We shall see."

He pressed his lips onto hers. She closed her eyes. Finally, she could let herself feel him without worrying what he would do next. She had been wanting this. Adrian was there for her at every corner. Part of her still couldn't understand what he saw in her, but she was glad there was finally certainty in how he felt.

She pulled him closer for fear he'd disappear and leave her waking up from a dream. He rested his forehead on hers and said, "I could kiss you till the end of time, but if we don't move soon, I doubt we'll get out of here."

"You have to watch yourself," she chuckled.

Outside the door, Benjamin was a few steps down the corridor, staring at the ceiling. He snapped his head back when Lia waved to him, beaming as he eyed the two of them. "Looks like something is solved, huh?"

Lia and Adrian exchanged a glance. "I guess so," she said, pecking Adrian on the cheek. He flinched. As Lia raised her brows, Benjamin laughed.

"That's OK, my King. I'm not telling anyone. Your little secret is very safe with me."

"Why does this have to be a secret?" she asked with a frown.

"Just for me to keep as a surprise for a little while? It will soon not be a secret anymore." Adrian winked at her with a warm smile on his face. Despite not knowing what he meant exactly, she nodded.

CHAPTER 21

LIA

As Adrian showed Lia around, the den was more complicated than she imagined. Walking through the corridors, almost every one looked the same; even the number of the lamps that looked like torches were equal. The walls were made of grey stones. There weren't any signs on most of the doors, and even their appearances were very similar. It reminded her of the gang and The Orbit, it seemed everything looking the same was the trend?

"You like it here?" Adrian asked, opening a door to a room with a desk holding a pile of books with a few chairs set on the floor. The room was brightly lit, the stone walls gave it the feel of an old castle.

"How do you remember the corridors and the rooms? Everything looks the same." Lia eyed the books. They were a mixture of history and biology books.

He chuckled. "Hm… You have a point. You will soon remember after spending some time here."

"It kind of feels like the base of the gang in the way that everything is indistinguishable for a newcomer."

"I'll be mad if you compare me to them."

"I won't want you if you are as dumb as them."

"Should I be grateful?"

"You got lucky," she beamed, stroking his hair. He leaned into her touch with a wide smile. Lia's smile, however, faltered quickly.

He asked, "What's on your mind?"

"How long was I down? Helen must be worried about me. I have to find her." Her heart skipped a beat, she scrambled to search her pockets, but her phone wasn't with her. She flicked her eyes to him.

"I already told her you are with me, but I think it will be great for her to hear directly from you."

Lia released a sigh of relief, pulling him into a tight embrace. "Thanks. Didn't realize you do know how to do some friend things."

He groaned, but the corner of his lips curled up. "Let's go call her." He held her hand, their fingers interlaced with each other.

"Can't we do it here?"

"We can do a lot of things here, but making a call is not one of them." He winked at her with a devilish smile. She rolled her eyes and smacked him in the chest, he laughed. "Don't you find something special here? I told you good observation is very important."

The room looked like a typical office room, but something felt out of place. She looked around the brick wall: there was an ancient map hung up, but the location seemed to be fabricated. Otherwise, nothing looked strange. He nodded at her expectantly.

"Oh. There's no windows here." Both in this room and the room she met him earlier that day were completely dark when the lights were off.

"Not too bad. We are underground, and there's no signal here."

"Then I suppose there's also no internet connection? How do you even survive? And who actually designed a place without a network?" Lia stared at him. *Such a caveman.*

He shrugged. "When I set up, neither internet nor phones existed. Can't blame me."

"Wait! How long ago was that? And actually how old are you? I don't think you've told me." Her eyes opened wide.

He leaned close, pecking a gentle kiss on her lips. "Probably longer than you could imagine. You never seemed to care."

Lia blushed, looking away. "Didn't think an old man like you would be interested in me?"

He rolled his eyes. "Who are you calling old? I also wonder what makes you that special. I guess you just know when it happens. Anyways, time to call Helen?"

"In fact, if you don't mind, I want to see her in person." Lia cupped his face in her hands, looking straight at him. He struggled to keep eye contact, wrapping his hands around Lia's.

"I'm sorry. Not now. Since your disappearance, William and Eric have been keeping a close eye on Helen and Patrick. They're not even allowed to leave the clan without being accompanied by one of them. Somehow your Elders think that someone is after magicians."

"They don't know I'm safe."

"You don't think I'm going to tell them, right? Although Helen knows you are safe, without being able to show you to them, she couldn't tell them."

"I can tell them I'm fine. So I can meet Helen."

"You think coming out from nowhere after

disappearing for a few days is going to cut it? They wouldn't believe a thing from you."

"They may find out about you…"

"I'm sorry, I can't take the risk."

"But us waiting here won't help either. They will still try to find me."

"I'm working with Benjamin for a solution. We'll go call Helen. After that, just take a rest, will you? You are still recovering. With Evelyn lurking around, I want you to be in your best shape."

Lia searched his eyes; he was determined. She sighed, nodding.

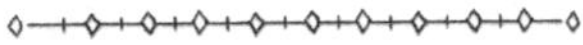

ADRIAN BROUGHT Lia out of the dungeon and into the city for her to communicate with Helen and for him to buy her tacos. Before he left the car, he warned her to not get out. With the tinted windows of the car, the outside was dim.

Lia stared at her phone while it came to life with internet connection. It buzzed for a few seconds, loading all the messages she hadn't received. Almost all of them were from Helen. The day she disappeared, Helen had sent a lot of messages wanting to know whether she was OK and where she was.

Scrolling down, Lia's heart sank. She wished she could have let Helen know she was fine earlier. Looking at all the emojis and randomly-capitalized letters, Helen must be very worried about her.

The frequency of the messages slowly decreased. Helen had given up messaging her, knowing something must be wrong and she probably wouldn't be able to reply if the messages weren't even delivered. Lia winced, those probably were a few terrible days for Helen to know nothing about what happened. Adrian did say he told Helen, but it was probably not the first thing on his to-do list. Lia couldn't blame him, though.

She snapped a photo of herself and sent it to Helen before slumping back in her seat. Now not only she had to deal with her power, but there was this woman named Evelyn that was after her. It didn't help when she also had to stay away from Helen. When would all this be over? Why was it so hard to live a comfy and easy life?

She stared out of the window, the afternoon sun dimmed from the tinted glass. Its cool surface sent a chill down her spine. It felt like ages since she had seen the sun and the trees outside. She never treasured all that until now. She reached for the handle of the car door, but her hand stopped mid-way. Was that a good idea?

There seemed to be no one nearby—maybe she could just get a breath of fresh air. She reached for the handle to push the door open, but it was locked. She leaned towards the panel, trying to fumble with the buttons until she found the one to unlock all the doors. But the car door was still. *Am I locked in?*

Lia jumped when there was a buzz; it was her phone, a lot louder than she expected in the silence and more of a shock when she was trying to do something forbidden. Helen had messaged her back, the screen filled up with emojis of all kinds. Lia smiled, releasing a sigh of relief. They updated each other on their current state. Helen seemed to be very happy to know she was safe. She was as pissed as Lia was for not being able to see each other.

A low thud of the car door closing interrupted her smile and texting. She jumped, almost dropping her phone. She looked up to find Adrian smirking at her, his blue eyes shining in the dim car.

"You scared me." She poked his chest. He chuckled,

sitting down before putting the takeaway bag on the console between them. Soon the car was filled with the tasty smell of freshly made tacos and other Mexican food. She beamed, reaching for a chip.

He grabbed her wrist. "Don't you dare to eat in my car, the mess you are capable of creating…"

Lia rolled her eyes, letting the chip drop back into the bag, puffing her cheek. "C'mon, it's just a chip. How messy can it be?"

"With you, everything is messy." He wrapped up the paper bag. "Had fun talking with Helen?"

"It would be better if I could call her, but she was worried that the Elders would hear." She sighed, putting down her phone on the seat beside her.

"You will soon be able to see Helen again. Pinkie promise?"

"Wait! What happened to the Adrian I knew, he wasn't into pinkie promises? What have you done to him?"

"Sadly, the Lia he knows is into it, no way for him to not bend down to her height."

"How dare you." Lia laced hers with his, but not without rolling her eyes.

"I'm telling the truth. Let's head back before the tacos get cold and before you spill food in my car."

CHAPTER 22

LIA

After Adrian drove them back to the mysterious dungeon and got them settled, Lia dug in, filling her mouth with the tasty tacos and nachos. It was great to finally have some food in her system. They were sitting on chairs in a brightly lit lounge room. Everything looked great except there's no television or video games.

"Are you sure you should eat that fast?" Adrian laughed, shaking his head. She rolled her eyes, her mouth too full to respond. He leaned closer, gently brushing away a flicker of spicy sauce on the corner of her mouth with his thumb. The touch sent a tingle down her spine. He licked the sauce off his thumb and winked at her as their eyes met.

"You're cute when you wolf down your food," he said. He picked up a chip, throwing it towards his mouth. Lia huffed, snatching it before it arrived at its intended destination. His eyes widened. "That's mine!"

"Not anymore," Lia stuffed the nacho into her mouth, smirking at him. "You're just showing off. Who really eats chips like that?"

He groaned, picking up another. "I thought you would be more pissed to have to stay here."

Who says I'm not?

"Nah, it is fine. I know you're just trying to keep me safe." Lia put away the wrapping of the taco back into the paper bag after finishing it, sipping at her soft drink.

"I really need you to be safe." He stared at the last chip on the table, his mind seemingly elsewhere. She snuggled up to him. He nodded, still staring. He almost jumped as Lia swept the nacho off the table into her mouth.

"What's on your mind? Obviously not this chip, huh?"

"Just thinking about us. Maybe I should have told you earlier."

"At least you have half a brain."

He nodded faintly, resting his head on hers. They remained pressed against each other for a while longer before they stood to clean up.

Afterwards, Adrian showed her more of the dungeon. Lia walked very close to him, wrapping her arm around his waist.

"Can you even walk on your own?" He rubbed her side.

"Fine. Of course I can." She rolled her eyes, taking back her arm.

He clutched her with a grin. "I'm not stopping you."

"You are insufferable." She huffed and leaned into him.

He gestured to the branches of the corridors. "There are a lot of rooms here. You will get to know them better as time goes on. Before that, don't wander too far. It would be hard to find you."

"Sure." She stared at the crossroad, flicking her eyes between halls. She had been trying to remember all the rooms he showed her, but she barely remembered.

Everything looked too similar, not to mention she found his company a lot more interesting than remembering corridors.

"You can stay here in the meantime, just to be safe," Adrian said, turning on the light in one of the many rooms. The walls were covered up with some type of material resembling wood. She traced the surface of the wall, along the pattern of wood, and the coolness of it sent a shiver down her spine. Either it was cold in the dungeon or the material was more like metal than wood. The wood did make the room a bit warmer than the bricks.

"Thanks?" Lia said half-heartedly, still looking around the room. After noticing the wall, she turned to the desk and chair set in a corner of the room. Both were made of wood. The bed by the other corner looked comfy and large enough for her to roll around freely.

"I hope you will like it here," He said.

Something feels off, but I don't know...

"Sure, thanks! Hopefully no one will find me."

"That's the goal." He smiled weakly with a faint sigh.

"Things will be fine, right?" She squeezed his hand.

He lifted their hands, kissing her knuckles. "I will make sure you're safe. Just take a rest. You better get in shape for whatever is coming."

Lia nodded as he tucked her into the bed. He leaned onto the wall next to the bed, staring blankly at the door.

Lia asked, "Something on your mind?"

He shook his head. "Nothing. How's your power feeling?"

She closed her eyes briefly, trying to catch signs of it. It was a small warm stream now and didn't feel threatening. "I think it's fine for now."

"Any pain?"

"Nope. I guess I am just a bit tired. I've had better days."

He nodded. "I still didn't know why you went into a coma. Things we don't know with our magic, huh? At least you are fine now. At least I'm not fooling myself anymore."

Her heart skipped a beat and her smile reached her eyes. She sure was glad he didn't push her away. "Will you stay with me?"

"If you mean in this room, not now, sorry. I have something to do, but I'll join you later."

She frowned deeply, staring at him. He gulped, then straightened and headed to the door. "I'll be back sooner than you know."

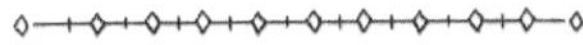

LIA LAY IN BED, rolling around. It felt great to finally have a glimpse into Adrian's mind and to know that he reciprocated her feelings for him.

The thought of a dark magician with equal power as Adrian coming after her life sent a shiver down her spine. After witnessing what Adrian could do in the gang's headquarters, she wondered what would happen when the two factions fought. Evelyn had her people, and she knew Adrian had his. Although she met some of his acquaintances at the bar, none of them were magicians except for Benjamin. If they were, they hid their power very well. Maybe those were people that had trades with Adrian.

As she learned her dark power, her senses became stronger, especially with detecting magical power. But it still required her to focus on feeling it in the air. Lia rubbed her temple, contemplating the chance of staying highly alert every moment to keep herself safe from other magicians.

No way. That seems too mind-numbing… But Adrian is keeping me here anyway…

She yawned. After walking around most of the day in the dungeon and finishing the meal, she was getting drowsy, but she wanted to find out more about the den. She flicked her eyes around the room, finally knowing why it felt off: there wasn't a clock. She reached to the bedside table instinctively, then she realised her phone wasn't with her. She'd given it back to Adrian as they went back to the dungeon.

Crap… This is going to be boring. Although without an internet connection, it is going to be boring regardless…

She rolled around on the bed, willing herself to sleep, to stop worrying about the ones seeking her life, but to no avail. Instead, she got up and paced around the room. Something was stirring in her stomach. She was pretty sure it wasn't the Mexican food she ate, but a hunch of some kind, making it hard to fall asleep. Before she knew it, she pushed open the door and peeked out to the corridor. Nothing other than the flickering light was outside.

Maybe I should go to the bathroom before trying to sleep. I think I may have remembered the rooms.

Carefully, she put on the sneakers she kicked off earlier and wandered along the corridors, worrying that a ghost may pop up.

She successfully found the bathroom and finished her business there. But on the way back, she may have mixed up a few corners. She pushed at a door she believed to be her room, but it was locked, the wrong room.

She looked around at the very similar corridors and doors, and sighed.

Good luck finding the way back… Why couldn't he make it a bit simpler… At least make the corridors distinguishable…

She was now wide awake. May as well get to know the

place. She wandered around, trying to find her way back. Most of the doors were locked, and the ones that weren't usually only consisted of a table and a few chairs, nothing noteworthy.

She walked until she was quite confident that she wasn't making any progress. She leaned on the wall.

Hopefully Adrian can find me... I don't even know where I am. Hopefully he won't be too mad to find me missing from my room...

It was then she heard a noise behind the thick door beside her. Someone was talking. She pressed her ear against the door, there were a few muffled voices.

"That seems to be the only solution." It sounded like Benjamin.

"I should have done it a long while ago." Adrian.

"I told you even before that girl appeared." Lia frowned at the voice she didn't recognize.

"Lia is not going to like it..." Benjamin said.

"Like it or not, she is going to live with it. I can't risk her. It's not like she'll know until then, and by then, there's nothing she can do." Adrian's sound muffled and soft, almost impossible to catch.

"Is it a good idea not to tell her? She would be very pissed," Benjamin said.

Lia pushed her ear closer to the door, hoping the words would come clearer. Her heart hammered in her chest, her palms sweating. If Adrian found her, she didn't know what would happen to her, but she had to listen.

"I can take care of the two on my own. She will be no wiser," Adrian said.

"Or should we do it instead? To spare you in case the girl really gets mad," the stranger said.

"She knows I'm the King. I will never get off the hook. She would be fine, I guess. It may take a while, but at least she would be safer."

"She's just an Elements' magician. What's the big deal? Why don't we just go with the pact?" Whoever that was, Lia didn't want to meet him.

Adrian cleared his throat awkwardly. "Her magical power is still valuable."

Wait! So Adrian got close to me simply because of my power?

Lia covered her mouth with her hand as tears welled up in her eyes. *Am I thinking too much? I really want to trust him…*

The unknown voice spoke. "Well, you are the Lord. Whatever you want, I guess. How about we just get rid of all the Elements? The other magicians wouldn't even know. Without William and Eric, they can't do a thing. Just to keep us safe from any revenge."

Benjamin said, "No way. There is that other magician we can't kill. Otherwise, Lia will never take our deal."

"My Lord, is she really worth getting out of the shade, breaking the pact, and making more of a mess than is already coming?"

Adrian said, "Whatever you think, I am doing it. I will kill the two off myself. William is no match for me, and Eric probably is even weaker."

So that's Adrian's solution so I can see Helen again?

Lia gasped and slapped her hand over her mouth, but it seemed to be too late. The unknown person's voice came. "Is there someone outside?"

"Who can there be?" Adrian said.

"I wonder…"

Lia ran off as there was a squeak of a chair from the inside. She dashed down the corridors, turning all the corners she could manage to reach, hoping whoever was looking out of the door wouldn't see her.

Despite panting quickly for air, her throat was tight. Pushing random doors, she cursed under her breath, until she magically pushed the right door to greet the comfy bed still waiting for her, the blanket she kicked aside still in its place.

Lia tucked herself into the bed, curling into a ball, struggling to stabilize her breath and heart. She winced, pulling the cover over her head. She grabbed the corner of the blanket, squeezing it with her shaky hands.

If Adrian is killing the Elders, I can't stand and watch it happen.

Her mind ran full speed, searching for ways she could warn them without Adrian knowing.

But if they know Adrian is coming, they will kill him.

She coughed from the choking feeling brewing in her chest. A lump formed in her throat. In the darkness under her blanket, faint footsteps came from the corridor, echoing closer and closer.

CHAPTER 23

LIA

The door opened and Lia lowered her blanket, peeking up just enough to see who it was. Adrian walked in with a faint smile on his face. He raised his brows at her. "Can't sleep?"

Lia shook her head, trying to calm herself.

It is OK. He won't know. Just act normal.

She said, "I heard your footsteps."

"Sorry." He whispered as he sat next to her on the bed.

"Is the something done?" she asked.

For a split second, his demeanor changed, and she barely caught the mischievous glint in his eyes. "It's going great. Nothing you need to worry about."

He caressed her face with his thumb, leaning down to kiss her on the forehead. "You seem tense."

Crap! Does he know I know?

"Yeah… It feels awkward not having a clock or a window here. I kind of… feel trapped." She searched his face, a pained look flashed through it.

"I can put up a clock if you want. But I doubt a window is possible with an underground dungeon."

Lia nodded. *Does he really feel something for me or is he after my power? Maybe I shouldn't have wandered around… I don't even want to know.*

"I was thinking about my power. I kind of got tired of it, not to mention it giving me lots of trouble. Would it help if I give you my power? You can take people's power, right? Will Evelyn stop hunting me down?" She frowned deeply, bracing herself for the answer.

He searched her eyes as if trying to figure out something.

Was that too obvious?

He sighed. "I won't say I don't want your power, but more than anything, I want you by my side. What were you thinking about?"

Is it too quick to doubt him?

She sheepishly looked down. "I don't know, sometimes I can't shake the idea that you're getting close to me just for my magical power."

He pulled her into a tight embrace, resting his forehead on hers. His warm breath on her lips. She could see herself in his eyes, lost in his gaze.

"I don't have any other plans for us other than keeping you safe and hopefully beside me. Your magical power will be good to have, but it's not my concern anymore. The power chose you. Getting to know you is the best thing that has happened to me. I doubt I want anything else. But for what I've done to you, I know trust takes time."

But you said…

Lia kept searching his eyes. Her arms ran up his back subconsciously as she hugged him back. Closing her eyes, his lips warm on hers, he kissed her with great passion, stealing the breath from her lungs. His hand tangled in her hair, pulling her closer.

When she pulled back, he was beaming, stroking her

hair. She snuggled by his side and he wrapped his arms around her, lying on the bed.

She let out a sigh of comfort, smiling wide. It felt great to be close with him. The thought of what she heard remerged. She flinched. He flicked his eyes to her.

No way, he can't know I heard something…

"I'm scared. Evelyn sounds terrifying. Someone you don't have absolute confidence in beating."

He gave a wry smile. "I will do everything I can to beat her. It is going to be fine. Don't forget, she is after you, scared of your potential. You are more than you know you are."

"Really?" she asked. Was he joking? His face was too serious to be playing around. She gulped audibly.

"As if it is not evident enough by me appearing for the deal with you in the first place?"

"How am I supposed to be that strong like you said? I sure don't feel that way." She frowned.

"Take your time. I will keep you safe until you can fend for yourself. Evelyn did mention giving me some time, but whether she keeps her word or not, I am not going to leave you alone." He kissed her gently, rubbing her side, the touch sending a shiver down her spine. "Now get some sleep, will you? You must be tired."

Lia nodded. *Yes. More so after hearing your meeting…*

He pulled the cover over her body, tucking her in.

"Adrian… are you leaving?"

"I can stay if you want."

She grabbed his wrist, tugging him. "Yes, please. This dungeon is a bit scary."

He chuckled, nodding. At once she wrapped her arms around him, feeling his warmth. It may be scary outside, but he would be there for her.

CHAPTER 24

LIA

The dream in Lia's mind slowly faded into the darkness of her closed eyes. Before she fully woke up from her sleep, she stretched, reaching out both her arms and resting them on the blanket beside her.

"Grr…" The blanket stirred. Lia flinched.

Did the blanket learn to talk without me knowing? She snapped her eyes wide open. Adrian was staring at her with half-opened eyes, smiling lazily.

He stifled a yawn, snuggling closer. "Getting up early, huh? You know you don't have to tell me when you get up."

She grinned. It still seemed unreal for her. He really was there and didn't leave her. It had been so long before they started trying something between them. She caressed his cheek. There must be a dumb smile on her face which she couldn't control.

"I am not used to waking up with you next to me. It's impossible for me to get up without waking you." Lia rubbed the arm he rested over her waist.

"Hm… I guess so." He reached up, nibbling on her

throat, his teeth sending sparks down her spine. She shivered. "Are you cold?" He pulled her closer.

"You know it is hard to feel cold when you stick to me all the time." She chuckled, resting her hand on his wrinkled white t-shirt, on his chest, feeling the warmth from him.

"It feels good, I hope?" He raised his brows, trailing kisses along her neck.

"Clingy, aren't we?"

"I don't know, somehow I feel the need to hold onto you. I have no problem staying here with you all day," he hummed, running his hand up and down her back.

"But you said there are things we have to get done."

Not to mention I have to know what you are planning to do with William and Eric.

"I guess so. Not before you train first." He let out a sigh, sitting up and turning up the dim light. Lia remained lying in bed for a few moments longer, looking at his back, staring at him as he attempted to fix his messed-up hair.

If only there was a window here. I bet he would look great in the sunlight. Not that he doesn't already.

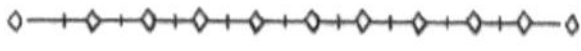

AFTER LIA GOT ready for the day, Adrian brought her down the stairs, heading for her training. "I didn't realize how many levels there are," she hummed.

"Just what's necessary to stay alive down here, I guess." He shrugged, running his thumb along the back of her hand.

"There was a time you stayed here?"

"That time is crazy. Luckily it was long gone. Had to try to not die." He pushed open a heavy wooden door.

From the dim light coming from the hall, she could only see the edge of some rubber mats.

"This is where I first met you here?" she asked, taking a few steps inside the room while he switched on the lights.

"Yes, one of the many important places here." He walked to the center of the room, Lia followed behind him. Their shoes left at the door.

On the walls hung different types of wooden weapons designed for practicing with others. At the door, before the rubber mat began, there were two benches, where Lia's sneakers tidily sat.

Adrian gestured to the floor for her to sit on. She sat with her legs crossed. He stood behind her, rested his hands on her shoulders, squeezing gently. She looked up at him, raising her brows. "Something on your mind?"

"Oh, just thinking back to what happened here before." He shrugged, shaking his head as if snapping himself out of the memory.

"Yeah. That was a great talk after a hell of a long wait."

He leaned down, kissing the tip of her ears. "Sadly, being a sweet talker doesn't exempt you from training. It's been a while since we've done anything. Let's see how you are faring."

Lia closed her eyes, getting herself ready to face her power. As she reached for it, the warm surge felt more controlled. It wasn't as hot as it used to be. There was still the urge to fight something, and she could still smell Adrian's magical power around her and got riled up slightly, but she resisted it. The power slowly rushed from deep inside her to the rest of her body, her limbs, then guided back to her core. She let out a sigh of relief as she opened her eyes.

"How are you feeling?" he asked, running his fingers

through her hair. She leaned back against his legs, looking up at him with a smile.

"Great, I guess. During my time in the clan, I found out that I can use the power up, so it bothered me less?"

"Yes, that's right. Although I would prefer you save it for future use, using some of it helps to feel less overwhelmed. I think the initial stage of your power is almost complete. Now it comes down to how you will deal with some triggers that may bring your power up."

"What initial stage are you talking about?" Lia frowned as he took a seat beside her.

"There are no samples other than myself for me to learn the whole process from. And I've never explained it to others before, so I hope I make it clear. At first the power comes up randomly, and the chance is higher when you use magic yourself or some strong magic was used near you. Failing to stop it in time before it really overwhelms you is irreversible, causing one to lose control of themselves and attack living things around them.

"At least for me, after a while, the power will come up less randomly. This is a stage where something outside of you will trigger it. For example, blood is a very prominent trigger. Also, the pain and suffering of people around you seems to work. But you have to get the power to work with you instead of taking control of you."

"How am I supposed to work with my power?"

He stared at her for a moment longer. It seemed to be something he didn't want to talk about. "You will be fine if you can contain it. If you really want to know… the origin can gain power from people's pain and blood."

Lia gulped audibly—the gang's men on the floor had been attractive in that moment. And she felt strange looking at the woman with a piece of glass in her face during the fire. The thought sent a shiver down her spine.

"It makes me feel like a terrible person… I am wanting them to suffer and their blood?"

"You should know it is nothing kind and fluffy from the name alone. It is just an urge. You are still the one making decisions. There are always different ways to go. It seems you are already pretty strong against it.

"Or maybe look at it as a way to gain power. When you get stronger, you can help more. The dark power is nothing different from a sword. It depends on how you use it. From what you did in the gang's base, I'd say you are much better than I could fare."

"You mean how I stopped you from tearing off the gangster's throat and sucking all their blood?"

"Yeah, it was very attractive, wasn't it? The amount of power around, just at your fingertips. Somehow you managed to resist it."

"But then why wasn't I overwhelmed?"

He remained silent for a while, as if trying to come up with an explanation. He stroked her knuckles with his thumb. "I have two guesses: one is that you weren't at this stage yet back then. Or, in the gang, maybe you were too shocked by me and Ben that you didn't know what you wanted, so the mere draw to the blood didn't take hold of you. The dark magic is not that different from the Elements' magic, after all. It is still down to the power of the mind." He was leaning on her shoulder, his breath shaky.

"Back in the day, when I knew nothing about myself, it was scary. A lot of what I knew came from Ariel. She was the one that enjoyed trying out new things while I never wanted to touch my magic. The combat magic and the bonds were discovered and mastered when she was there with me. After she was gone… all I cared about was to make others take my magic and help my fight against the

Elements. I suppose there is more I don't know, but what I know should be enough for you to stay alive."

"I see how Ariel helped you a lot."

"It is a miracle I didn't scare her away. She's very brave. I… You know how to use a sword, right?" He pulled away and stood, gesturing at the weapons on the wall.

Maybe he wasn't ready to talk about that yet. Lia nodded, looking closer to the wooden swords. He picked up one of them, handing it to her. It weighed almost the same as the one she used in her training with William.

He picked up another sword for himself and took a step back into the center of the room. "Let's see what you've got."

Guess he's not ready to talk about it yet.

Lia poised herself, holding up her sword, its tip facing him. "I know you are an old guy, but how much are you still into swords?"

"Very much. I am very into all kinds of weapons and all kinds of things I can use as weapons. Did you forget how good I am with crossbows?" He winked, advancing with his sword.

Their blades clashed and Lia tilted hers to the side, stabbing at him. Something tugged at her leg, she stumbled. She rolled her eyes at him. "You used magic with it. That's cheating."

He sidestepped, evading her advance. "That is doing the job effectively."

"Whatever you like to call it." She lifted her sword just in time to block his slash. Starting her attack at his waist, but he raised his blade with a clean movement from his wrist, he knocked off her sword. In the split second it took for her to register what happened, he patted her on the side with his sword.

"You should let the master teach you the way with a sword." He grinned.

"Confident, are we?" Lia rolled her eyes, her hands sore from how he forced the sword out of her grip. He wrapped his arms around her and pulled her close, their bodies pressed against each other. Her breath caught, dropping the sword and hugged him back. "What is this for?"

"I think I deserve a prize." He smirked, leaning down to rest his forehead against hers.

"You are insufferable." Lia tried to deadpan him, but the corner of her lips curled up against her wish. Her heart hammered in her chest as his breath warm on her lips. She couldn't tear her eyes away from his blue eyes. She stroked his cheek.

Their lips met. The kiss sent a shiver down her spine, feeling his lips tender and warm against hers. She closed her eyes, getting lost. *I really can do this all the time. He's so attractive when he acts all cocky.*

She ran her hands down his back, feeling the warmth from his body. Her other hand lost in his hair, pulling him closer to deepen the kiss. His hand roamed her, the touches sending sparks along the way. She kissed him with greater force, pushing him half a step back.

"Satisfied with your prize?" Lia raised her brows as she rested her hand on his chest, his heartbeat strong and comforting.

"Could there be something better?"

"It depends…" Her words were interrupted by a quick kiss.

His eyes darkened, his Adam's apple moving up and down. "Stop being such a tease. Things I want to do to you…"

But this is more fun than you will ever know. Just look at your face.

"What's stopping you?" She smirked.

He pulled away from her with a groan, shaking his head. "Not now. I still have things to do."

Things? As in planning to kill William and Eric?

"I kind of want you to stay here with me…" She flicked her eyes down to the floor, holding his hand.

He sighed. "I also want to, but there are things I need to get done before we can have some fun."

"Can I at least go message Helen? It will get boring with only myself." She put up her best cute puppy eyes. He gulped, shaking his head as if trying to shake himself out of her gaze. She tilted his chin to meet his eyes.

He took a glance at his watch, nodding to the door. "Maybe later, I will bring you out a bit if you want. I really need to get going,"

"When can I actually see Helen again?"

He halted mid-step, but he schooled himself quickly. "Very soon. Just be patient, will you?"

"How soon is very soon? You know you seem to have a definition about soon that's very different from the rest of the world's." She rolled her eyes, crossing her arms above her chest and pursing her lips.

He eyed her with amusement, staring at her for another moment. Lia struggled to keep eye contact, wondering whether it was meaningless to press him for more information.

"Less than a month," he said with a solemn face, walking out of the room. Lia fought to stay calm as she followed him.

Now don't act strange. Just be normal. You can do it.

"That's great! I can't wait to spend some time with her."

CHAPTER 25

HELEN

"These are quite some ideas you've got here." Helen stared at the pile of paper on William's desk. Eric was next to her, seemingly as surprised as she was. It was the day after Lia contacted Helen. William seemed to be tenser as the days went by.

William said, "There's still no hints of where Lia is. Knock on wood, I even went to search for records of dead bodies recently discovered, but there's nothing. I guess that's a good thing. But whoever caught her hasn't reached out either. It doesn't seem to be about money. It seems more and more likely it was done by the dark magicians." He frowned deeply, clenching a fist.

"Are you sure they are behind Lia's disappearance? Or rather, are you sure they are still living?" Eric folded his arms, his brows knitted.

"I don't know. Who else do you think did it? I don't think the hostages losing memory is really a coincidence. If it was the people that tried to kill Lia, we would have found her body already. Killing her would be easier than holding her hostage, knowing we will be searching for her." William rubbed his temple, his body visibly tense.

Helen gulped, her palms drenched with sweat. She wanted so much to tell them that Lia was safe, but they wouldn't trust her, not to mention she had no way of keeping Adrian out of the story.

"These are the next batch of locations?" Helen asked, pointing at the pile of paper.

"Yes. Maybe we will finally find something." William let out a heavy sigh.

Helen flinched as she saw Benjamin's bar and the ice cream shop Adrian's people opened in the list. She flipped to other locations as fast as she had been looking at each of them. Soon Eric and she went through all the locations William thought were worth looking into.

Eric set down the pile of papers and asked, "You two have already tried some of these, right? How did it go? If it really is the dark magicians, won't they find out about us hunting their tail if we really go to all these places and hide even better than before?

"Unless we nail the first time, there's no point searching one by one. They are smarter than that. We are in the open and they are watching in the shade if they really exist."

William rubbed his temple. "Well, last time, we found nothing. I have no better plan. Maybe if we are subtle, we stand a chance. They are hiding and should have no idea whether we are searching for them or not."

"When should we start? I can't wait to get Lia back," Helen asked. It seemed William had his heart set on doing the search anyways. There was no point fighting over this.

"Maybe now. You and Eric will get part of the list while I will go for the rest."

"Sure, I think we can do that, but how about Patrick?

Are you going to go with him?" Helen asked, while taking the pile of documents in front of her, luckily it included Benjamin's bar. She feared if William was going there, he would find out something. But Eric was equally smart. And regarding searching for dark magic, Helen had no idea how good the two were.

"I don't know whether I want to include him or not. I worry he is a bit too quick-tempered. I think it is best to leave him out until we actually fight the dark magicians," William said, rubbing his chin.

Eric's eyes narrowed in thought. "I think he would be angry to be left out. But you're right. Going to inspect them is dangerous enough without knowing where the dark magicians are. If he randomly attacks, there's no telling if they would outnumber us."

"Then should I pretend to know nothing if he asks?" Helen asked. Her heart beat quicker—now there was one more thing she had to keep secret.

"It will be for the best. He will know later. If he doesn't understand, that's still fine. Better than putting everyone in danger." William stood and got ready to inspect the list in his hand while Helen followed Eric out of William's office.

Helen got into Eric's car, and they headed to the first location. "Do you think we will find the dark magicians like this?" Helen asked, staring out of the window.

"Honestly, I don't think so. They are smarter than this. But I don't have a better plan. It is a lot easier to hide than to hunt. If they exist all the time, I don't understand why they never strike. I would hope they don't exist, but hope is... not that reliable."

"How will we know if dark magicians are really there? Or are we wasting time on nothing?" Helen held up the sheet of paper with Benjamin's bar. It contained very little information about it, as did all the other sheets.

"It is all feeling, unless they fail to hide their magic, which doesn't really happen. More likely you will know when they glare at you with the red eyes when they stab you to death." Eric's jaw tightened, as did his grip on the steering wheel.

She remembered clearly how Lia's eyes glowed in red as she shot blasts at her, and how she jumped on her. Adrian's red eyes when he yanked the gang members' heads off was just as scary. Her hand reached up to her chest, where the meteorite monster clawed down before, the touch sending another shiver down her spine. But Adrian saved her life.

"Here we are," Eric lowered the window on his side, peeking out. Benjamin's bar was down the road, on the opposite side to them. Helen swallowed. What if Eric found out about Benjamin? Whose side would she be on?

Helen dreaded getting out of the car. She waited for Eric to get out, but he didn't. "Are we going in?"

Eric shook his head. "The dark magicians know us, at least me and William, so I can't get close to them. Luckily, I also know most of them, unless they've added new members. Maybe I can sniff out something from here. The dark magic has a strange feeling attached, like the unearthly thing it is."

It was only the afternoon. The bar looked to be closed, but the door was open. There wasn't light from the inside. She had only been there a few times when they planned the attack on The Orbit. The parking lot nearby was empty. She closed her eyes briefly, trying to catch some noise from it, there wasn't any. Even with her magic, she didn't feel anything. Maybe it was too far away. It sounded like nobody was there.

They stayed there for almost half an hour. There were a few passersby walking along the street, but none seemed to be paying attention to the bar. Helen leaned on the car door, resting her elbow on it, having nothing to do than stare blankly out of the window.

"It seems nothing is happening… Don't you think we're too early for a bar?" Helen asked.

"Maybe. I don't feel anything. No scent of magic whatsoever." Eric crossed his arms, checking the paper.

"Are we out of range? I don't feel anything either."

"It's in my range. There's likely nothing inside."

Helen resisted a frown. Benjamin should be inside if the door was open, or was he hiding his power from Eric?

"Maybe I should go in and take a look," Helen said. *Maybe then we can leave before Benjamin or Adrian actually show up.*

Eric asked, "Are you sure?"

"I mean… we are here anyway. Or are you just playing to William's plan?"

Eric rubbed his forehead with a wry chuckle. "Actually, yes. Sometimes I don't understand him. After all these years, he should know better. If the dark magicians got her, there's no chance we would save her. If it wasn't the dark magicians, we are wasting our time."

"Then why did you agree to do this? Who do you think took Lia?"

He drummed his fingers on the steering wheel and sighed. "I have no idea. But what dark magician would pull Lia from William's side? Even though they are strong, in that proximity, really? If they are after Lia, there are a lot more chances to do it without William around. I'd look into the other gangs in the city. Maybe it was those people that stabbed Lia before. Those aren't dark magicians."

"I see. Have you talked to Mike?" Helen wanted to tell Eric that the gang in The Orbit was already beaten, but she wouldn't be able to explain why and how she knew.

"There's no string to pull there. Sadly, all our time in Zitannas is spent connecting with those government parts and everything above ground. I have no idea how to even start. Maybe you can just go in so we can report back to William."

"Sure." Helen nodded and got out of the car. The afternoon sun felt warm on her skin and she took a deep breath. *You know they won't hurt you. You've been there before.* But she couldn't stop worrying about Benjamin being inside and coming out to greet her.

Getting closer, Helen took in the entrance before slipping inside. The counters were still arranged the same way as they were the last time she was there. She squinted, trying to search for someone, but no one was there.

"Hey, anyone here?" she asked, her voice echoing in the empty bar. The smell of alcohol lingered, but there was no response. The hair on the back of her neck stood; something felt odd. Not to mention someone should be there if the door was open.

Helen pulled out her phone, wanting to call for Benjamin when his head popped up from the tiny storage room door. His hair was messy but he smiled weakly at her, waving.

She took a few steps to him, her brows furrowed in concern. She whispered, "Is something wrong?"

"We aren't open for business as you know. No dark magicians are around." He winked.

"You know I'm supposed to be here to catch you." Helen raised her brows. She didn't tell them yet, but he seemed to know their plan.

"The King has more eyes than you could guess," he said. He gestured at the empty bar. "Just do whatever you need to do. I am holding back my power so Eric wouldn't feel me around. Stay safe, will you?"

Helen nodded, her mind still wondering how Benjamin knew. "You don't look very good."

"I'm fine. Just had a discussion with the King about things and got tired. Not to mention suppressing my power is tiring."

"Where is he?"

"He knew you were coming and left. Probably has no interest in getting slapped again." He chuckled with a glint of amusement in his eyes.

"I didn't think he would tell you."

"You didn't go easy on him, did you? I saw his face." He gave her a knowing look with a smirk. "Anyway, just get going before your Elders barge in."

She nodded, turning to the bar and taking a few photos of the counters, the chairs, and the wine displays. She soon left, not wanting Eric to worry about her. Outside, the sun was welcoming. She let out a sigh of relief.

She settled into the car. Eric raised his brows at her. She said, "I took a look. It seemed like just a regular bar." She sent the photos to Eric's phone. "Took a few pictures just in case William asks. See for yourself."

He pulled out his phone, scrolling through the photos. "As expected, I guess. At least we can show William we were there. Anyone inside?"

"Yeah, a bartender was there tidying things. Just a human. At least I didn't feel anything."

He didn't seem to be paying his attention to her though. Instead, he kept staring at the photos. "I see."

"Is there something wrong?" Helen raised her brows as Eric stared at the photo of the darts machine.

"Nothing. I just don't know what I could even do. Knowing the dark magicians... Well, if Lia was dead, we'd probably see her body in front of the door of the clan. I hope that won't happen." He scrolled to another photo, apparently trying to take his mind out of what could have happened to Lia.

Did Adrian do that to other magicians? Helen swallowed and sank into the seat. She wished she could tell Eric that Lia was safe. It wasn't her plan to keep lying to them. Maybe she and Lia would think about something soon.

CHAPTER 26

LIA

It should be early in the morning, or is it late at night? Lia shook her head, opening her eyes to stare at the brick ceiling above. There was no way to tell without a window. She sat up, staring at the clock on the wall, but it didn't help. She sighed, reaching out for her phone. The screen lit up to show it was around noon. She got out of bed. The conversation with Adrian a few days ago never left her mind.

"It will be great to see Helen in person," she said.

"Very soon. Just be patient."

"How soon is very soon?"

"Less than a month."

Lia took a sip of water from the glass on the bedside table. She had to do something. Otherwise, things would turn ugly. It should be fine—there was still time. She just needed to think of a way to stop Adrian, and possibly also William. It couldn't be that hard. She laughed at herself. Adrian was almost the scariest fighter she had seen, and with his history with William, it wouldn't be that easy for them to not fight.

She paced around the room with her hands on her waist, her brain working quickly. All she knew was in a month, Adrian would attack William and Eric, but how were the Elders doing about her disappearing? She had to get in touch with Helen first, maybe the two of them could come up with something, and then…

The door squeaked open and Lia flinched. Adrian was there, holding up a takeaway bag. "Hungry? Got you lunch."

Maybe she had to try to not make him suspicious first.

"Sure! What've you got?" She smiled, hugging him and pecking his cheek. They took a seat by the desk, taking out the food. "Wow! You got fried chicken. Not a bad choice!" She beamed, picking up a piece.

"Just not bad?" He raised his brows, taking a sip of his soft drink. Lia mumbled with half a piece of chicken in her mouth. Adrian laughed. "I can't hear you when your mouth is full."

"Not stroking your ego anytime soon." She snorted after she swallowed. "By the way, can I go out for a while today?" Her heart raced, hoping it wouldn't be hard to get through him.

He stared at her for a moment longer than she expected before shaking his head. "With Evelyn hunting you, I don't think it is a good idea."

"Please? I'll be very safe if you go with me. You aren't that easy to beat, right?"

He turned away, busying himself with the fries. "Of course I'm not easy to beat. But I don't want to risk you. Please be patient. We can go out together soon. You can even meet Helen."

"What will be different in a month's time? You will have beaten Evelyn already?" Lia busied herself with an onion ring.

It took a while before he said, "Just… it will be safer by then."

"Why?"

"You will know." He frowned slightly, likely not intending to tell her anything more. Lia sighed silently.

"OK… I hope it would work out."

"Me too. I'm trying everything to make sure you will be safe. I can't stand the thought of anything happening to you, not even the chance. I will not allow that to happen again," he said with a solemn face, his jaw tight. He gripped strongly on the soft drink cup, it buckled slightly.

Luckily, the fried chicken hid her gulp. She took a sip of her drink, pretending nothing happened. *Happen again? Ariel was killed by William… Is that the thing he is fighting to avoid? This is not going to end well.*

They finished the rest of the food in silence. As they packed up the trash, Lia nudged him. "Hey, I understand why I should stay here. Can you at least show me around again so I don't have to stay in this room all day? I'm still worried that I will get lost in this big of a maze if you aren't here with me all day."

"Of course. I'm sorry there's no internet here. I should've at least told you where to get some fun."

They took out the trash and Adrian led her down the corridors holding hands. She took the time to remember the route to the training room.

"I think this should be more familiar to you, seeing we have been here a few times." He turned on the lights; they were back in the room with rubber mats. Lia nodded, looking at two ends of the corridors, trying to distinguish them.

Adrian laughed as she was still confused. She huffed, rolling her eyes. "Why must it be that complicated?"

"Actually, it is in reverse. It is so simple here everything blends in," he said, crossing his arms with a smug smile.

"Of course you'd think that. You built it."

"Don't you think it would be fun to go on an adventure here? Feel free to walk around. It is not really that big, so you should be able to figure it out."

"Then I hope you won't find out about me getting lost. Is it really OK if I walk around? In case there are places I can't go? Like how you may have a few skeletons buried somewhere?"

Like how I heard about your secret plan?

"Skeletons, really? Who would do that in their home? It's fine. Even if I tell you not to go somewhere, being someone who causes trouble all the time, you will still find your way in." He spread his arms to his side and shrugged.

Lia growled, smacking his back. *Great, so you can't blame me for finding out something.*

They kept walking until they arrived at a heavy brick door, but there wasn't a doorknob. At the center of the door, there was a silvery sign of a wolf. Adrian gestured at the door. She pushed it, but it remained still.

"I know this door is not meant to be pushed or pulled. You can just tell me." She squinted at him as he fought to stifle a laugh.

"It's just fun to see you struggle. Anyways, I think you should be able to open it. I remember making it for magicians in general, so we will try." He gestured for her to rest her hand on the wolf.

She followed, the wolf cold on her hand. There were tiny tingles like static electricity. She jerked back her hand, looking at him. He nodded reassuringly. She rested her hand on it again. The tingles were still there, but with the expectation for them, she kept her hand there. After the initial touch, the wolf sign felt calming. There seemed to be some kind of magic in it that spoke to her power.

"Now just will it to move to the left. Focus on channelling your power into the sign."

Lia closed her eyes, focusing on the wolf. The whole door seemed to be in her hand. She willed the door to move, and when she opened her eyes, it had moved away. She stared at the door, rubbing her eyes.

"You aren't that bad" He chuckled, walking inside and gesturing for her to follow. As they walked in, the door closed behind them so the room was completely dark. Adrian snapped his fingers and the lights turned on. "The light is the same; you just will it on."

"Are you sure this is just willing it to light?" She pointed at his fingers.

"Well, isn't it fun to act at times? It helps to keep secrets in check." He winked and snapped his fingers again.

"Other rooms are the same?" Lia raised her brows. She remembered him reaching for the switches in others.

"No, this one is special. Only magicians are allowed here. The door is activated by magic only."

There was a time humans were here?

"Why?" This room was filled with bookshelves. Under the yellowish light, they looked more antique than they probably were. She walked up to one of the shelves.

"You will soon see." He stood next to her, picking out one of the books and showing it to Lia. It was a guidebook about summoning magic.

"Does this really work? Or would the average person think it is just a joke?" She furrowed her brows.

"When the first human who had too much time on their hands actually tried it, things would go down before you know it. Although not every human has the potential for magic, there are enough of them to disrupt the balance." He flipped open the book, reading from it, "With the focus of the heart and the call from the core, one shall wield the gifted power. In the blink of an eye, substances can be created, and in time, it fades."

Lia frowned deeper. "It is my… our magic? Or the way of the Elements' magic?"

"Someone compiled ways the average person could check whether they're a magician or not."

"Still, it doesn't look dangerous enough to warrant this kind of security. What's so bad with having more magicians?"

He flipped a few more pages. "Try this. 'It is believed that magic can be transferred by blood and of blood, both life-granting and filled with blessings.'"

"Um… I don't know about the correlation of the Elements' magic and blood." Lia ran her fingers through her hair, shaking her head.

"You see, the author can't distinguish our magic from that of the Elements. The Elements' magic can't be transferred nor built without the foundation in the person from the beginning. Think of what the humans would do to a magician for their power if they read this and believed it. Luckily, this and magic are more like a secret to humans now. Think of all the chaos it could cause."

Some power-hungry humans could kill magicians for their blood. "Who wrote this?"

"I am not sure. It could have been someone working closely with the Elders of the Elements, or just a random person putting together myths. There are quite a few of these books, but this is the only one left. Or so I think." He shrugged, putting the book back to the shelf.

"There was a time when it wasn't a secret?"

"Smart, huh? Yes, a long time ago, most people more or less knew about it. It took a lot of work to finally put the cat back into the bag. Even now, outside of Zitannas, if people see magic, they are going to remember it."

"So no one outside knows?"

"Some do, but magicians are smart about it."

"There are magicians outside of you, Evelyn, and the Elders?"

"The world is large. Though everyone is very careful. Now, as far as I know, most magicians only become one after they are decided to fit beforehand. Most humans wouldn't discover their power even if they had it."

"How did you guard something that big?"

He chuckled, shaking his head. "In ways you wouldn't like. So maybe don't ask. It was a long time ago."

There weren't a lot of things she didn't like, she could guess. Probably included killing. At least it was a long time ago. "So, all these books are about magic?" There were eight shelves, every one of them taller than her and almost filled with books.

"Not really. Some are completely made up, just like those in bookstores. I put them here in case someone did break in so they don't find the real thing. I've been an expert of making up things for years, so it is only reasonable for me to have some of them here. It was so long ago, done as part of the effort to make magic seem ridiculous and fake for the outside world." He followed her gaze, looking at the shelves. "All the lies and stories I had to make up are tiring to think about now."

Like how the gang thought the strange sound could defeat magicians?

Lia trailed behind him, glancing over the spines of the books. "I suppose you brought me here so I can come back later?"

"Yes, you can have fun reading here. I'm pretty sure

you can figure out what's fake, and you may actually learn a few things."

"Didn't know you were such a nerdy guy." She smiled, linking their arms.

"For a long time, books and paper were the only ways to record things. You do know that, right?" he huffed a humorless chuckle.

"Oh yeah, I always forget how much of an old soul you are," she chuckled.

He groaned, messing with her hair. "That has nothing to do with being old and I am not old." She smacked his shoulder, pushing away his hand before fixing her hair.

"The other rooms aren't as interesting. But you can walk around as you like. I've locked up everything you shouldn't see anyway." He leaned closer to her with a smirk.

"Hiding things behind my back, huh?" Lia cupped his chin, pulling his face close.

"I'm keeping some surprises for you." He planted a kiss on the tip of her nose.

Yeah… when I know William and Eric are dead, it sure will be a surprise. Not letting that happen, sorry not sorry.

CHAPTER 27

LIA

Adrian wasn't going to let Lia out of the dungeon— she'd have to do it herself. In the next few days, Lia explored, getting to know most of the rooms. She pushed on every door she could lay her hands on.

Adrian wasn't around, probably perfecting his plan to attack the clan. If he was working hard on his end, there was no time for her to slack off. Back in her room, she drew herself a map of the dungeon, marking down the rooms, and more importantly, the stairs leading to different levels. There was still one level she had yet to explore; maybe she would do that tomorrow.

If she was going to help William and Eric, she had to get out of the dungeon. It seemed there was no way Adrian would agree to it. She didn't dare ask, no point risking what he would do when he knew what she knew.

She traced her fingers on the map along the route that would take her to the stairs going up. Adrian never brought her up there. Before she figured out what to do, she didn't need more attention from him.

The faint sound of the doorknob turning startled her.

She barely stuffed the map into her pillowcase when Adrian walked in, yawning and rubbing his eyes.

"Have fun walking around?" he asked, sitting on the side of the bed and taking off his shoes.

"Yeah, I went to the library and the books are interesting." Her heart racing, hoping he wouldn't find a thing suspicious. He nodded, seemingly oblivious.

He lay on the bed face up, resting his head on his crossed arms. "That's good. I'm worried that you will get bored."

What makes you think I'm not?

"I don't know how long I can stand this underground secret facility, though…"

He turned to her, wrapping his arms around her waist. "I'm sorry. I promise this will end very soon. I told you less than a month, right? Maybe sooner."

Her heart skipped a beat; it would be time for her to move things forward. "I guess it's more bearable when you're here with me." She laid down next to him.

"I wish I could be with you all the time, but there are still things to be done," he sighed, nibbling on her earlobe.

"Tomorrow? Although we had training yesterday, can't hurt to have an extra session."

"I… sorry, I have something else to do tomorrow. But the day after tomorrow, I promise."

If he wouldn't be here the next day, maybe she could sneak outside. If she was fast, no one would know. Her heart raced despite her wish, and he looked up with furrowed eyebrows. "What's wrong?"

"I… I just want to spend more time with you, but you are always busy…" She stared down, averting his gaze.

"Tomorrow night, we'll have dinner together. Whatever you want. Deal?" A pained look flashed on his face as he toyed with her hair.

"Can we go out to have dinner?"

Please say no… Don't tell me you will be fighting William that soon…

His face fell and he shook his head. "Have some patience. I will get you takeaway like before. Or if you want, I can cook you something."

"You are lucky I like food and I like you."

He growled, nibbling on her throat under her chin. "Is there a reason I'm listed behind food?"

She chuckled, pushing on his shoulders. "Jealous?"

"You better give me an answer." He tickled her side and she squirmed, trying to grab his hands.

"Hey! Stop it! Fine, you are better than food! Happy?" She playfully shoved his chest.

He laughed, shaking his head. "It seems I can't help but feel good with you around. It's too hard to be angry."

"I guess that's a good thing."

I probably will need that if I fail to sneak back in time.

"Lucky you," he beamed, stroking her cheek with his thumb.

She spent the night going through her plan in her mind while trying her best to keep a straight face. He fell asleep quickly after he hit the pillow. She couldn't tear her eyes away from him, resisting the urge to stroke his hair. She liked how peaceful he was when he was asleep, much better than when he was stressed.

Sorry, Adrian. I can't let the Elders die. Please forgive me. If anything, I will try not to let you know until the last moment.

CHAPTER 28

LIA

"Hey." Something nudged Lia gently and she stirred, opening her eyes. Adrian pecked her forehead with a smile on his face. "I'll see you at dinner time, OK?"

The next day came sooner than she hoped. She faintly nodded, pulling him closer, kissing him on the lips, stroking his cheek. He let out a small moan, hugging her close. They remained wrapped in each other's arms for a while longer before he finally pulled away.

"I have to go." He got out of the bed, lifting her hand to kiss her knuckles.

Lia sighed. "Sure. I will try to find something to do." Adrian nodded, putting on his shoes and grabbing his things before heading out.

She sat up as soon as the door clicked closed. Her brain felt tired after all the planning, but she needed to remember the route if she was to pull this off. Holding up a map wouldn't help.

She only had to get out of the dungeon and message Helen; it couldn't be that hard. Adrian for sure wouldn't be happy about it, but he didn't need to know. If she came back quickly, before Benjamin brought her food She got out of bed and dressed, laying the map on the desk while she tied up her hair.

Adrian was the one working behind her back first, she didn't have to feel bad about what she was going to do.

She gripped her phone tightly and slid it into her pocket, giving it a pat before pressing an ear against the door, making sure Adrian was long gone.

The dim corridors were still empty and cold as they always were. But now, they seemed even creepier. It took much more force and determination for her to step out of the room. At each corner, she made sure to check for anyone. Although it seemed only Adrian and Benjamin were there, this place felt a bit too big for just the two of them.

Soon, she arrived at the stairs and took a last peek down the corridor she came from, relieved that it was empty, without even a trace of magic. Keeping her steps quiet, she walked up the stairs, her heart beating quicker and quicker as she climbed. She made her way through two more floors before she froze as there was a hushed voice down in the corridor.

Adrian and Benjamin were chatting, seemingly deep in conversation.

Lia carefully continued up the stairs, but then there was a hand on her shoulder. Crap! When she snapped her head back, Adrian was glaring at her.

"May I ask where you're going?" He scowled, standing a step lower than her. She swallowed, her mouth dry.

"Just walking around trying to find something to do? You said I could figure out this place." She averted his gaze.

"Go back, will you?" he said with a cold and commanding voice, gesturing at the stairs behind him.

Lia gritted her teeth. If she went back, he wouldn't let her have the chance to go out anymore.

She took a deep breath. He moved sideways, giving her the space to head back. She kicked him in the chest, pushing him down the stairs while dashing up. Hopefully, he wouldn't kill her.

Her heart thundered in her chest. She could hear him shouting after her, but she kept running. Soon the stairs ended, revealing another corridor—she was close to the exit.

Someone from behind grabbed her waist and tackled her to the floor. She tried to pull away, but he was too strong. She closed her eyes, bracing herself for impact to the floor, but she landed on something soft. When she opened her eyes, she was in Adrian's arms—he was the one who took the impact. He grabbed her tightly, staring daggers at her.

"Did I not tell you to wait for a while?" he grunted.

Lia struggled to free herself, yanking at his arm, but to no avail. She hauled her ice shards, getting ready to shoot at him, when a sharp chill spread from his arms through her body.

No, not now! She kicked around, fighting his grip, but her strength left her quickly. She fought to stay focused as her vision slowly blurred. Her limbs felt heavier and heavier until she lost the power to fight and the world blacked out.

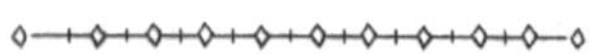

Lia found herself lying on something soft and comfortable, a stream of warmth came from her hand through the rest of her body. She felt her own breath once again. She opened her eyes. Adrian was holding her hand, his eyes glowing in red.

Back to square one…

"Feeling better?" he asked.

She pulled her hand away from him, turning her back to him and pulling the cover up her face as a sob escaped her. Tears fell down her face, her cry muffled by the blanket. Better play it well for the next chance.

"Please, Lia… I know you want to spend some time outside. Let me do my work first, OK? There's nothing more I want than your safety."

He rested his hand on her shoulder, but she turned away from his touch. "Leave me alone…"

"Lia…" he pulled at the blanket, yanking it off her. She flinched, averting his gaze. "Can you please not do that again? Stay here until things are settled, OK?" A pained look flashed through his face. He reached out to stroke her cheek, but she slapped his hand away.

He sighed, getting out of the bed. "Whatever, you are staying here. I will bring you your meals when it's time." He headed to the door when Lia sat up on the bed.

With a shaky voice, she asked, "Are you holding me prisoner now?"

He halted without turning around to face her. "That's one way to look at it. This won't last for long."

"Wait! Adrian!" She dashed for him, but he closed the door in her face. She reached down to the doorknob, but it was locked from outside. She willed for an ice beam to break the lock. When she tried, a strong electric shock pushed her back a few steps. She fell to the floor, staring at the door with her eyes wide. It had to be his magic, how dare he do this to her.

"ADRIAN!" She clenched a fist, nails digging into her

palms. There was no response from the other side of the door.

Why... why must he keep me locked up in here...? Did he already figure out I know his plan?

Lia dashed at the door again, but whatever magic he casted on the door bounced her back. She groaned as she landed on her elbow on the floor. It hurt. She sent ice shards at the door, but her attacks were deflected, sending them flying back at her. She barely evaded her own blast.

Dammit! Adrian, I hate you!

Lia punched the floor, getting up, pacing the room. *There must be something I can still do. I have to get out of here!* She shook her head, breathing deeply, trying to clear her mind. She was so close to getting out successfully, but now she was locked in by his magic. There seemed no way she could break through. Even if she could, he would know at once and had ample time to just wait for her at the exit.

Could there be more than one exit? She rubbed her forehead. *Nah, the problem on hand is how to get rid of this stupid magic.*

She walked up to all the walls of the room, touching every inch and knocking lightly. There didn't seem to be a secret door.

Anger simmered in her stomach. Adrian couldn't do this to her. Who did he think he was? He didn't get to decide for her what would happen, and he also didn't get to kill the Elders whenever he wanted to. She punched the pillow on her lap mindlessly. *It seems the only way to get through the magic is to convince Adrian to take it away... He probably won't...*

As her mind raced through ways she could get out from the dungeon, but solutions seemed to be limited. She focused her mind on the magic around the door, trying to identify it. Maybe she could find a way to crack it.

She had no idea how long had passed with her sitting

and staring at the door when she heard faint footsteps outside. Lia slid under the covers, pretending to be asleep.

The door clicked open. "Hey…" Adrian walked in with the smell of cheese and pepperoni. "Want some food?"

Under the cover, she could barely make out the muffled sound of paper bags and a box. She pulled the cover over her head, hiding herself from his gaze. He walked over to sit beside her, but she rolled away from him.

"Still angry?"

She buried her head in the pillow, not wanting to see him. She didn't even want food. What did he think she was? Just a puppy he could bribe with food?

He reached out to her shoulder over the cover, and she flinched at his touch. He took back his hand. "Don't want to see me, huh…? I guess that's what I deserve, then… I just hope you will understand where I'm coming from."

Lia's head remained down on her pillow as it became wet from her tears. *I know how much you want William and Eric dead, but now that I know, I can't stand and watch. Whatever they did to you, they helped me a lot…*

If she could knock him down, maybe she could escape. Then she remembered how the gangsters died. This wasn't a good idea at all. She already kicked him on the stairs; it was better to not push her luck any further. Not to mention he was much stronger than her. She set the plan aside.

"I got you pizza…any interest?" he asked, but there was no answer.

They remained in silence. She could feel the bed moving slightly as he shifted his weight around. Even under the blanket, she could feel his intense gaze on her. He nudged her shoulder gently. "Are you asleep?"

She remained silent.

"I guess you don't want me here…sorry. I'll leave the

pizza. When you want some, you can have it…" He got off the bed and shortly after, the door closed.

As soon as he was gone, Lia popped her head out. She glanced at the pizza box before staring at the door again. She launched a small ice shard at it, but it bounced against the magic, breaking before it could hit. She sighed, shaking her head.

Up until now, Adrian thinks I want to get out because I am bored here. He doesn't know the real reason I want to get out. Maybe I can use this…

She got up, walking toward the door. She tried again to reach for the doorknob. The magic sent a spark through her hand. She gritted her teeth, trying to push through. The magic was strong, as if she was trying to punch through a thick pillow, and she couldn't seem to get through the field and reach the knob. It sent a burning pain through her the harder she tried. As soon as her resolve fell, the force field knocked her back.

Ok… This is it. Hopefully, this will go well.

Despite her body shouting at her, she took in a deep breath, facing the door again. She launched at it, and the magic threw her onto the ground. Nausea stirred inside her. She bent over on the floor, squirming as her body twitched from the strong force.

Gathering all her strength, she pushed herself up again and rammed herself at the door, at his magic, again and again. Her head throbbed with pain, probably the magic would for real knock her out some time soon. She tried to dash at the door, her legs were heavier than she expected, she stumbled.

She closed her eyes as she anticipated the blow from the magic. Instead, she bumped into something with a low thud. She should have bumped into a wall or something, but she felt nothing. She snapped open her eyes. *Did I knock off the magic?*

Instead, from her still blurry vision, Adrian's face was in front of her, his eyes filled with guilt and pain. Lia tried to push herself away from him, but she was too weak. He pulled her closer to him, his arms wrapped around her waist.

She opened her mouth to talk, a choking feeling stirred her throat. She coughed, tasting her own blood, before closing her eyes, panting and letting him hold her.

"Lia… What are you doing? Staying here is bad enough that you'd resort to this?" Adrian asked.

In the darkness, she was lifted and set carefully down on the bed. She slowly opened her eyes as the comfy pillow and blanket surrounded her. Both Adrian and Benjamin were looking over her, their faces filled with concern.

The world was still spinning. She shook her head, tears running down her cheek. "I… can't… I can't even breathe here. Trapped… suf… focated…" She rolled around, turning her back to them.

"You know I don't want this for you," Adrian said.

Benjamin walked over to her with a glass of water and she took it, clearing the taste of blood in her mouth. Benjamin sighed. "It must be scary to be in a dungeon without a glimpse of sunlight… or fresh air."

"I… know… but…" Adrian shook his head, crossing his arms. Lia grunted, pushing herself from the bed. Adrian pinned her down on her shoulders. She stared at him with blank eyes, barely holding herself together. He had no idea how much she wanted to punch him in the face if she didn't have to appeal to him. He gulped, averting her gaze.

She closed her eyes again, giving herself the room to breathe. "At least give me a window or something? Waking up to walls and complete darkness is not working for me… Maybe you should tie me up with those chains again. It's easier than me trying to kill myself with the magic you set up."

"My King, you still remember the days we hid here? It drove half of us almost crazy. Is it too much to demand Lia to stay?"

"Benjamin, I didn't ask you here to…" Adrian trailed off as Lia looked into his eyes, tears welling up in hers. "I mean… you know there's no window underground."

"You can lock me up in your office? At least there's a window," Lia said, her voice shaky.

"I don't know, it may be more dangerous there." Adrian frowned deeply, hesitant.

"If you don't mind, I can keep watch of Lia. I am confident to at least drag on in case someone thinks they can trespass me. You won't be far away," Benjamin said, looking between the two of them.

Adrian raised his brows. "You are talking about around the clock?"

Benjamin nodded. "I can do that. I guess that's the best. I can cast the magic and still get work done in another room. Of course, that's if you two don't mind."

"That's all fine with me. Just get me a window somewhere and some fresh air." Lia looked at Benjamin, mouthing a "thank you" and a grin.

Adrian pulled back from the bed, rubbing his chin. "I guess it is for the best then. If something happens to Lia, Ben, you know what will happen."

"Of course. I know, my King. You can rest your worries. Have I ever failed you?"

Adrian's voice was cold. "You better keep your record straight." He reached for Lia's waist. At the touch, a stream of warmth rushed into her and the throbbing pain subsided. The spinning world came to a stop. She wrapped her arms around him, pulling him into a deep kiss. It would be better for her to not keep annoying him.

"You make it hard to focus on my magic." He chuckled.

Lia let out a sigh of relief. "Thank you. I really need a break from this dungeon."

"Sorry… I should have thought of my office earlier. Ben should be capable of protecting you." He averted her gaze, staring at the pillow beside her sheepishly. She rubbed his back, stroking his hair. He leaned into her touch, nudging her with his nose. "I hope you aren't still angry with me?" he whispered.

"You aren't the brightest, but not that bad, I guess." She smiled. "Also, you are kind of heavy."

"Oh! I'm sorry." He rolled off her onto the other side of the bed before getting up. He helped her out of the bed, wrapping an arm around her waist, guiding her out of the room.

It was then that Lia remembered Benjamin's existence. She blushed, looking around the room, but he was nowhere to be seen. She raised her eyebrows.

He shrugged. "Ben? He was already outside."

"Oh, I thought…"

"While I have few problems letting him see us hugging each other, he won't want to see."

Lia blushed even more, playfully shoving his chest. Outside the room, Benjamin was a few steps down the corridor. He looked up as they approached, shooting them a knowing look.

The moment they walked out of the dungeon into the warm sunlight, Lia took a deep breath, closing her eyes and taking in the fresh smell of the soil and leaves. The chirping of the birds sounded more pleasant than she ever realised. She spread out her arms, feeling the warmth from the sun. She turned around to find Benjamin and Adrian looking at her with smiles on their faces.

"What? The first time you two see me?"

Adrian let out a relaxed sigh, shaking his head. "I found myself missing your smile so much."

"I do smile when you actually talk to me and spend time with me."

"I guess I simply enjoy seeing you happy." He chuckled, hugging her tightly enough to lift her slightly off the ground.

She hugged him back when Benjamin smirked at her, standing a few steps behind Adrian. She blushed bright red. Benjamin shook his head, looking away from them.

Lia closed her eyes, snuggling into the crook of Adrian's neck as he stroked the back of her hand with his thumb.

They got to Adrian's car a short distance away from the entrance to the dungeon. They were in a forest, probably quite some distance from the city center. Behind them, the entrance to the dungeon blended in with the surroundings on a larger boulder. A few steps away, she had already lost sight of the door.

Benjamin beat Adrian to the driver's seat. "How about you two go chill in the back? I am very concerned about everyone's safety."

Adrian cleared his throat. "Just to be clear, I have no problem still driving my own car."

"So, you would rather drive than sit in the back?" Benjamin tilted his head to the side with a teasing smile.

"Fine… If you want to drive, I'll let you," Adrian huffed, opening the car door to get in the back with Lia.

She leaned onto Adrian, savoring the warmth from his body. He wrapped his arm across her waist. She closed her eyes, faintly feeling the rise and fall of his chest. Although the damage done by the magic was healed, she was still exhausted. She blinked, her eyelids heavy.

Time for me to take action, finally.

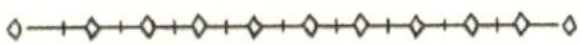

As soon as Adrian opened the door to his penthouse, Lia rushed past him, sticking herself to the floor-to-ceiling window in the living room, staring at the shimmering sea view outside. Her palms on the window, she never thought she would miss the view so much. It felt like ages since she looked through this window.

A pair of arms wrapped around her from behind and she shuddered. Adrian's breath warm in her hair, her neck. His body pressed against her. She grinned, rubbing his arms.

"I don't know, Lia. I may care about you a bit too much," he whispered.

"Yeah? Too much to lock me up in a dungeon?"

"I can't risk you. The dungeon is where I find safety, hiding away from the rest of the world. But I guess what works for you is more important."

"I know you care about me. Lucky me, huh?" She chuckled, leaning back into him.

"Are you still angry?" There was a glint of worry in his voice.

Lia shook her head. "If you had kept me locked up down there, I would be."

"Great."

She remained wrapped into his arms, feeling his warmth on her back. Looking at the sea from the window, she could imagine herself inside, swimming in the cool water around her. She closed her eyes, getting lost in the moment. They stood by the window until Benjamin's voice came from the kitchen together with the smell of cheese.

"Hey, I'm coming out with pizza!"

Slowly Adrian took a step back, his fingers lingering on her waist before he finally let go of her. She turned around, meeting his intense blue eyes. With a smirk, she kissed him gently on the lips. Before he could kiss her back, she pulled away.

His eyes widened, raising his eyebrows at her. "What does that mean?"

"It means I still like you, but I want my pizza first." She ran off to the kitchen table.

He shouted behind her, "Really? Why must you put all kinds of food before me?"

Lia took a seat by the kitchen table when Benjamin set down the warmed-up pizza. Adrian soon followed, sitting next to her.

Benjamin grinned as he cut the pizza into pieces. "I rescued this poor thing before we left. Luckily it is all freshened up after staying in the oven."

She took a piece, beaming as the cheese and tomato sauce filled her mouth. She didn't realise it had been hours since she last ate.

Benjamin tilted his head to the side, winking at them. "Should I go somewhere else so you two can get comfortable?"

"It's fine, Ben. You can stay here." Adrian almost choked on his soft drink. Lia laughed at him.

"Great!" Benjamin took a slice for himself, taking a big bite. "You will never know how happy I am to see you finally stop fighting."

"When I said you could stay here, this is not what I meant." Adrian rolled his eyes, but the corners of his lips curled up.

"Whatever you want, then. You are the King—it's your call as always. I will zip my mouth and eat my pizza." Benjamin gestured to zip up his mouth with his hand, winking at Lia. She averted his gaze as a stream of heat reached her cheeks.

Adrian huffed, chewing down on his slice. Lia shivered as Adrian's gaze landed on her and she turned to him, carefully making sure the piece of pepperoni didn't fall from her pizza. His face was serious. "For real, Lia. Don't try to get out anymore, OK? I will try to be here more. Whatever you need, Ben will get for you. You get your window and your breath of fresh air. Don't make it difficult on any of us. You'll be able to go out very soon."

Lia nodded, snuggling up to him. *Except I am still going to do what I need to do... Even though I don't even know how I can do it... Is there even a way for him to not fight with the Elders? Hopefully, with Helen, we can think of something.*

After they finished the food and cleaned up the kitchen table, Adrian and Benjamin went into the office to discuss something. Benjamin cast his magic onto the door, and she was dismissed.

Lia plodded down on the bed, staring at the ceiling, resisting the urge to sneak to the office door to spy on them. Probably they were talking about keeping her in check and maybe continuing their plan to kill the Elders. She wanted to keep them safe, but she had to find a way to also keep Adrian safe.

Maybe she shouldn't try to listen; she already made Adrian angry by sneaking out of the dungeon and forcing him to let her out on the same day. It wouldn't be good if she got caught eavesdropping.

At least she had her phone. She let out a sigh of relief, when it connected to the network. Luckily, Benjamin's magic didn't affect the signal. *Lucky Adrian doesn't seem to remember I have this.*

Her phone buzzed like crazy from all the messages. It lasted so long Lia had to stuff it under the pillow, for fear Adrian would hear something. She didn't know whether he knew she would find Helen. *He better not remember. I can't even imagine how I would get him to give me back my phone.*

After the buzz died down, Lia took a glance at the messages. There were messages from Helen, and as she scrolled through them, her breath caught. Seemingly while Adrian was planning to take out the Elders, they were also actively searching for the dark magicians and trying to take them out.

Slowly, you can think of a way to do it, now just let Helen know she can contact you. You two can work out something. Remember to breathe. It will be fine.

She closed her eyes briefly, pulling the blanket over her head and trying to ground herself. She almost got under control when there was the sound of the doorknob turning. She jumped, sitting up on the bed just in time to see Adrian peeking in with his eyebrows raised.

"You scared me! Learn to knock, will you?" She forced a smile, tucking her phone under the pillow, hoping the blanket concealed her movement.

He seemed to be taken aback. "Oh, sorry about that. Just want to see whether you are feeling better now that you're not underground anymore."

She let out a sigh of relief, nodding at the window. "Very much so. Being able to look at the sky is a lot more therapeutic than I imagined."

"That's great. I really love to see you happy." He walked in, sitting by her side. She snuggled to him, leaning on his shoulder. He wrapped his arm across her waist, pulling her close.

They remained wrapped together for another moment before he sighed, rubbing her arm. Lia looked up at him with a light frown on her face. His smile faltered. "I have to go. Soon, we'll be free to just spend time with each other. I will be back tonight. Due to a certain someone, my schedule for the day is falling behind."

Lia stuck out her tongue and chuckled. "You are fighting Evelyn already?"

He flinched at the mention, shaking his head. "There are some things to be done before we take care of her."

"What are they? Can I help?"

His demeanor changed for a split second before he schooled his features. "Nothing to be worried about. I can do it on my own. I'll let you know when it is done." He gently squeezed her hand before kissing it.

Of course you aren't letting me help.

"Just stay safe with whatever you are doing, OK? Without knowing what you are up to, I get worried something will happen to you."

"I'm not a rookie like you. I will be fine." He pulled her into a tight hug before standing from the bed and heading to the door. "Ben will be here to keep watch over you and to keep you safe. Let him know if you need anything."

"Sure!" Lia walked him to the door. He hugged her once again before he left. Was it wrong to feel at ease when he was gone? The door clicked close, not only did it physically separate the two, it seemed to also close something for her. Well, Adrian was never an open book since the beginning.

She turned back to her room. Benjamin was standing nearby, raising his brows. She froze. "Something's up?"

"Not really. I guess it's just fun to see you two together. I thought of the time we first met and now. Kind of crazy, isn't it?"

"I guess so?"

Maybe it would be easier to get something from Ben than from Adrian.

"You know what Adrian is up to? He seems to be really busy?" she asked.

He chuckled, gesturing to the office. "He's the King. Of course he ought to be busy."

In Adrian's office, Lia took a seat on the chair facing the window, where she used to sit when she was in training. Benjamin stood awkwardly on the side, running a hand through his hair as he sat on the couch by the door frame.

Lia turned the office chair to face him, tilting her head sideways in question. "Why don't you sit here?" She gestured at the chair behind the desk.

"Well… I don't dare sit there, just in case. Don't want to risk pissing the King off." Benjamin spread out his hands beside him, smirking.

"I didn't know the rules were that detailed." Lia eyed Adrian's empty chair.

"It's just a habit now. He actually doesn't care that much now., but I don't feel comfortable doing that. There's something you shouldn't do, just to play safe. But I guess you get plenty of leeway with him."

"He is the one trying to lock me up. And it feels terrible being underground. Do you think running into his magic is that enjoyable? I have no choice." Lia frowned.

There was a flash of something in his eyes for a split second. "I know. Things you would do to get him to bend over for you, huh? Maybe you should know he seldom changes his plan. Consider yourself lucky. I also know you are smarter than we may have expected. Please know that we are simply trying to help you."

"Actually, I am very capable of helping myself." Her

heart hammered in her chest. There's no way Benjamin knew her intention, right?

"Not with what he—" Benjamin awkwardly cleared his throat. "Not with Evelyn. You've never seen something of that scale. Our time before facing her is limited, so we are just trying to get prepared."

"Can I help?" Lia asked.

The mischievous glint flashed in his eyes again, the hair on the back of Lia's neck stood.

"We can manage it. You don't have to worry at all."

"Is that something I would get angry about?"

He flinched, his smile faltering for a split second before he schooled himself. He shook his head. "I don't know what he is doing. But I am just researching Evelyn, so nothing you would be angry about."

"Given how close the two of you are, you have no idea what Adrian is up to?"

He chuckled dryly, seemingly a bit forced. "You think the King has to explain himself to me? Feel free to do whatever you want, as long as it doesn't require leaving. I have stuff to catch up with before the King gets angry with me."

Fine, I'll try again later. "Sure, I will just spend some time with the sea view outside." Lia walked out of the room and Benjamin closed the door behind her. On the way to the window in the living room, she walked by the door. There was the low humming of a magical forcefield around, she could feel the spark when she slid by.

Standing by the large window, she looked around the living room, her memory rushing back: the time when she started exploring her power, how she seemed to get along with Adrian at times, how he pushed her away, and how they fought each other about their relationship. Those seemed to be so far in the past.

She turned to the window, the sea calming. With each breath, she slowed her mind, focusing on the pressing matter on her hands.

There was finally internet. Now she just needed to find a way to one-up Adrian's plan. She spent a few more minutes by the window before retreating back to her room. She made sure to lock the door before she sat by the desk, taking out her phone from below the pillow. She messaged Helen.

> *Finally you can get hold of me!*

The reply came back quickly.

> *LIA! YOU CAN'T BELIEVE HOW HAPPY I AM! Please tell me this is not a dream!*

> *C'mon, this is not a dream. You can go pinch your face.*

> *I couldn't find you before. What happened?*

> *Let's just say he doesn't get internet where he kept me.*

> *Really? I can't imagine that kind of place exists. Where were you? In a cave?*

Lia rolled her eyes; she could imagine how much Helen was laughing at the message.

> *Of course, spending time with grumpy dinosaurs. Important things first, William really is looking for them?*

Helen sent a bunch of crying emojis before the text.

> *Yes… I am trying my best to delay their progress, but I don't know how long I can drag it…*

Lia sighed heavily, typing with shaky fingers.

> *Sadly, A is doing the same. He doesn't know I know. At least that's what I think. He wants the Elders dead.*

> *Really? What should we do?* Helen must be worried as there were ten messages of only scared emojis in a row. Lia rolled her eyes.

> *Although I can find you now, I can't get out of the penthouse. Ben locked the door with magic. And you also can only get out with William next to you?*

> *Correct. I can sneak out. But a magic on the door…*

> *Not to mention Ben is too strong for me to beat… Can you do something on your end?*

> *I will see, how much time do you think we got?*

> *At most two more weeks before A will strike. The Elders?*

> *As soon as they find out… I don't even know…*

Lia sighed, rubbing her temple.

> *We will screw both of their plans. I will find a way to get out. Same for you.*

Helen sent back an OK sign.

Lia took in a deep breath. She would have to wait, at least until Benjamin was certain she wasn't going to escape anytime soon.

CHAPTER 29

Helen was sitting in her room in the clan, facing the desk, toying her hair with her fingers. It had been a day since Lia messaged her after she escaped a boring dungeon. Helen hoped she could come up with a plan quickly.

Adrian was planning the same thing William was. Only, Adrian seemed to be capable of doing things more efficiently; he already knew where the Elders were while William was still trying to figure out where Adrian was.

Now she and Lia had to stop both Adrian and William. When compared to Lia, she could at least sneak out of the clan. But she still had to find a way to provide help to Lia. It was not like she could just show up at Adrian's penthouse and barge her way in. Even with Lia, they probably couldn't beat Benjamin, not to mention Adrian may be there. And what would they do after getting Lia out?

Helen rolled her eyes, sitting back and crossing her arms behind her head. She already messed up William's documents a few times, mixing in irrelevant details and swapping the reports. But she couldn't keep doing that, otherwise, only a dummy wouldn't find her suspicious.

William wasn't that dumb; he would soon find out. Benjamin's bar wasn't going to vanish into thin air anytime soon. As much as the dark magician could hide their power, there was still a chance William could sense it.

She twirled her hair thinking about things she had no idea how to do and their importance. She sighed heavily, picking up her phone and scrolled mindlessly through the social media site she frequented. As she cursed under her breath at the advertisement, waiting for the skip button to show up, something about it caught her eyes.

It was a short advertisement video she usually wouldn't pay any attention to. "Just for today! Get your sleeping schedule fixed! This all-natural stress relief is what you need! Send us a message to order!"

Helen's eyes lit up—maybe she could find something like that. Not at all what the advertisement was selling, but maybe something that could divert Benjamin's attention enough that his magic would fail. If the dark magic was not too far from the Elements' magic, if Benjamin was unconscious, the magic would fail. She jolted up, knocking over the chair.

She quickly texted Lia, and her reply came quickly. Lia was onboard. Helen shoved the phone into her pocket and ran to the library. She wasn't sure what she could come up with, but if she was to use her magic in some way, that was the place to go.

As Helen approached the entrance to the library, she took a deep breath. She wasn't quite a fan of books, but if this was the only way, she had to do it. For Lia, Helen could get that bit of patience to dig through the piles of books.

Helen walked past rows of bookshelves, trying to find

the books for her magic. When she walked past the counter, Sophia wasn't there. Helen sighed. She walked past the books on the history of magicians, myths about unknown creatures, and even how to fix a car, but she didn't seem anywhere near the guidebooks for magic.

Maybe there weren't such books. If there were, Eric would have taught her more about her magic. She shook her head, knocking on her forehead gently with her hand. *Come on, Helen. You said you would be patient for Lia. You haven't even been here for an hour. Keep it up!*

She turned around a corner with her eyes still on the row of shelves behind her.

"Whoa!" Helen halted just in time not to bump into Sophia. "Sorry."

"It's fine. What are you looking for?" Sophia smiled warmly, putting down the book in her hand onto a small cart beside her.

"Thank goodness I found you. By any chance, do you know of any books about nature magic?"

Sophia paused a bit too long before she said, "Sure." She led Helen down the rows of bookshelves. On the way, she asked, "Why are you searching for a book like that? Isn't William taking care of your training?"

"He doesn't have my kind of magic. And I don't know any other magicians, so books may be my best bet. There could be some more tricks for me to learn. The dark magicians sound scary, so I thought maybe I should learn something new to help tackle them."

Sophia's smile faltered slightly, but she schooled herself. "You think dark magicians exist? William has been taking books out, but staying in here most of the time. I don't know a lot. Do you know how the investigation is going?"

"Like you said, I think he is still trying. He sometimes looks confused. I'm not sure if he's found anything solid yet. I tried to help, but I don't even know what dark magic is like, I doubt I am of any help..." Helen shrugged. Sophia nodded with a solemn look.

"Do you know about the dark magicians?" Helen asked.

"Mostly from rumors and myths, like you. I don't even know if they really exist. All the books about magic other than ours seem to be a mix of fiction and history." Sophia shook her head, fixing her braid.

"I don't even know whether I want them to find them or not. Nonetheless, getting prepared would never go wrong." Helen sighed, peeking half-heartedly at the shelves they walked past. Finally, they walked to a row with different guidebooks, separated into different types of magic.

Sophia gestured at the bookshelf. "I just hope everyone will be safe, I guess. The Elders know what they are doing. I think you can start at whichever seems interesting to you."

Helen couldn't shake the feeling that Sophia was avoiding her gaze by looking at the books. Maybe she was too anxious because of Lia and everything happening. Hopefully Sophia wouldn't tell William she was there. It was almost the team's knowledge that she had no interest in books; and she was worried that would be suspicious.

She thanked Sophia and took a closer look at the books. Trailing her fingers along the spines, she rubbed her chin with her other hand. There were quite a lot of books about the nature magic, making it hard to pick one out. There were even books written in languages she didn't know.

There had to be a way to sort out the one or two she may need. She frowned at the rows of books. A bit frustrated, she decided to close her eyes and just pick one at random. Her hunch had been quite accurate anyway.

She took a deep breath and picked one. The spine felt like cloth. She opened her eyes at an illustrated handbook of different types of plants. She raised her brows, pulling out the book. It was titled *100 Types of Medicinal Herbs*. The title looked nothing magical, but if her hunch picked it, she should at least take a look.

The library was quiet as she wandered to find a seat. Sophia had disappeared into the sea of books again. She arrived at a sofa, opening the book. There were beautiful and detailed illustrations about different kinds of plants with handwritten text nearby that pointed out how to differentiate the plants and their uses. Helen flipped through the pages. While it was amazing how people in the past could draw with such detail, it seemed to be nothing close to what she needed. The plants were beautiful, but it didn't seem like she would get a chance out of the clan to actually find them.

Helen flipped through the pages and was getting ready to pick another book, when she got to the last part. It was a page with only one sentence: "To the savior of our village, the one who brings everything when there is nothing."

From nothing to everything? That sounds magical.

On the next page, there was an illustration of a woman with wavy light brown hair, sun-tanned skin and beautiful brown eyes. The woman gave off a similar vibe to Lia. If the picture was accurate, Lia's hair was a shade or two darker than this woman. The woman had her hand held out, and above it, a few plants floated. She was standing on barren land with a few farmers in old-fashioned clothes sitting on the ground around her, looking upset.

Helen read the description under the illustration. "*Our village doesn't deserve her. None of us know where she came from.*

There was nothing left when she arrived. We tried to chase her away, having no food for another mouth. But we were so wrong. She saw our land, reached out her hands, and our land that gave nothing in the year was filled with harvest and all kinds of plants."

Helen's eyes widened. Maybe that woman was a magician like her. Maybe she could also create plants.

On the next page, the same woman was drawn to be talking to a few teenagers around her. There was a bag in her hand, her other hand holding up a plant Helen didn't recognize. The caption below read, "*I am blessed to be able to learn from her. As she described the plants and taught us, she always pulled them out from the bag. This must be some kind of magic, or she was sent from the Gods to save our village.*"

The following few pages included some notes on what happened when the woman was in the village with the author of the handbook. The book detailed how she taught and how the village was revived, written and collected when the author was learning under her. She was with them until one day she disappeared, and none of the villagers saw her again.

Helen sat back after finishing the last page about the mysterious woman. She drummed her fingers on the table, supporting her chin with the other hand. Her eyes lit up as she remembered Adrian creating a sunflower from nothing a while ago, when she was there watching Lia's training. If Adrian was using the nature magic instead of the dark magic, then she could probably do it too.

She looked around her, switching to a seat by a corner in the library, making sure Sophia wasn't around. There's no telling whether the librarian would be on her side and wouldn't tell the Elders. She'd prefer the Elders knew nothing about what she would be doing. She opened the book again, at a random page, there was a plant with pale green jagged leaves and purple fruits that looked like tiny cranberries. Helen opened her hand with palm up, furrowing her brows.

It probably worked in similar ways she'd already been using her magic. She held out her palm, focusing her power. She stared at the illustration, picturing the plant in her hand. Slowly the plant appeared like when she summoned the vines. There was a tingle from her torso to her arm, then to her palm. Her heartbeat quickened as the plant slowly appeared. After the plant fully formed, Helen let out a relaxed sigh, holding the plant in her hand.

It seemed to be working. The plant looked almost identical to the one in the book. Its fruit was meant to be sweet and the author added them to bread. It could increase appetite, or at least the book said so.

Helen picked one fruit off the stem. It was the size of a blueberry. She sniffed at the fruit and, closing one eye, put it into her mouth.

The fruit was juicy and sweeter than she expected. If this was working, then she should also be able to create more types of plants.

Helen flipped to another page. There was another plant that looked like the branches of a Christmas tree. Seemingly this plant's leaves should be sour when they are raw and upon cooking, the sourness would leave and they would taste like rice.

This was unheard of for her. While she was a nature magician, she wasn't very keen on learning about plants. Helen scratched her head, setting the book down on the table. Could she only create a plant that existed? Or could she create something from pure imagination? She started to dream of a new type of plant, holding up her palm.

Um... I guess its leaves are red, the color of tomatoes. They are round like a lotus. Maybe it will taste like celery. I guess it will also have small white flowers that look like broccolis. She closed her eyes, trying to imagine such a plant, picturing every detail of it in her mind before willing it to appear. She took a deep breath, it was harder than before. Her hand shook slightly, but she kept focusing on her palm.

Finally, a leaf and a small bunch of flowers that looked like what she imagined appeared. Both confused and excited, she took a small bite of a leaf. She winced; it tasted more like celery than celery did. Maybe she should cook it. She stuck out her tongue, shaking her head.

It seemed creating an existing plant was easier than imagining a completely new one, not to mention she needed the plant to perform a certain type of duty for her.

She traced her fingers along a page with a dark green vine that looked just like the ones she used to trap monsters. The text on its side said that the leaves of the plant could make a beast fall asleep in minutes, or seconds if the juice was extracted.

Did Benjamin count as a beast? Maybe she could use that. Now she had to find out a way to get the juice from the plant. Helen took the book with her, heading back to the shelves. She scanned through the rows, searching for one she needed. She could use a potion book, or maybe it would be a cookbook. She walked around the shelves until her eyes went back to the empty spot she pulled the illustrated handbook from. The book beside it was called *Introduction to Herbs*.

Helen took it, flipping through the pages. It turned out to be another book like the one she found earlier, filled with pictures of plants and their descriptions. She put the book back in its spot and looked at the book next to it. *Using Medicinal Herbs*.

She grinned. That one looked like the book she needed. Looking at the index, it turned out to be more than she expected, including a list of potions she could make with different plants. She chuckled when she read a line of smaller text under the index page that read *"No magic required."*

She lifted her brows. Did it mean people in the older days knew about magic? Or was it just a joke?

There were a lot of potions she could make. She wondered why no one told her before. She scanned the index until she reached *Types Of Sleeping Potions*. A few required some type of bugs. She winced, quickly looking for something not as scary.

A few potions tasted sweet, used when young babies had problems sleeping through the night. But something sweet may make it difficult to use without Benjamin knowing. Something tasteless would be more convenient.

She flipped to the next page, skipping over a potion that was green until she finally reached one that was colorless, had no special taste, and wouldn't give off any kind of smell. She read the description: it was used to hunt large animals, with a warning to be careful of the amount used, otherwise the game would make whoever ate it also fall asleep unless treated with another kind of herb.

She reached for her phone to take a picture of the recipe, but then remembered that it was at the entrance of the library, as required by the Elders. She grimaced, why was she always a follower of rules? She stared at the list of herbs. She thought of borrowing the book, but then set aside the plan. She didn't need Sophia knowing her interest in herbs and potions. Maybe old-fashioned pencil and paper would work better.

Helen walked over to the counter. Sophia wasn't there. She looked around, making sure nobody was watching before she snatched a piece of paper and a pencil. If Sophia thought she was using potions on the Elders, she wouldn't have a chance to give it to Lia… Maybe she was a bit too paranoid, and Sophia actually didn't find her suspicious at all, but she'd rather be safe than sorry.

She headed back to her table, quickly copying every detail of the ingredients needed and the procedures. It took a bit longer than she would like to search for the plants she needed from the illustrated handbook.

Helen took the books back to the bookshelves and put them on the emptier side so she could come back to them later in case she missed something. She picked up her phone by the entrance, typing in the name of the first plant, but no results came up. She frowned and moved out of the library, to the corner of the corridor where no one was there. Staring at the list, she made sure she got the spelling right. She tried with the next plant in the list, but still, there weren't any search results coming back. Either the book was fake or those plants weren't known to humans. Seeing how almost no one knew about magic either, the latter seemed to be more convincing.

At least she kept the books somewhere she could go back to. It would be a nightmare to search through the shelves again. She headed back inside, and, finding another seat, she scribbled on the paper, trying to capture the image of the plants.

She groaned, rubbing her forehead at the messy strokes. Drawing wasn't a thing in her skill set. Not to mention the black and white of the pencil and paper wouldn't help visualize the plants. Maybe she should sneak her phone inside and take pictures. But what if she missed something and needed to come back?

Was there a chance she could sneak these out? Apparently, William didn't have security codes with the books. No way he could remember every book in the library anyway. It wasn't like he would need such a book anytime soon—he wasn't even a nature magician.

She scooped up both books, walking toward the exit until she turned a corner and saw Sophia with her head down. Helen's breath caught. Before Sophia saw her, she hid behind another shelf, walking the other way.

The exit of the library was in sight when someone called her from behind. She flinched.

"Hey, Helen. Had fun reading?"

At Sophia's voice, Helen had no choice but to turn around. She forced a smile, there seemed to be no point hiding the books. Sophia had to be blind to not see them. *Chill. Sophia doesn't know much. Just act normal.* "Well, I did find out a bit more about my magic. Isn't it fun to always learn more?"

"Of course, it is. Who's to say no to more power?" Sophia said. There was something in her eyes that chilled Helen's blood to ice. "I see you have two books there."

Helen resisted the urge to run away. "Well, yeah. I was thinking maybe William could teach me about them."

"I think he would want to make a record of who borrowed what," Sophia said, her voice cold. Something with Sophia didn't feel right, and it probably had nothing to do with getting caught sneaking books out.

"Oh, even if he told me to come? You know how tense he's been with the dark magicians."

"I still have to record everything. No point risking him being angry, right? He is not going to like missed records. Just make my job easier?"

"OK." Helen sighed to herself. She was going to follow Sophia to the counter when her phone rang. Her eyes widened in shock. It was the signal for an emergency case. "Well, I guess I have to hurry. How about we fill that in later? I am not going anywhere. I bet William would be madder if I am late than if I don't check these out." Before Sophia could answer, Helen grabbed her phone and dashed out of the library. Sophia shouted something, but Helen ignored her. *Thanks William.*

Once Helen got to her room, she locked the door and finally relaxed. She set the books down on her desk, mixing them in with her comic books. She pulled her phone to check the message. It turned out Patrick was quicker than her to respond. He probably was bored to death, too.

Sophia hadn't seen which books she'd snuck out with, so Helen planned to just return them later. Sophia probably wouldn't care enough to search the shelves to track them down. If William asked, she would just come up with something, but he probably wouldn't care anyway. Given her track record, William should be fine with it. And given how William cared about the dark magicians, he wouldn't care even if she burned down the library. Hopefully, by that time, her plan was completed. Adrian and Lia seemed to be the bad influence for her to break rules.

Just as Helen was about to open the book and get started, loud and rapid knocks on the door made her jump. There would be no way William already found out about her, right? She hurried to the door. "Coming!"

Patrick was outside, and Helen let out a sigh of relief. "What happened? What's the hurry?"

"William told me to come for you. We are needed at the office."

She pulled out her phone, checking the message again. It was the yellow signal for sure, which meant William was only looking for one of them, not both. If he needed both of them, he would have usually sent a red or an orange one instead. "I thought you already responded?"

"I did, but he told me to go get you, too. I don't know why he didn't just call both of us in the first place."

"Whatever. Let's get going."

The two of them hurried down the corridor. William's office door was half opened. They exchanged a look. Patrick's brows furrowed. "I closed the door when I came to get you."

Helen took a step forward, knocking on the door regardless. There was no response from the inside. When she pushed the door, William wasn't at his desk. The two of them walked in, leaning on the bookshelves on the side.

Helen asked. "Where is he? You sure we are wanted here?"

"A hundred-percent. He was here just a while ago."

"Anyways, any idea why we are wanted?" she asked. He shook his head.

It has to be about Lia or the dark magicians…

"Did you break any rules?" Patrick asked.

Helen rolled her eyes. "Asks the troublemaker." She shot him a pointed look. Patrick stuck out his tongue with a smirk.

A while later, William barged in with Eric hurrying behind him. William dropped onto his chair, scowling at Eric.

Eric shook his head frantically. "C'mon, William! Do you know what you are talking about? This is not as easy as you imagined. You really think he won't fight back? No matter how much we surprise them, he will still put up a fight. We don't even have an idea how powerful he is!"

"If we wait any longer, he will get even stronger. I'm not going to let them hold Lia hostage! They could have already killed her. We have been tracking them down for years—are we giving up now? If we let them loose, you really think we will be safe? You know how much he hates us."

Helen looked between them with a frown. She'd never seen them argue before. Although none of the words made sense without more context, she could infer that it was about the dark magicians. She exchanged a glance with Patrick, his brows knitted tightly as he shook his head.

William turned to them. "I tracked down an old enemy of ours, of all magicians. But it will be very dangerous to fight them. You two can decide whether you want to join or not. Be prepared to meet the hardest fight you will ever see."

Helen gulped. This wasn't good. Now she was almost certain who the old enemy was. She didn't know much of what happened between Adrian and William, but from Benjamin, she knew they weren't on good terms at all.

A flash of what happened in The Orbit surfaced in her mind, sending a shiver down her spine. Adrian and Benjamin were scary fighters. If William really was going to fight them, it would be really bad.

Despite Helen's effort, William had still found something in the end. She should have seen it coming. She thought of the friends she met in Benjamin's bar—would they also get killed in the crossfire? That better not happen.

"How strong is the one you are talking about?" Patrick asked.

"I suspect he is stronger than me, at least my equal. We may also meet his minions," William said.

Except Benjamin doesn't think you are their equal.

"Must we fight them?" Helen asked. When William glared at her, she gulped and continued. "I… I mean are you sure they took Lia?"

William sighed. "I am not sure, to be honest. But regardless of whether they are the ones taking Lia or not, we still have to defeat them. Now that I finally located them, I don't need them to run away again."

Helen wanted to convince William not to, but she didn't dare to challenge him. If he found out she was hiding something, it wouldn't end well. The silence lingered for a while.

"Let me know before next week. We will plan by then," William said, dismissing them. There were only three days left. Helen and William left, but Eric stayed, seemingly wanting to further discuss with William.

"Do you think it is a good idea?" Patrick asked, toying with his hair.

"I... don't know. Dark magicians sound scary."

"Agreed. William didn't tell me much, but I think he knows what to do. He always does. Well... though his plans don't always go right."

"Are you going to join?" she asked.

"If they are that dangerous, then I guess I should try to bring them down, but I am a bit worried, seeing how I don't even know how strong William is. But at least we have both Eric and William?" Patrick shrugged. The two slowly made their way out of the clan, parting ways by the corner.

Her plan with Lia better work before everything came crashing down.

CHAPTER 30

LIA

Lia took a seat on the couch in the living room. It had been a few hours since Helen messaged her about the potion. Success or not, Helen would probably let her know. As soon as she knew there was a sleep potion, she made a plan and told Helen. It was a huge bet, but her options were limited. Hopefully there would be time to make sure everything would work.

She stared blankly at the bare wall; Adrian didn't even have a television there, not to mention a video game set. Although she was doing nothing, her heart was racing. Her eyes went to the locked entrance, then to the locked door of Adrian's office. Adrian had come back, but he didn't talk to her much before he went into the office with Benjamin. They had been in there for almost an hour. Apparently, it was something she couldn't know, like always.

Having seen how quickly Adrian could come up with a plan like what they did with the meteorite monsters and The Orbit, he would attack the clan soon. They probably wouldn't be talking about keeping her safe, seeing how she'd been behaving herself. At least they never caught her messaging Helen. At least she'd lasted for a day without doing anything.

Helen agreed with her plan, though warning her how crazy it sounded. Lia sighed, wishing for another way to stop them. She still had to wait for Helen to give her the potion for her plan to go smoothly. She resisted the urge to reach for her phone in the room, she couldn't bear the risk of Adrian seeing her with it. In case he decided he should take it away from her. To hell with her safety.

If Adrian or William were able to exercise their well-crafted plans, a lot of people would be affected. If they had been fighting for years before, and countless magicians already died in the process, letting them fight on their terms would be disastrous. She stirred her soft drink with the straw before taking a sip. The ice had been melted for a while. She put her legs up on the arm of the couch, lying down.

After quite a long while, she startled at the sound of the office door opening. The two of them walked out with coy smiles on their faces. Lia gulped; that didn't look like a good sign.

Adrian came over to her, pulling her into a tight embrace and rubbing her back. She hugged him. "Something happy happened?"

"Very soon." He ran his fingers through her hair.

"What will that be?"

"You will know. Just stay here and watch it unfold." Adrian gently kissed the tip of her nose. Lia faintly nodded, her eyes flicking to Benjamin. He winked at her with a reassuring smile.

I know you two are trying to take care of me, but I really doubt I will like what you are planning…

Benjamin went out to grab the three of them dinner

while Adrian headed into the bathroom for a shower. At this chance, Lia snuck into his office. *They must have finalized the attack on the clan, I have to know when…*

She scanned the documents on the desk, but the pile seemed to have nothing to do with the clan nor the Elders. Her heart racing, who knew what Adrian would do if he found her inside his office. She flipped through them anyway. Out of the corner of her eye, there was a scrap piece of memo-sized paper with something scribbled on it. She turned back to other documents, but something about the note caught her. She took another look, and it seemed to be shorthand words or something. Lia cursed under her breath for not bringing her phone with her.

There was still the sound of running water from the bathroom, but her time was running out. She closed her eyes. Despite her hand shaking, she held onto the paper. Somewhere in her mind, she knew it had to be important. Adrian was too tidy with things; he wouldn't keep something useless lying around. She took in a breath, staring at the scribble. Slowly the rest of the world seemed to fade and the markings danced in front of her eyes. She began to hear something in her mind. She slapped her hand over her mouth.

"*Really? Just a forcefield around the clan?*" Benjamin asked.

"*Not even a forcefield. Just a lousy spell. I can break it in seconds,*" Adrian said, his voice cold.

"*Then everything is nailed down?*"

"*I guess so. I can't believe you convinced the two of them to come back.*"

"*Well, I told you they would. They are far too interested in putting an end to the Elements. When are we going? I don't know how long she will agree to stay here.*"

"*Next week. You said they would be back by then, right? I want the stack on my side. You have to keep watching her. There's nothing those nasty Elements can do in a few days to stop us."*

"Great! But I guess it's time you start planning what to tell her. She's not going to like this."

"I know… but she will have to accept it as is. There's nothing she can do."

"Agreed, my King."

The voice slowly faded from her mind as her heart hammered in her chest and her mind raced. Was this also something with her dark magic? Before she could give it more thought, the shower stopped. She quickly put down the paper to where it belonged and rearranged the documents in the best way she remembered. She rushed out of his office into the kitchen just in time to hear the bathroom door opening.

Lia opened the fridge, trying to busy herself. A pair of arms wrapped around her waist. She froze. Adrian was smirking at her, hugging her from behind.

She let out a sigh of relief, straightening, and turned to him, with an audible gulp.

He raised his brows at her. "What's wrong?"

Lia's eyes trailed down his bare chest, his towel was hanging from his shoulder. He was in a pair of shorts. She blushed, but couldn't tear her eyes off his muscular frame. "Um… nothing."

He tilted his head sideways, looking down at himself. He took a step back, drying his hair with the towel, flexing his biceps. "I am too used to being here by myself. Sorry about that."

"I know this is not simply your office for long." She winked at him, he was a bit too good looking for her to tear her eyes from.

He leaned closer to her with a cocky smirk. "Like what you see?"

She rolled her eyes, trailing her fingers down his chest. He had to be working hard for that body. "I guess you don't look that bad." He shivered under her touch.

He snorted, turning away from her and leaned on the kitchen table. "Are you that hungry? Benjamin is already getting us dinner."

"I guess I am bored. And when I am bored, I like to find some snacks. Who would have guessed you don't even have a television here."

"Why waste my time on those things?" He shrugged. His hair was almost dry, he made his way out of the kitchen, Lia followed him.

"You had no problem playing video games with me all day before."

"With you, it's different." He picked up a fresh t-shirt from the armrest of the couch, putting it on. Lia grinned, hugging him from behind. He smelled like mint from his shower. Her heart skipped a beat as she rubbed his abdomen, he sure was well trained.

If only we weren't hiding things behind each other's back… But you are too cute to get mad at…

He patted her hand. She could feel him smiling. There was the sound of keys at the door. She reluctantly let go of him. Benjamin was back with dinner.

Adrian and Benjamin seemed to be in a great mood. There were those sly smiles on their faces. No matter how handsome Adrian looked, it didn't sit right with her. Not in the current situation. "You two seem to be really happy, huh?" Lia raised her brows.

Benjamin blinked and said, "You know I'm always happy to see you two not fighting." Lia blushed slightly, rolling her eyes.

Adrian forked up the spaghetti and chuckled. "What's

wrong with being happy? When chaos isn't around, that's good enough for me."

She tried a few more times, but despite her effort, they wouldn't leak a word. *Nevermind. I already know of your plan. And I have a better one to trump yours.*

They packed up the wrappings of the food. Adrian offered to take them out. Lia furrowed her brows. "You aren't staying for the night?"

He awkwardly cleared his throat. "You are quick, huh? I have to be back in the dungeon. Unless you want to come with me?"

At the mention of the underground base, she shook her head. "No way, I'm not getting close to there. Who knows whether you will lock me there again."

A pained look flashed through his face, he nodded faintly. He kissed her goodbye, hugging her once more before he left.

At least I can feel free to contact Helen now.

Benjamin was watching her from the kitchen. She raised her brows.

He shrugged and his smile faltered before he returned to the office.

Lia stared at his back until the door closed behind him. He seemed to be troubled. But he was happy just a moment ago. It probably wouldn't be smart for her to go ask him; curiosity wouldn't help when she already knew the things she needed to know. May as well lay low until she could carry out her plan. She thought of the scribble and what she heard when she focused on it. While she didn't know why or how, what she heard felt real.

She headed back to her room, reaching for her phone under the pillow. She lit up the screen to see a message from Helen, her face fell even more.

CHAPTER 31

HELEN

Helen let out a heavy sigh after chatting with Lia through text. The clock was ticking; she had to finish the potions quickly. She made sure she had locked her door before settling down at the desk. The two books she snuck out from the library were there waiting. She scanned the books again, making sure she was on the right page of the illustrated handbook and reading about the right plant.

She held out her hand, focusing on the dark green plant she needed. She closed her eyes to bring it alive in her mind, but the thought of William and Adrian fighting each other kept interrupting. She didn't need those at the moment. It was about the plant, the stems, and the leaves.

Slowly a dark green vine appeared on her hand and she set the section of it aside, starting her work on the other plants. One by one, she laid the plants on her desk. She took in a deep breath, reading through the procedures.

She took out the mixing bowl she took from the lounge, putting it in front of her along with a knife she'd taken as well. She carefully cut off the top green layer of the vine, revealing the almost transparent flesh. With a tiny spoon meant for sugar, she scraped the inside of the vine into the bowl. Mashing the flesh for its juice.

Then Helen picked up the pinch of leaves, tearing them into smaller pieces, dropping them in as well. As she tore the leaves, a strong smell of fresh soil on a rainy day filled the air. Helen winced. There was no way the end product had no odor nor taste… *I never expected to need some cooking skill to make this whole thing work… I guess it is more interesting than I expected.*

After adding a few more fruits and leaves into the bowl, she stirred it together. The different colored leaves and the strong smell of a few of them slowly blended, cancelling each other out as the odor slowly faded. She referenced back to the book, measuring the right amount of water. Soon, everything was mixed well. Helen stared at the mixture with a frown.

Is it done? I think I should give it a try. Helen let the mixture sit while she hid the two books and leftover plants, making sure no one would see them.

She got a small spoonful, cupped her hand and fanned the air towards her. The potion had no smell, but it made her drowsy. Her eyelids grew heavy. *I guess this means it works.*

She poured most of the potion into a vial. According to the book, the amount she made was enough to knock out an elephant. She set the vial away safely, collecting the rest into a paper cup. She returned the mixing bowl and everything she'd used to the lounge, carefully washing every last bit of the potion and traces of plants away. Luckily it was late in the night, so she didn't bump into anyone.

Back in her room, the vial stared back at her. This better work, otherwise all she could do was to warn Lia before William would barge into the bar. She traced her fingers along the cold glass surface of the vial, hoping for the best. She messaged Lia to let her know when she would put out the vial for her to get.

It probably wouldn't be easy while Benjamin was watching Lia and would stop her from leaving the penthouse. Lia urged Helen to relax a bit; she seemed to be confident.

Helen set her phone on the charger and got ready for the night before lying down, staring at the ceiling. Her heartbeat a bit too fast for her to fall asleep. She peeked at the vial, barely seeing the glint of the glass when the lights were off.

Benjamin, it is your fault for being on Adrian's side.

CHAPTER 32

HELEN

Helen woke up to the brightly shining sun, squinting as the light pushed through the gap of the curtains, warmly kissing her skin. She opened her eyes with a wide smile on her face. It seemed to be a good day for the plan.

There weren't any messages from Lia. In the state they were in, no news was probably the best news. She walked over to the window, looking down, it seemed to be a perfect day. A great one for the plan she had in mind.

It was still early in the morning, around seven. She doubted William was already up. Since the Elders kept her and Patrick in the clan, this place somehow turned into a hostel. The nostalgia was here again. Back when she was in college and pulling pranks around with Lia had been remarkable and fun. After they got this settled, maybe they should go back to that now that they had more people outside of the clan to prank.

She changed out of her pajamas into a pair of jeans and a t-shirt. Before she could second-guess the plan, she stuffed the vial of potion into her pocket, trying to stop herself from touching it every minute to make sure it was safe.

Patrick wasn't a concern; he wouldn't be up until training time, probably waking just in time to get breakfast.

Helen scratched her head when it came to Eric. It seemed he usually got up a bit early, but would he be busy with work that early, she didn't know. Maybe she should check whether he was in his office. She clenched the vial in her pocket, or maybe she should come back earlier after putting the vial out instead. She headed towards the exit of the clan.

Walking down the corridors, she quieted her steps. While there seemed to be no one around, the low echoing voice of her shoes on the floor was louder than she intended. She was already in a pair of sports shoes, but she was still worried. She jumped at the elevator's noise when it announced its arrival.

Can't you just stay quiet? Maybe I should take the stairs…

There was the sound of someone talking when she turned towards them. Her breath caught as she ducked behind the smoke-proof door leading to the stairs. The sound was on another floor.

Helen caught a few words, and it sounded like the person was talking on the phone. Helen listened closer, trying to make out who it was. She was still in the clan anyways, even if she got caught, she would still be fine.

"Yes… we're prepared… no wiser…" It sounded like a female's voice, but it was muffled. It could also be another magician. Helen remembered William meeting a few people she didn't know. It was probably someone William called in to fight the dark magicians.

Crap! Then I really have to hurry!

She quieted her steps, walking down the stairs. Her heart raced even faster when she finally reached the door.

I hope William's magic really only detects strangers from outside…

Helen sucked in a deep breath, pushing the door open. There was no sound nor anything special. No one seemed to be coming after her. She ran through the parking lot, blending herself into the streets.

She caught a bus right before it left, heading to the large tree on the hill where Lia and she always used to go. At least that was the case before Lia found out about her dark magic power and was kept under Adrian's watch. She ran up the gentle slope.

The tree and the surroundings were tranquil. Birds were singing and the leaves were rustling. The grass was thicker in the springtime. Helen leaned on the tree, levelling her breath.

It is OK. No one's around. Now I just need to hide the vial somewhere only Lia will find out. An Easter egg hunt, anyone?

She walked around the tree and found a few piles of leaves. She toyed with her hair, raising her eyebrows. *I should hide it somewhere so it will be easy for her to find an excuse to check it out.*

There was a small gap on the tree. She pulled out the vial, measuring it. She nudged the sides of the tree to make a bit more space to fit it better. She took a step back. The lid of the vial matched the color of the tree, it seemed invisible unless someone was to look very closely. Lia should be able to find it if she searched.

Helen took a picture of the tree and circled where she put the vial in red. After she sent the photo to Lia, it was almost half past eight. Time for her to head back before someone found out about her absence.

She hurried down the hill to the bus stop. Luckily the bus came soon enough. While she felt more at ease after half-delivering the vial to Lia, her heart was still racing, hoping she would get back to the clan without anyone knowing.

When the bus arrived, as soon as the door opened enough for her to slip through, she jumped off. She hurried towards the clan, she halted as she approached the parking lot. That was the only open area where if William was watching from the inside, he could see her. She couldn't see anyone in the windows, so she dashed across the clearing, pushing the glass door in. The whatever magic William mentioned seemed to really not detect her.

The lobby was empty as always, she ran up the stairs, barely making it into her room when someone knocked on the door. She jumped, her eyes wide. She took off her jacket and shoes before opening the door.

William was eyeing her. *Did he already know… I hope not…* Helen swallowed dry, daring herself to look up at him. "Good morning."

"As a trend, you never wake up earlier than the assigned training time. There's no day I don't need to wait at least ten minutes before you would open the door if I came earlier than your first assigned task."

She better come up with something good, and quick. "Well, there is this famous person you probably never heard of on social media that started a twenty-one day at-home workout challenge. It is a live session, so I can't miss it. Great for me and good for you not needing to wait." Helen forced a smile, trying to make it look natural.

William snorted and rolled his eyes. "Whatever, Patrick is feeling sick today. Do you want your training earlier?" He looked oblivious to her lie. The tension in her shoulders dissipated slowly.

"Sure. I'll come in a second." She nodded. William's

eyes flicked to Helen's phone on the bed for a second before he turned to the arena.

Closing the door behind her, Helen let out a sigh of relief. She wiped off the sweat on her forehead, reaching for her water bottle and heading down to the arena before William could become more suspicious.

CHAPTER 33

LIA

Lia woke up to a buzz from her phone, she flinched, snapping her eyes open. *Dammit! Did he…* She let out a sigh of relief when she remembered Adrian wasn't next to her, so he wouldn't have heard the noise. She frowned as a surge of sadness stirred in her chest. The sheets were cold without him. Whether her plan worked out or not, he would probably be pissed. Would he push her away again?

If only we aren't working behind each other's back… Otherwise, I really want to wake up with you by my side…

Lia reached out, patting the empty space next to her. She sat up, reaching for her phone. She grinned when she saw the picture of the tree, knowing Helen had been successful. Now it was just a matter of whether she could convince Benjamin. That would hopefully be easier than convincing Adrian himself.

When she got into the living room, Benjamin was already sitting on the couch with a bagel in his hand. He beamed at Lia, waving at her. She smiled back, sitting next to him.

"Morning." His voice slightly muffled from the bite of bagel in his mouth.

"You are early today as always?"

"Have to be earlier than you, I guess. That's my only job in the meantime."

Well... It is fine if you want to take a break from your so-called job...

"Adrian?"

Benjamin's demeanor changed slightly. "Oh, I guess he is still asleep in the den. I think he worked late yesterday. It is very easy to over-sleep there." He winked at her, taking a sip of his coffee.

Lia nodded faintly. "Is he coming anytime soon?"

"Um... I don't know. Maybe you should ask him yourself."

"How am I supposed to ask him?"

"I guess you're right... The den..." He pulled out his phone, glancing at the screen before setting it on the coffee table, he shook his head.

"It's OK..." Lia sighed, despite feeling a bit at ease. *Am I feeling happy he is not here? Well, this is kind of messed up...*

"Anything you have to do today, Ben?"

"Other than keeping an eye on you, nothing's on my plate." He took another bite of his bagel, gesturing at the paper bag to Lia. She reached out for the bag, taking out a bagel with smoked salmon and lettuce in it. She beamed.

Benjamin chuckled. "I knew you'd like it."

After she brushed her teeth, she returned to the couch. They remained in a comfortable silence as they finished their food. Lia sighed again as she wiped her fingers clean after eating. He raised his brows at her.

"You think I could go out for a walk? While I am very happy to not have to stay in the dungeon, it still gets boring. There's nothing other than some books to keep me occupied, which I ain't a big fan of. Can you go out with me?"

Benjamin tilted his head sideways, as if deep in thought. "If only you weren't dating my King, I'd be happy to go out with you. Seriously though, I don't think it is a good idea. He would be very mad."

"He doesn't have to know."

"You are not wrong, but I can't really hide things from him." He gently knocked his temple. "Where do you want to go anyway?"

"The tree where I accidentally called you when Adrian was still pushing me away. Today seems to be such a nice day, I want some nature and some fresh air. It's not even crowded, and if someone really tried to attack me, you will be there. Please? Can you take me there?" Lia furrowed her brows, shaking Benjamin gently on his shoulder. He frowned deeply, rubbing his chin.

"C'mon, Ben… Just an hour is all I need. You can still keep an eye on me. Adrian told you to keep me safe, but he didn't say you have to keep me safe in his penthouse. I promise I'm not trying to run away or anything." Lia leaned closer to him, looking into his eyes with her best cute eyes. He gulped with a conflicted look on his face.

"Wanting even more after we agreed to let you out of the dungeon, huh?"

"You know I used to take a walk in the park every day. It is hard to stop a routine and even harder when there is nothing to do here. It's not like anyone would attack me when you are around, you would kick them real hard." She looked down on the ground, faking a sob.

He sighed heavily. "Fine. You can stay under the tree for just an hour, don't ask for more. The King would kill me if he found out." He gestured at his neck, sticking his tongue out.

"Sure! I won't bring you any trouble." She jumped from the couch, hugging him on the side. *At least for now, that is… You can't blame me.*

He patted her arms. "I retrack, this will get me killed sooner than bringing you out. The King really has to know nothing."

"Sorry." Lia chuckled, dancing back to her room to get ready.

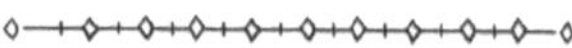

"I DON'T EVEN KNOW if this is a good idea," Benjamin said, shaking his head as the two of them walked up the hill. Lia's heart hammered in her chest, her palms drenched in sweat.

"You will know how great a tree is soon." She forced a smile, looking around at birds flying around, taking in a deep breath of fresh air filled with earthy smell. It was great to feel the sun on her skin without it being filtered by the window.

Walking up to the tree, the scene looked the same as Helen sent her. As both of them knew, the tree wasn't a popular place for people to go. Lia circled the tree, pretending to be looking for a good spot to sit. She soon found the small gap in the tree and took a seat near it, blocking it from Benjamin's view with her body. She now just needed a reason to reach for it, or something to distract him so that he wouldn't catch her.

She leaned back on the tree; she had an hour after all. Benjamin took a seat beside her. He rested on his arms behind his head, squinting at the sky. "Have you ever thought about ants walking on the tree you are lying on?"

Lia rolled her eyes. "Must you spoil the mood? I don't see them. I am good to pretend they don't exist."

"Really? One would think ants and all kinds of bugs are common in the wild. Think of ants crawling on the tree and getting on your arms."

Lia shivered, the hair on her skin stood. She sat up, moving away from the tree, glaring at Benjamin. He laughed.

"Why do you think ants won't climb on you?" She hissed as he was still leaning against the tree himself.

A mischievous glint flashed in his eyes. "I'm not as sweet as you. I am perfectly safe."

She huffed and smacked his shoulder. "Whatever. You think it is a good idea to try calling Adrian? Maybe we should find out what he's up to."

Benjamin looked her way, tilting his head to the side. He pulled his phone. "I guess you are right. If he isn't in the den, we should head back."

While he was busy dialling, she quickly pulled the vial and stuffed it into her pocket. She was just in time when he looked at her and shook his head. He said, "Either he forgot to turn on his phone or he's still in the den. I think we can stay a bit longer if you want. The full hour for you." He seemed oblivious to the vial. "I also missed going out like this. It is kind of boring when I have to stay indoors to keep an eye on you." He let out a content breath with a wide smile on his face.

"I've told you the tree is great." *Sorry Ben... I hope Adrian won't make it too hard on you later... But I really have to bet on this...*

She closed her eyes, enjoying the tranquillity around her, the rustling leaves and the gentle breeze brightening her day, relieving every bit of tension inside her. Just what she needed before she carried out the rest of her plan.

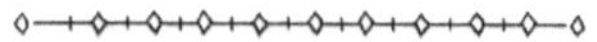

THE HOUR they agreed on soon passed. Benjamin got up and helped Lia to her feet. They headed back to Adrian's penthouse. In his car, Lia slowly tensed up, rethinking her plan. "When will Adrian be here?"

"More likely late tonight." Benjamin kept his eyes on the road while Lia kept her gaze outside of the window. *At least it would be easier with Adrian away. It is tonight or never…*

CHAPTER 34

LIA

For the rest of the afternoon, Lia rolled around on her bed. It would be better to wait till after sunset for her plan to work, but the anticipation made her stomach churn. She tried to ground herself by reading a book, but she couldn't focus on the words. When she read the same sentence for the sixth time and still couldn't register it right, she gave up, resorting to her bed.

From time to time, she kept an eye on Benjamin. He seemed to be in a good mood, staying in Adrian's office, often humming a song or two. There was no sign Adrian would be back soon. Lia took that as good news.

Around late afternoon, the time she agreed with Helen quickly approached. Time felt to be moving slowly when it was far away, but rushing to her when it got close. Lia headed into the kitchen with the vial in her pocket, peeking into the office to see Benjamin with his head down in his laptop, sitting on the couch by the door.

Lia stood in front of the cupboard, eyeing Adrian's selection of beverages. He had good taste, and all the money he wanted to spend on drinks. She traced her outfit with her hands, running her finger along the hem of her t-shirt. *Just act normal, will you? Ben wouldn't know if you don't shout with odd gestures. Breathe in, breathe out… You can do it!*

She closed her eyes briefly, convincing herself it was the only way forward. She took a bottle of scotch that was already opened, pouring it into two glasses. Her hand shook slightly, luckily not enough to spill the drink. After she poured it, she looked toward the office again. Faintly there was the sound of keyboard smashing inside, Benjamin should be busy. She retreated into the kitchen, breathing so quickly and shallowly she could faint at any time.

C'mon, you are doing it anyways, let's get going!

Lia's eyes narrowed with determination as she took another second listening to noises from the office. There wasn't anything worth noting. She pulled out the vial from her pocket. If only she could come up with another plan. Hopefully Benjamin wouldn't be too mad when he woke up from this.

She unplugged the vial, adding all of its contents into one glass. She stared at the glass as the potion dispersed. It soon disappeared completely, mixing with the drink. She fanned the air above the glass; it smelled like how scorch should be. Benjamin would be no wiser.

She took the two glasses out, setting them on the coffee table before knocking on the door to the office. Benjamin's head poked out from the door, he raised his brows. "I thought we already had tea and we agreed on a late dinner?"

"I just wanted a drink. Wanna join me?" She smiled, despite her heart racing. She hoped he wouldn't hear her heartbeat.

"That's kind of random." He tilted his head to the side.

"I guess I am too happy with going out today, I think we deserve a celebratory drink? You said your only job is to keep an eye on me, right?" She rubbed his shoulder, putting on her best cute face.

"Um… I still have something to do…" He frowned, shaking his head. "Maybe later?"

Lia's face fell, she looked down. "Are you also too busy to keep me occupied?" She snaked her arm around his waist, and he flinched. She moved closer to him, leaning on his shoulder. "It's just one drink."

He swallowed. "What drink do you get?"

"Just a scotch." She shrugged, turning away. "When Adrian decided to lock me up here, he should have been ready to part with some of his drinks. I really hope to have a tiny celebration for the two of us, you know? Before he is back, since he won't like what happened."

He chuckled. "Fine. I can still work under a glass, but one only."

Lia's heart skipped a beat as they went to the living room, taking a seat on the couch. She made sure she handed him the right glass. She tried her best to put up a genuine smile and kept herself from staring at the glass too much.

They lifted their glass for a toast. Lia beamed. "Thank you for letting me have some outdoor time."

"It's my pleasure."

They downed the drinks. Lia kept her eyes locked on him as he set down his empty glass. His face twisted slightly, and he snapped his head at her. Lia leapt backwards, her eyes wide.

Helen said the potion had no taste and would knock him down quick?

He raised to his full height, glaring at her. "What did you add?" He jumped forward to grab her, but Lia was one step quicker. She escaped his first attempt, hiding behind the couch, away from his gaze. Benjamin's eyes turned red.

"I don't know what you are talking about. I just poured it out. Is something wrong?" As her limbs began tensing up, she threw a cushion at him, interrupting his hold on her. She put more distance between them, heading to the kitchen. Her heart was thundering, her legs felt weak, almost rooted to the ground. Running away from his reach became difficult.

Wait, is the potion not working for dark magicians?

He growled, leaping for her, wincing. There was a strong wave of magical power in the air that made her shiver. He stumbled, bumping against the kitchen table. With a low thud, he fell on the floor.

Lia's breath caught. Instinctively she wanted to check whether he was alright, but what if he was faking defeat? She couldn't risk it. She rushed into her room, picking up her phone and pulling on her sneakers before heading to the door, wishing putting Benjamin down could really knock out the magic.

Having past experience with the magic, her heart skipped a beat as she reached for the doorknob, anticipating a shock, but there was nothing stopping her. She grinned, sneaking out, running towards the elevator while sending Helen a message alongside with the social media post she already prepared.

CHAPTER 35

Helen got the message from Lia, her heart skipped a beat. *Yes, the potion worked!* She grabbed the items she'd already packed, rushing to William's office. She barely slowed down by his door, knocking rapidly. Her heart raced, hoping William was inside and wouldn't ask too many questions while hoping the plan Lia came up with would work.

"Come in," he said, the sound muffled by the door.

Helen slammed the door open and rushed in. He was typing something on his computer, but he stopped to look up at her. Helen waved her phone at him. "Lia seems to be out there!"

He shot up from his chair, staring at her. "What?"

She pointed at her phone, showing him Lia's post. "There's something from Lia! Maybe she escaped from whoever captured her!"

Without a glance, he waved Helen off from her phone. "Whatever that is, let's get going." He grabbed his jacket, leaping to the door. "Where is she?"

"I'm not sure, but I can see the sign of the park where

we fought the monsters, where I…" She trailed off at the reminder of the attack, her hand instinctively went up to her chest, although she couldn't feel the scar over her clothes. She followed William, who was rushing down the stairs, not bothering to wait for the elevator.

"Let's go there. Try to call her," he said. They ran out of the building, getting into his car.

Helen dialled for Lia as William speeded along the road. The traffic was slightly sparse for a weekday. All she could see was the road ahead and how William ignored the red light as long as there wasn't a car coming from the other side.

"She didn't pick up…" Helen lowered her phone, looking to William. He groaned, shaking his head, his eyes trained to the road.

"Never mind. We will find her," he said.

"Maybe she's busy hiding," Helen said, looking out of the window, making sure William couldn't see her face. He hummed in agreement, flying through another red light.

CHAPTER 36

ADRIAN

Adrian snapped his head up as he lost track of Benjamin in his mind. He frowned deeply, barging out of his office in the dungeon. Benjamin didn't call him the King for no reason; he could always tell what his people were feeling, especially if they became unconscious. When he wasn't with Lia, he had part of his mind on Benjamin, tracking him closely in case the two of them needed help.

He got into his car, speeding along. His mind raced as he stomped the pedal, gripping the steering wheel tightly.

No way Benjamin is going down without a fight. Did Evelyn come early? Dammit! I shouldn't have thought she would hold her promise.

"Can this damn car go any slower?" he shouted as the car in front of him seemed to snail along the road. He punched on the horn, honking at the car, but it seemed to have no effect on the driver.

Adrian peeked to the other side of the road; no cars were coming. He cut over, speeding past the car in front. The bright headlights of an oncoming vehicle shone through his windshield. He moved back over just in time to avoid a crash.

He got out of his car, barely remembering to lock the car doors before running up the stairs into the corridors heading to his penthouse. The door was unlocked, wide open. He gritted his teeth, heading inside.

"Lia! Benjamin!" He scowled at the faint smell of the scotch. *Did that dummy knock himself down with alcohol? Dammit, Benjamin doesn't even drink much… He's smarter than that.* He glanced at the two glasses on the coffee table. One was empty and the other still half-full. The cushions were scattered on the ground and the couch was out of place. A fire of rage simmered in his chest. He took a few steps in and could feel Benjamin's presence nearby.

"BENJAMIN!" Adrian rushed into his office, but nobody was there. He scanned his desk—there was no sign of someone searching his place. If he saw Benjamin later, that jerk wasn't seeing the sun for another day. He rushed out, catching a glimpse of something on the floor heading to the kitchen.

"Ben…" Adrian's heart skipped a beat, his jaw tight. He leaped over the cushions. Benjamin was lying on the floor, face down with his hand outstretched as if trying to catch something. There was no sign of a fight other than the messed-up cushions and couch, and no trace of magic nor the smell of blood.

Adrian turned Benjamin around, feeling for his breath and his heartbeat on his neck. He let out a sigh of relief that Benjamin was still alive. He looked around once more, his chest tight at the absence of the attacker. No way Benjamin had gone down without a fight, his warrior wasn't that bad at the job.

He took a glass of water from the sink, pouring it down on Benjamin, but he had no reaction to it. Adrian winced, hopping over to the coffee table, picking up the two empty glasses. As he sniffed at both of them, something clicked in his mind. Gritting his teeth, he stormed out of the apartment.

Dammit Lia! Must you go this far to run away? Do you have any idea of how many out there are seeking your life?

CHAPTER 37

LIA

Getting out of the building, Lia headed for a bike parked nearby. She cracked the lock with an ice shard, mouthing a sorry to the owner. There wasn't a better way to get to Central Park, where Helen would meet her and they would stay until their plan was completed. Adrian lived too far away to walk there.

She was panting as her legs fought to carry her forward. William would be driving, and so would Adrian. She better be quick so that Helen wouldn't get into too much trouble.

In the streets, at a corner, a strong heat came from her side, approaching quickly. She put up an ice wall at once. There was a loud crash as steam hissed from the ice wall. Deep within the alley, she couldn't see who shot at her. She jumped off the bike, shoving it to the wall nearby.

She held her hands to the side, wielding her. "Who are you? Come out!"

Another fireball shot at her. She blocked it off with an ice blast. Someone in a hood emerged from the alley, running towards her. Lia dashed off, heading for a spacious place to get a better view. She ran down to the bank of the riverside, the nullah for water drainage.

She turned to the man once there was enough room for a fight. She shot ice shards at him and he dodged, sending a few fireballs in return. She took a step to the side, shooting at him again while closing their distance.

Who is this guy? Did Evelyn send him?

Lia took a closer look as his hood came off, revealing his face as he moved away from her blast. He was a man looking to be around Lia's age. She frowned, unable to shake the feeling that she had seen him before.

They took shots at each other and it seemed to be a standoff. Lia gritted her teeth; she had no time to waste. Helen would have called William and Adrian would soon know of her prank on Benjamin. Before she got caught by either side, she had to be in the right place.

"Who are you? Did Evelyn send you?" she shouted.

He answered with a hoarse voice, weaker than she expected. "I don't know anyone called Evelyn. How about you just surrender to end this mess?"

"Then who sent you? I don't have time to waste on a rando!" Lia focused her power; she didn't wish a painful death on anyone, but it seemed the strange dark magic she used in the gang's base would work.

"I'm no rando. I'm sorry you didn't kill me in the hotel. I'm not going down without trying." The man shot fireballs at Lia again, and she dodged. Her breath caught at the mention, faintly remembering the showdown with the gang. It seemed a few magicians had escaped while she was busy stopping Adrian from drinking every drop of the fallen men's blood.

Lia rolled her eyes. "If I were you, I would hide far away. What makes you think you will win on your own when your whole gang failed."

"You left me no choice," the man shouted, launching a fire blast at her. Lia pulled up an ice shield, blocking its power. "Because you killed Bob, the other branches are here to pick the rest of us off. Maybe your little life would earn me safety. Even not, it would be satisfying to get revenge."

So he doesn't really care about killing me, but his own life, huh? I really don't have the time to waste.

Lia stared at him, summoning the dark power inside her. As she focused, she seemed to stare through the ice wall, feeling the man's limbs connect to her will. She gritted her teeth as she threw the man backwards, groaning as he landed. Lia rose to her full height, staring down at him.

Maybe we could use some information about Bob and the gang. Adrian seemed to not know about them a lot.

"How about I give you a counter plan for your little life?" Lia said. The man's eyes widened in shock. "How about you do what I say and I promise you a better chance to live?"

He snorted. "Why would I take it and why would I trust you?" He tried to shoot at her, but Lia locked his arm with her glare. It was a strange feeling like when she first learned to ride a bike on her own, and like how she first used the dark magic herself in The Orbit. *This psychic force thing is easier than I expected.*

"One, you can't defeat me. Two, you really think the gang would spare your life if you killed me and wouldn't claim it for themselves? If I were the other branch, I would kill you regardless."

The man groaned, he stopped fighting Lia's hold on his arm. He turned to the side, seemingly in agreement.

"How about you help me so I can appeal to the man himself? Maybe he will spare your life."

Of course, my plan will work… It has to work… Just take my offer, will you?

The man rolled his eyes. "Why would I agree to that?"

"I could have ended you here, but there's something I want from you. If you want to stay alive, you better do as I say. You've seen the man who trashed your little boss's operation. Whether you can kill me or not, he would be coming after you. You need a reminder on what he is capable of doing?" She glared at him, daring him to say anything. She glanced at her watch, who knew how long she still had…

The man gulped. "What do you want from me?"

Lia took a step back and the man stood, fixing his hair as he stared at the ground. She crossed her arms. "You better not screw up to keep your little life safe. I am heading to Central Park. You know where that is?"

"How can I not know where it is? C'mon."

"Make sure I arrive there safely." When Lia ran off, the man followed her.

"Why are we going there? And who else is after you?"

"You will know by the time we get there. Stop asking questions." Lia kept running through the streets, not looking back. At least the park was close enough she didn't need to steal another bike. She took a peek at her watch again. *Probably the traffic won't slow them enough…*

Lia's heart raced, both from running at top speed and from worrying about her plan. Her heart was also heavy as she regretted keeping a random fire magician that threatened to kill her. There's no promise he wouldn't try that again. While she had no doubt Adrian would go after the man should anything happen to her, maybe she shouldn't draw the conclusion too early. After tonight, who knew what Adrian would be thinking about. Her breath caught at the thought.

At a crossroad, something caught her eye in a side alley. Before she could turn and look, someone grabbed her waist, pulling her into the alley. She lost her balance, falling back on whoever grabbed her.

Adrian! Her eyes widened; she couldn't get caught here. "No!" She gripped his arm, trying to free herself.

Adrian's familiar voice echoed in her ear as he hissed, "What do you think—?" Before he could finish, he screeched in pain and jerked his arms away. They were on fire. Lia elbowed him in the abdomen, putting distance between them.

He glared at the fire magician, shooting an ice blast at him. Before it landed, Lia raised an ice shield, blocking it off while shooting a beam at Adrian's knee. His still-burning arms must have slowed him. She managed to freeze his leg. He lost balance and fell to the wall with a grunt.

"Let's keep going!" Lia nudged at the fire magician, who flicked his eyes at Adrian before following Lia.

Behind her, Lia could faintly catch her name. Adrian was shouting something at her, but she had no time to stop.

I'm sorry, Adrian… You will understand later. Don't blame me. You never told me your plan to kill the Elders either…

"Who is he?" the fire magician behind her asked as the park came into view from a distance.

"Someone you should never shoot at again. But you are safe with me, no worries."

Lia arrived at a lamp post in the park and leaned on it, panting and gasping for air. She wiped the sweat off her forehead with the back of her hand. The fire magician was staring at her with raised brows. She said, "Go hide somewhere and stay safe. If that man shows up, remember not to shoot at him from now on. Oh, and your name?"

A glint of amusement flashed through his eyes. "Call me Terry. So, I should just stand somewhere else?"

"Yes. Don't get killed. I will call you, so don't go too far away." Lia looked up to the lamp post and reached for her phone, taking a selfie with the sign of the park behind her. The man stared at her for another moment before he left.

With shaky fingers, she sent the photo off to social media. She needed him to be in the park like she planned.

Lia found a spot further away to hide with the lamp post still in sight. She focused her power, hiding her breath and magical power away from detection.

CHAPTER 38

ADRIAN

"Dammit..." Adrian grunted, leaning on the wall of the alley, holding his right arm with his other hand. His both arms were still red hot, sending jolting pain through his body. He put out the fire, but his arms were weak and heavy, as if he couldn't lift them an inch. He winced, feeling the burned flesh stained by his sweat, sending another throbbing pain down his spine.

The leg Lia froze wasn't something to be cared about; it would soon take care of itself. He closed his eyes, willing and channelling his magic to his right arm. He sucked in a deep breath, drawing his strength from his acquaintances that took his deal before. That goddamn fire magician! He slowly pulled the energy he needed. It tickled as the burnt flesh gradually regenerated and the pain subsided.

He barely caught his breath, the sweat on his forehead getting in his eyes. He snapped his eyes closed, rubbing them with the now healed arm. His left arm screamed in pain from merely the touch on the wound, he shivered.

It had been a while since he got hit by any type of

magic. He cursed himself under his breath as he healed up that arm. The burn from a magic was much worse than its natural counterpart. The fire magic, as with other magic, lasted as long as the one casted it willed it to, or until it was put out. Even so, the damage lasted much longer and was more severe, taking more power to heal it.

As Adrian pressed on his injured left arm, the rage sent his blood boiling, his jaw tight. His body shook as he glared at where Lia and the disgusting magician ran off.

Lia… What the heck are you doing? Who the hell is that fire magician?

As his arms regained mobility, he stretched his fingers with a deep frown. He shook his head, trying to calm himself.

Luckily I don't die that easy. Though, if I got burned to death, maybe it wouldn't be that bad.

He shuddered; he didn't need the reminder of Ariel at the moment, though the thought already sent another pain through him.

Wait… Did Lia knock Benjamin out and teamed up with a fire magician to shoot at me? Did something happen without me knowing? He winced, something in him ached, making him nauseous. It was a familiar feeling that made his gut twitch, a feeling he hated and thought was long gone.

Maybe Lia would rather hang out with the Elements than stay with a devil that would lock her up?

He leaned against the wall. His legs felt numb as he gasped for air. *Lia… What is happening…* His vision blurred as tears welled up in his eyes, his rage and strength seemed to have left. Maybe he should just leave. Maybe she agreed to try with him just to keep herself safe and for this chance to escape. He should know that; it would be hard to push him away when he was that much stronger and life-threatening to her. If she didn't want him around, why should he still bother her?

Maybe for Lia, after everything, she'd already left him. He chuckled wryly at himself. Who did he think he was? Why would someone like her want to have anything to do with a devil like him? He should've known since the beginning. She was too kind and too pure for his world.

He pushed against the wall, shakily standing. He was heading back to his car when his phone buzzed. He lit up the screen to see Lia posting the picture of herself in the park in front of a lamp post. It was stupid that he set up a notification for her. He stuffed his phone back into his pocket, getting back on track when he thought of something.

If those that were really after her didn't know before, they now knew where she was. His heart skipped a beat as an image flashed in his mind: her dead body in the park the next day. Evelyn would have no problem making it the ugliest body he ever imagined.

He shivered, maybe he should at least take a look. If the photo was indicative of where she was, it wouldn't hurt to go there. He did tell her he would protect her even if she didn't want a relationship with him. Better honor his own words. He already left her alone with the stupid power before; he wouldn't survive anything happening to her again. When he beat the monster the first time they met, he didn't ask for permission either. Hell, what kind of devil ever asked for permission?

◇—┼◇┼◇┼◇┼◇┼◇┼◇┼◇┼◇┼◇—◇

ADRIAN PACED THROUGH THE PARK, holding up his phone. He had been walking around, but he couldn't find her. He tried to call her, but she didn't pick up. *She has to be around.*

The scent of magic is near. And that fire magician, he better wish I never see him again.

His stomach twitched, all his instinct shouting for him to leave. If Lia found a magician to shoot fire at him, who knew what else she had planned. *Is everything just an act? Just to hand me to Evelyn or whoever? Did she even feel anything—*

Adrian rolled his eyes, shutting down his thoughts. *I only hope she will be safe… Who cares what will happen to me…* He leaned against a lamp post next to the entrance of the park, putting his phone back into his pocket with a frown. There was no sign of her. He frowned, staring blankly at the bushes and trees in the park.

"Adrian…"

Hearing his name in an unfamiliar voice made him jerk, snapping his head to the man standing a few steps away from him. Adrian raised his brows with a wry smile, taking a deep breath in. "William, finally. The inevitable, huh?"

William stared at him with wide eyes and gritted teeth.

Is this what Lia planned? I should've known… That girl… is more trouble than I expected. Why am I finding that attractive?

"I would guess you are here looking for Lia?" Adrian straightened, his arms crossed above his chest. William took a step back.

"So you still exist… Just as I guessed." William clenched his fist, his body tensing.

"Of course I am. Try harder next time. I am planning to end you before you know it. And I think you have a similar plan. But seeing how someone trumped both our plans, this is what it is. Should we get started with our fight now?"

There was a tug in his stomach. *Did Lia run away just for me to meet William? Or was it just my own imagination and she meant to turn me in? But William seriously thinks he could kill me on his own, alone?*

William huffed, staring daggers at him. "I… I wouldn't mind, unless you need some time to prepare?"

"I have no problem if we start now. But as this is probably the last night we will see each other, how about we catch up after all these years? It's not like either of us will run away." Adrian smirked, tilting his head slightly. The moment he saw William, he was confident he could overpower him. Unless he did something stupid, William wouldn't see another day.

What am I doing? Just finish him!

It had been years since he saw William face to face. Maybe he just wanted to know what happened. It would be fine; he could get rid of William later. An hour or two wouldn't change anything.

"I guess that's not a bad idea, letting you live for a few hours more." William rolled his eyes and turned, leading the way. Adrian followed him.

It felt somewhat comforting walking along the streets with William a step ahead of him for a reason Adrian couldn't put his finger on. Maybe it was the relief after all the years hunting each other down while hiding from each other at the same time finally coming to an end.

The night felt quieter than it really was. Soon, there would be no one stopping him to be with Lia. That was if she would still care about him at all. He sighed silently; she would be very mad if he killed William. A few leaves crumbled under his shoes. The leaves were dead, crushed into pieces.

William stopped by the entrance of a cafe, looking back at Adrian. Adrian nodded solemnly, looking up at the sign.

"You want coffee or tea? This is so not you, William."

"Don't pretend to know me!"

"As a matter of fact, I do. But I guess things changed over the years." Adrian shrugged as he pushed open the door. They took a seat inside the comfy and tranquil cafe, with soft music playing, the brief peace before the storm.

255

CHAPTER 39

LIA

Lia peeked out of a thick bush, watching the back of Adrian and William as they walked out of the park. There was no sign of them getting into a fight, and she let out a sigh of relief. She straightened, stumbling a few steps and cursing her numb legs after squatting for a while. Finally, she reached a bench by the roadside and sat, the cool breeze in the night blowing through her hair. She leaned back to relax. It seemed her plan worked. Hopefully the effect would last.

She pulled out her phone, calling Helen, who soon joined her on the bench. "I can't imagine they aren't already fighting. Does this mean your plan is working?"

Lia shrugged, a wry smile on her face. "I hope… Maybe I guessed right about their relationship. At least it is better than them clashing at each other with full teams."

"I guess so… At least there's a chance they can talk instead of in a team fight, that is no place to slow down."

Lia nodded. The thought of the two fighting sent a shiver down her spine. Her eyes lit up as a reminder slipped into her mind. "Helen, I have someone to introduce you to. I may need your help again." Helen raised her brows at her, confused.

"Hey! Terry? You can come out! Are you somewhere?" Lia cupped her hand around her mouth, looking into the park. She scanned a few more bushes like the one she had been hiding under, then flicked her eyes to a few larger trees. She ran her fingers along her hair, a slight frown creeped up her face.

She jumped at a tap on her shoulder. Terry was now next to her. She let out a sigh of relief. "Whoa! Didn't realize you were there."

Terry nodded, sinking his hands into his pocket. "They don't know me. It is easier to hide under the radar for me than you two."

Lia turned to introduce Terry to Helen, but Helen was standing a few steps away from them, poised and scowling. Lia raised her brows. "You know him?"

Helen hissed, "Of course I do. He's from the gang. He fled when we got the upper hand. How come you are with him, Lia?"

Lia raised her hands in front of her, between Helen and Terry. "Hear me out. Yes, he tried to attack me, actually not even an hour ago… But I convinced him to help me and he knows something important about the gang."

"Really? How did he help you? You sure he isn't waiting for a better chance to kill you?" Helen glared at Terry, he averted her gaze, staring at the ground.

"Actually he shot fire at Adrian, burning his arms," Lia chuckled wryly. *I'm so sorry, Adrian…*

Helen's eyes widened as she flicked her eyes between Lia and Terry. "Well… that's intense… I guess I am not the one you need to appeal to."

"I know, that's why I need your help. While I am

confident I can convince him on my own, I don't want Terry to be a surprise for you when the time comes, and it would be great if you can help." Lia reached for Helen's shoulder, giving her an encouraging squeeze.

"Then what's the information so important Adrian would spare you despite you injuring him?"

He gulped. "I… I understand why you don't believe me. I helped her so I can live. Not the best reason, I know, but it is much harder out there than the two of you under the Elders."

Helen rolled her eyes. "Who is to say you won't stab Lia in the back when you know it could help you survive?"

"I… I understand your concern, but I can't beat her anyway. Probably can't make you trust me. Um… maybe some backstories help? Bob was the only one I heard of that would keep a magician around. I have nowhere else to go… Your clan is not very accepting." Terry rubbed his hair with a heavy sigh.

Lia had no idea there were magicians outside of the clan before she met Adrian, and it seemed magicians that had no affiliation with both also existed.

"It sounds like you are just here for a ride. No, I don't think this is a good idea. Adrian is not going to be OK with this." Helen scowled, shaking her head.

Lia hid Terry behind her arm. "He really knows something we need." She turned, nodding to him. A mischievous glint flashed through his eyes as he met Lia's gaze.

He said, "As someone under Bob for quite some time, I know something. There are more branches of the team from different cities. Now that Bob is dead and the team here was almost wiped out by the two of you and the two men that barged in, the others are trying to get this city under their belt. They are trying to kill all that's left of Bob's men."

Helen scowled. "Why should we care about your little gang fight? Why don't you just go and fight for your life?"

"I… I don't know the reason why, but it seems all branches are very keen on killing or capturing Lia. When Bob was commissioned, the money was very handsome. I heard now the bounty has at least doubled. It is an amount I can't even dream of."

"You mean they are still after Lia's life? Even after a branch of their counterpart was wiped by four strangers?"

Terry chuckled wryly and shrugged. "There's only money in the world I live in. The leaders like Bob won't care. But I heard a few top magicians from other branches also came specifically for Lia. Someone offered them unlimited magical power should they succeed in bringing her down."

Well, this sounds close enough to what Adrian originally offered me… I guess that someone has to be Evelyn. And I don't even know much about her.

"You have some idea who they are and how they will deliver unlimited magical power? It is not something you can deposit into a bank?" Lia asked.

He shook his head. "I don't know, but from another long going rumor, it seems there is a kind of magic that can control magical power. But no one knows how it works and no one seems to have ever seen that kind of magic before."

He flicked his eyes to Lia, taking a step back. "Actually, speaking of magic no one has seen before, the man that came with you to The Orbit seemed to have it. I've never seen that kind of magic and how he survived the crossbows."

Lia nodded with a chuckle. "Yeah, he is scary. If you

didn't know yet, he is the one that gets to decide whether you can stay or not. So… let's hope he will take you."

Terry cursed under his breath. "Well… I kind of remember him and maybe I should use my brain before shooting fire…"

Lia patted his shoulder and he flinched, snapping his head up to face her. "He will be fine. You stand a better chance burning him than letting him catch me. Otherwise, as soon as he knows you tried to kill me, it will be the end of you."

"Terry? So, you are saying you will help us beat the branches and that's why we should keep you?" Helen didn't seem to buy what Lia said.

"Yes, that's if he… Adrian? If he will keep me, I will for sure help you. But if he doesn't… I will have to fight for my life."

Lia shrugged with a wry smile. "I would urge you not to try. There's no way you can fight him. Not to mention when I try to appeal to him, another man will also be there who is also a very strong magician and very keen on keeping me safe. So… I doubt you stand a chance."

Terry sighed, slumping onto the bench. "I am just saying, you would be able to kill me already…"

Lia looked to Helen, lifting her brows. Helen shook her head at her, tugging her aside. "Can I have a word with you privately?" Lia nodded, asking Terry to stay while the two of them went a safe distance away, making sure he wouldn't hear a thing.

"Really, Lia… you think this is a good idea? I don't think it is worth it to piss Adrian off even more. You know he is probably already mad about us going behind his back and pulling this plan. Now you think he will agree to take someone that tried to kill you? C'mon."

Lia leaned on the tree behind her. "I just want to know

more about the gang. They are after my life. I think Terry can be helpful to us."

"I think Adrian would figure out what Terry knows very soon. He may already know. I know Adrian probably has a hard time rejecting your requests, but you really think this is a good idea? Right after you knocked out Ben?"

"Actually, that is *we*. I didn't do it on my own."

Helen rolled her eyes, shaking Lia's shoulder. "Yes, it is *we*, and that is an even bigger problem. You know he hasn't liked me since the beginning. How are you expecting him to listen to us?"

Lia grabbed Helen's wrists, moving them off her shoulder. "I will do most of the talking, but I hope you will help convince him."

Helen sighed as she freed her wrists from Lia's hands. "Sorry, Lia. I don't think letting Terry stay is a good idea. He's just… another variable in us keeping you safe. And you could be imagining he could help. What if he is just going to lie about everything and misguide us? If you really are keen to convince Adrian, the most I can do is keep my mouth shut."

It's not that I think Terry has no reason to stab me in the back, but I think he is smart enough to see the better option. Maybe Adrian would also like an extra hand in fighting Evelyn.

"That will do. Thanks, Helen." Lia squeezed out a smile, her brain running at full speed, trying to come up with something to say that would convince Adrian. That's if he still wanted to talk to her. Not to mention she was still worried what would Adrian be doing now that he met William at a time and place he never expected.

You two please stay safe… Please don't kill each other…

CHAPTER 40

ADRIAN

I nside the comfy cafe, the barista served Adrian and William their drinks. Adrian took a sip of his coffee, trying to stay focused. The gentle and light-hearted music of the cafe was playing in the background, the smell of coffee and bread filled the air. He took in a deep breath, setting the mug down on the table. Despite the pleasant environment, his stomach stirred, the tension building up in his shoulders.

"What do you want to know?" William glared at him, his fist on the table, clenched tightly.

Adrian took another sip from his mug. Drinking coffee that late in the night probably was a bad idea, but he needed some caffeine in his system. There were a lot of things he wanted to know, there were even more he wanted William to know.

Why do I still care what he thinks?

Adrian raised his brows. "There's nothing you wanted to know about me? About what happened?"

"I... I thought I killed you. How?" William frowned, gripping his mug.

"Let's just say you killed someone else. How… how did it feel, driving the blade into my chest?"

"Satisfying, knowing you couldn't kill anyone again." William's voice was cold. The bitter words stung. Adrian sighed, staring at his mug. Was he expecting a different answer? They fell silent.

William said, "The celebration was great, and the following few days were as great. But then it felt empty. You may not believe it, but I missed our fight, I missed… the time before our fight." He pinched the bridge of his nose.

"For what it's worth, I never intended to kill you or anyone, it was… difficult for me…" Adrian sucked in a deep breath, pushing what was welling up inside him down. He remembered the last time they drank and chatted in an old bar. It was a happy chat, but it was a long, long time ago, and the memory had almost faded.

If only that lasted…

William scowled. "Lia was with you, right? The day with the fire? The way she struggled on the ground, the look on her face, how she disappeared under my nose. It was you all along…"

"She was. I cannot afford her not to be. I wanted to help her. So what happened to me won't happen again." A pained look flashed through Adrian's face.

There was no forgetting the day that was burned into his mind. It was great weather, and they were outside making sure the merchants were safe on their journey. Well, the robbers didn't agree with that. Yes, he dashed for William, wanting nothing more than his blood. He couldn't help it; he lost control of himself. In his struggle against his own body, instead of reaching for William's throat, he managed to run into a tree, knocking himself out. Apparently, William didn't think he tried to not hurt him.

Since that day, things had changed. He was still in the fog, not knowing what happened. He was scared of himself. He wanted to talk to William, but he'd avoided him like the plague. Before he knew it, other magicians tried to kill him in his sleep. He barely made it out alive. Of course, they were scared, he also had no idea what happened to him. But nobody cared, those magicians were after him since that day.

Wherever he seemed to have fled, they would always find him. He was forced on a journey of hiding in the shadows, fighting people he thought were close for his life. He managed to be with the person he loved, but they were still behind his back. Then they found her...

William scowled. "Well, I guess I should have known seeing Lia that day. It wasn't just a heat stroke by any means. I had no idea she has dark magic. Even if I knew, I wouldn't do it to her... Lia..."

"If you'd known it, you would. I have no doubt. You would kill her on the spot, if not torture her to death just to locate me. Must I remind you that we knew each other much longer than Lia's been alive, yet you did what you did. Speaking of which, with what you had with Ariel, why the hell did you do that to her?"

"I... you... Can you tell me what happened to you? I tried to find out, but... there's nothing to study." William frowned deeply, averting Adrian's gaze.

"You are avoiding my question."

"I... Give me some time first?"

"It took me a while to figure out what happened. In simpler terms, what you called 'the dark power' took over me. Ariel helped me finally stabilize myself... As soon as we did that and I finally was safe to everyone... you burnt her alive. I know you hated her for running away with me, but seriously?" Adrian bit down the fire in his chest. Maybe it was his wild guess, but William surely did that because she ran away from the clan, from him, for a loser.

William's eyes widened, he choked on his drink. "I… I'm sorry."

"You should be… With the first blood spilled, our war was inevitable. My girl that you burnt, sadly, was the tipping point. You asked for a war, I delivered." Adrian put up a fight for his life, for Ariel while William fought to keep the Elements safe from his wrath. It didn't end until William thought he killed Adrian.

He tried, outside from fending off whoever sent by William, trying to kill him, he reached out, wanting to explain what happened. William wouldn't listen, the Elements had their heart set on spilling his blood. It was inevitable. The only thing that kept him alive was to bring justice for Ariel the only way he could. In the end, nothing mattered. She was still dead…

They fell into another silence. Adrian shifted in his seat. The past was back again, confronting him in full force. Wouldn't it be easier to just battle it out and be done with William? Why was he even here? The soft music in the cafe still dangling in the background, awkwardly seemed to be from another world.

William took a sip of his drink before sighing heavily. "What were you doing all these years? After I thought I killed you? Why weren't you trying to kill me?"

"Something creeped up that needed my full attention. Then, my people wanted peace, seeing they weren't being hunted anymore. If my people want peace, it is peace they get." Adrian took a mouthful of his coffee, leaning back on his seat.

After another long silence, Adrian looked at his watch

and stood. "I guess it's almost time. I suppose we will finish the unfinished outside?"

William remained seated, he lifted his chin, meeting Adrian's eyes. "This may come off as strange, but must we fight? I… I mean, you showed up only after all those years, why? Why don't you hunt us from the shadows? If you wanted peace, why would you show up?"

William will be gone very soon, so may as well…

Adrian looked at him, hesitating. He huffed, pushing down the bubbling tightness in him. "You were useful until I tried getting a deal with Lia. She turned out to have the same power as me. I am not letting her suffer. Knowing how you will treat her, I have to do something." His eyes narrowed with determination, glaring at William.

"I really am not going to hurt her. But I don't understand why you would help her." William stared back at him, his gaze intense, as if he could see through him. Adrian swallowed, fighting himself to keep eye contact.

"I am just after her power," Adrian said. He shivered, his words colder than he expected. Luckily Lia wasn't around, or she would be upset. He did feel for her, but he wasn't sure whether he wanted William to know.

William raised his brows. "I don't believe that. You don't run around doing charity work. And if she already joined you, no way she was in the clan until you picked her away in the fire. It had to be going on for a while longer. Do you have feelings for her?"

Adrian flinched, the tip of his ears warmed up. "Why is that a guess? An Elements' magician, huh?"

William sighed, shaking his head. "You do realise we go way back, huh? From what I know about you years ago, you'd never care about anyone, until you care about them. Then you go all in. And… I am sorry I used that part of you to want you dead."

There was no hiding when he'd spent decades living with William and the rest of the clan back in the days, William did know a lot about him. Adrian narrowed his eyes as his resolve built. "Yes, I do feel something for her. There is no way things will go down right. Even if I convinced her to leave the Elements, you would be on my tail. That is not how I want Lia to live. Our fight is as inevitable as our war in the past."

"If I let you have her, would we still fight?"

Adrian's heart skipped a beat. Shouldn't William be eager to slit his throat? "You aren't in a place to negotiate. You stand no chance before me." He leaned closer, towering over William. "Seeing you just have hours left, I'm telling you this. My old enemy wants Lia dead. You want both of us dead. The last thing I need is for you two to join forces, or for you to backstab me. So you are going down, then Eric. For the years we knew each other before our war, I will do you the mercy. I won't kill any Elements unless they turn on me. I will honor my promise."

William's eyes widened. "So you know who wants to kill her? I am also after them."

"I'll make sure Lia is safe. You can rest in peace without worrying," Adrian smirked with a stern look.

"If someone is your old enemy, they must be strong. Let me help." With a shaky hand, William gave Adrian's shoulder a squeeze.

Adrian's eyes widened. This was the last thing he expected. Was William buying time just to kill him when he wasn't paying attention?

"I know what you're thinking, Adrian. I know apologizing probably won't cut it, but I think I should take up the responsibility of our past bloodshed. After I knew you were still around, I thought about everything. At least everything I know of…

"In fact, I'm the reason for the war and for how my fellow magicians all died… For a very small part of me, I was worried about your strange power. I told them what happened with you, and I added quite a few things… I wanted the attention you got… I was selfish to want the ruling power of the clan. I… I could have stopped after you left, but I sent everyone after you. For some time, I lost track of you, but I insisted on hunting you down… I knew you loved Ariel… and I also knew she chose you… I'm the one who made the decision and actually killed her. In the end, I drove you to fight back, resulting in more deaths.

"Don't let me repeat my mistake with Lia. I already left you fighting the dark power alone, and made it even harder for you, hunting you down at every turn. I don't want to leave Lia alone, although I know she has you and would be fine.

"And… as outrageous as it may come off, I… hope to make up with you. I thought you became a monster, but it turns out I was dead wrong. There were years I hated you, disappointed at what you'd become, the version I imagined in my head. Then I saw myself, especially after I killed you. I'm the one driving you to the corner with others, mostly people you knew. If you were a monster, I would be the bigger one."

Adrian froze, stunned. His long-gone memories rushed back to him, the days when they learned magic together, when they fought over who should get the honor t0 hunt down the beast that attacked the village. The day his dark power first creeped up, making him kill a man near him, the day he tried to kill William. The day that magicians he knew and considered as friends came after him, William leading the way.

Before Adrian could react, William came around the table and pulled him into a bone-crushing hug. "I'm sorry. I'm the one teaming up with others, making up things about you. Because the high Elder always favored you… I turned everyone against you without letting you have a chance to explain yourself. You don't have to take my apology, but know that I am sorry for what happened.

"I really want to help. If you want to kill me after beating whoever your enemy is, that's fine. If you think I will harm Lia or you and you want me dead now, just do it. I'm OK with it."

Adrian found himself tearing up, but he blinked them back. He tensed up at the warmth and dampness on his shoulder. He didn't know what to do. After some time, though he couldn't tell how long it had been, he slowly came back into his senses and pushed William away.

"You really think I'm accepting your lame excuses? I don't know what's in your mind, but I'm not going to believe someone who tried to kill me for at least a century or two. Maybe stabbing me in the back later on will be more enjoyable?" He glared at him, not caring about William's remorseful face. He didn't want to leave everything in the past alone. William killed Ariel and murdered his life in the Elements. He wasn't going to be shaken by those pretty words.

"I… I guess you're right. If I were you, I probably wouldn't believe it either." William let out a heavy sigh, his shoulder slumped, flicking his eyes at the floor. After a moment of silence, he lifted his chin. "I'm not fighting it anymore. Just keep it brief, OK? And leave the newer ones alone. They have nothing to do with all this."

Adrian snorted a humorless laugh. "Of course, I'll leave them alone. You don't have to worry. I'll treat them very well." He reached out, grabbing William on the top of his head. William flinched, his face twisted in pain as

Adrian raided his mind, robbing the power of his life out of him.

All of William's memories and emotion played in Adrian's mind as he turned it into his power.

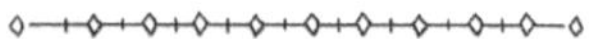

"GOOD WORK, HUH?" Someone patted William on the shoulder. He shuddered, nodding faintly not sure whether he really heard the words. He stood by the charred metal pillar, staring blankly at the pile of burnt stuff on the ground. A surge of pain hit him in the chest. Before the tears escaped him, he pointed to the side, at the nearby building.

"Do go search for him. He has to be around." William fought to keep his voice straight. Whoever was beside him left.

He had no idea what he had done. His throat tight, his vision cleared as the brewing tears fell. The chains were on the ground. The woman he once cared so much of was gone, he was the one killing her. He swallowed.

Shaking his head, he cursed under his breath. *Blame the devil. Ariel… you chose him, right? Why…? If you stayed, you know we could have everything we want. Not only did you run away for him, but you also took the magic from him. Why?*

It pained him when he threw the torch, hoping Adrian would come save her, but he didn't. William's throat tightened. Whatever he was thinking, she was dead, because he was jealous of Adrian. The bitterness lingered in his mouth.

Adrian had to be in town. When he caught him, the devil wasn't escaping anymore.

William made his way closer to what was left of Ariel, the charred ash painful to see. He kneeled, picking up every bit of it into a pouch. His heart hammered in his chest. *I am not sorry. You know he is a devil. You know we are not leaving him alone. Ariel… you picked your own fate.*

Still the load was in his chest, he sighed. He straightened, scanning the scene. Everyone had already left the clearing. When the drama ended, the bystanders were gone.

He went to the countryside the next day, his eyes puffy from crying through the night. None of his men managed to find Adrian. Maybe that disgusting devil had already left. William shrugged, gripping the reins tight in his hands. Did he kill Ariel for nothing? Or was it just his frustration about what Adrian managed to steal from him?

The Elder already liked Adrian, even though he was the rando that came out of nowhere. Ariel chose him and left the clan behind… She knew William felt something for her, but she still left. If William remembered right, she left the day before the Elder would pass him his crown. The bitterness in his mouth was hard to bear.

Regardless, he looked around. The forest was quiet, as if birds also were also hiding from his anger. Amidst the trees, he picked the strongest one. He stopped his horse and got off. He took out a metal box, his hands shaky. What was done was done. Now he had to come up with another way to pull out the devil and put an end to him.

He untied the shovel from the side of the horse, digging a hole by the tree. He took the metal box, kissing it before lowering it to the grave he dug. Every shovel of soil he put over the box pegged another shot of pain in his heart. He gritted his teeth. Before others found out he buried 'the dark magician everyone should hate', he had to head back. All the magicians were there waiting for him, the Elder.

◇—+◇+◇+◇+◇+◇+◇+◇+◇+◇—◇

ANOTHER PIECE of William's memory flashed into Adrian's mind as he dug deeper.

William was sitting alone in a very noisy bar. Everything still looked old. Though there was no way for Adrian to know the date, it felt to be sharper than the memory of William burying Ariel, so it was probably closer to the present.

"Cheers! Happy we finally did it?" Eric beamed as he lifted his glass of beer. William shuddered, yanked out of his thoughts. He pulled himself up, forcing a smile. He clanked his glass with Eric and they took a sip of their drinks. "You don't look happy." Eric raised his brows.

"You're thinking too much. How can I not be happy? Finally the devil is gone." His heart hammered in his chest; faking happiness sure was tiring. He had had enough in the past week. The music was too loud, and he had to stay until most of the others left.

Eric didn't seem convinced, but he shrugged. "OK, I suppose there are still things to be planned now that he's gone? If only we could have killed him when you burned that woman, it would have saved us a lot of lives."

"There are no 'ifs' for the past. There's only now and probably the future to worry about. And while I am sure everyone is happy, don't you think this celebration thing is going on a bit too long?"

"C'mon. Have some fun. Nothing dangerous can happen to us anyways. Although I know you've never been one for festivals and fun, you should see this as a big win." Eric patted William's back before he left.

William stared at his retreating form for a while before he slumped back on the counter, setting down his beer. Was it wrong to not feel happy now that the devil was dead? He stabbed into its heart and burned it. "It", huh?

There was a storm inside his stomach. He already got what he was after; the high Elder already confirmed him as the successor and everyone respected him as the leader, yet something felt off. He swallowed. Maybe it was the alcohol, but the world seemed shaky.

Almost everyone that was there when Ariel was killed were dead. Most, if not all, were tortured to death by the devil. And the devil himself was also dead by now. It felt empty. William bit the inside of his mouth. It was the devil, Adrian's fault. Yes, it had to be. If he wasn't dead, more magicians would be dead... Well, a lot of them were already dead.

What brought Adrian to his land that day? He knew they would kill him, right? Adrian seemed to want to have a few words with him, and he replied with the blade stabbing through the devil's chest and the fire that burned him like Ariel was burned.

Maybe he should've at least let Adrian talk. Once upon a time, they were friends that would talk about everything together.

◇—+◇+◇+◇+◇+◇+◇+◇+◇+◇—◇

ADRIAN SNAPPED his eyes wide open, staring at William struggling in his hand. Despite his thoughts, he let go of him. William stumbled, falling back on the chair, holding his head as he bent over on the table, moaning.

"I wasn't expecting that." Adrian chuckled wryly. "In the end, I was the only person you wanted dead, until you actually killed me off, huh?"

"I... I don't even know how to feel. It is me after all... I created all the mess. I could never figure out why the high

Elder liked you, and I… if you have no use of me, just do me the mercy. Know that I really want to help Lia. I don't want to do the terrible things I did before anymore." William was still holding his head in his hands, his voice filled with pain.

Adrian's blood ran cold, and his heart seemed to have a mind of its own. "If you really wanted to help Lia, I guess I will let you try. Seeing how she really wants you to live. Don't make me regret it."

Why am I doing this? Why…

William snapped his head up. Despite panting for air, he nodded frantically. "It is enough. I wasn't expecting you to ever forgive me. I'm taking what I can. You won't regret it. I will see to it." His smile was infectious, but Adrian schooled himself.

It is just for Lia's safety…

Despite still shaky, William stood, pulling Adrian into another hug.

Adrian flinched, frowning deeply. *Dammit, Lia. What have you done to me…? Ariel… I'm sorry. Please don't hate me more than you already do…* He remained standing awkwardly, letting William hug him. William pulled away, looking at the ground. Adrian sighed, moving to leave the cafe. He was always in debt to Ariel, why was he that much of a jerk to her?

CHAPTER 41

ADRIAN

Outside, Adrian spotted Lia and Helen hiding in the street adjacent to the cafe effortlessly. He cleared his throat, bringing William's attention there. Being discovered, the two sheepishly walked up to them.

"That was a fun stunt you two pulled up?" Adrian crossed his arms, glaring at them. The glare soon disappeared; he was tired of all this. Why did he agree to keep William and Eric alive? Why did Lia have to be so important to him? Why couldn't he get mad with her even though she set up all this?

Well, if this was her plan, maybe the fire magician burning him was part of it, and maybe she wasn't leaving him for the Elements.

Lia leaped, hugging Adrian and leaving a trail of kisses from his ear to his neck. He blushed, looking between Helen and William. Helen laughed. William looked away.

"I told you that talking through things is better than killing each other." Lia poked his nose, he rolled his eyes, hugging her back.

He didn't know what to feel. Everything seemed

unreal. Lia seemed to see that and said, "I'm sorry I forced your hand. I couldn't think of anything better to do."

Lia didn't know what happened in the past. Maybe he shouldn't blame her. His woman was just trying to help, like she always would. He patted her back and nodded. Hopefully Ariel would be OK with this.

His heart skipped a beat when he remembered Helen and William were there. They stood close to each other with very annoying sly smiles. Adrian said, "C'mon William, we still have details to hammer out if we are to make things work."

"How about we leave that for another day? Seeing how Lia would get angry if we are still here." William flicked his eyes to Helen, and the two shared a knowing look. Lia blushed, holding Adrian's hand tight.

"Um… I guess I will agree to that." Adrian found his cheeks burning and he ran his hand over his face, trying to hide the bush.

Adrian nudged Lia to leave when she tugged his elbow. "Wait. I still have something to tell you before we leave." Lia smiled coyly to everyone.

He raised his brows at her. She turned to the alley, calling, "You can come out now."

Adrian stared at a man that looked to be a similar age to Lia came out from the alley. He fixed his messy brown hair as he walked towards them, his eyes fixed on the ground.

A fire started up inside him, his arms twitched. There was the spark of magic in this man, that damn fire magician. He glared at the man, clenching a fist.

Who is this jerk who dared to shoot at me…?

A nudge from Lia snapped Adrian out of his thoughts, and he flicked his eyes at her, scowling. Lia stroked his fist with her thumb, her shiny brown eyes captivating as always. He raised his brows. *You better have a good explanation for all this.*

The man stopped a few steps away from them. Lia looked up to William and Adrian, gesturing at the man. "This is Terry. A fire magician. He had valuable information that would help us a lot. Not to mention he's helped me a lot."

Adrian sneered. "Of course he did. Setting me on fire must be fun." The rage he felt earlier came back to him, very ready to tear the magician in front of him into pieces.

Lia tugged him with remorse. "Hey, don't blame him. I told him I would appeal to you if he could escort me to the park safely. So when you grabbed me, he shot at you. I'm sorry. When I knew both you and William had a plan to kill each other, and I couldn't let that happen." Lia traced her hand up Adrian's arms, gently stroking him, her touch sending a chill down his spine.

Despite wanting to get angry with Lia's stunt, the anger and the tension inside him slowly faded. Something about her made it difficult to get angry. He also knew it was almost the only way that could stop him and William getting into a real fight. If he'd gone to the clan with his team, there would have been no chance to talk. The fight would escalate as soon as they met. He still didn't know how to feel about letting William go for what he had done, but for now, it was what it was.

Adrian took in a deep breath, tearing his gaze from Lia's beautiful brown eyes to the fire magician. He was toying the seam of his hood, shifting his weight between his legs. Adrian asked, "You, Terry? What is so valuable you have that I should spare your life?"

Terry cleared his throat awkwardly. "I don't know whether you will find it valuable or not, but as you killed Bob and most of us... people in our team, some other branches, began moving here, fighting to dominate this city. They are trying to kill off every one of Bob's men to get total control of the city. You are the devil, right? You know Zitannas is kind of special."

Lia flinched. Adrian eyed her, not knowing why she was nervous. He flicked his eyes to William, who was frowning deeply with his arms crossed. He seemed to have no idea what Terry was talking about, as he should. Adrian turned back to Terry. "Fleeing for your life, huh? I do not care about your little life nor the other branches. You better have something more interesting for me. You tried to kill Lia, but she defeated you. Then you loser said you would help her, right?"

The man took half a step back, his head hanging lower than before. Adrian rolled his eyes despite Lia snuggling up to him. He folded his arms across his chest. Lia whispered in his ear, "Please, Adrian. He could help with fighting the gang. I think we can use more hands in fighting Evelyn, whoever she is."

"This is stupid."

"But he helped me enough now that you agreed to not fight William. For that, give him a try?"

He flicked his eyes to the fire magician. "For what you've done, I can spare your life. But if you want something more, you better have more to contribute."

Terry looked up to Adrian, then he glanced briefly at Lia, speaking with a shaky voice. "Who is commissioning for Lia's life, I don't know. But I know the offer is still out there. The branches that are trying to set feet here are also after her. It seems whoever commissioned had a very tempting offer for her death. They are probably trying to figure out the city before launching an attack. Bob's remaining men are hiding."

Adrian stood tall as Lia tightened her grip on his hand.

He exchanged a look with her. She was frowning. She shivered, hiding herself partly behind his arm.

Terry looked genuine. Adrian could always raid his thoughts, so he would know quick enough if Terry was lying.

"What is the offer?" Adrian asked.

"I don't know what's in it for the big guys, but the offer for us on the lower level is already a very handsome sum of money. And for magicians, there's the rumor of unlimited magical power. Usually when there are casualties when hunting down our target, the price will hike to get over most people's budget. But Bob sent almost a dozen men after your woman. There has to be a very large gain for him to warrant those losses. Not to mention he actually stayed to fight you head on. Maybe you don't know. We knew you were coming, and there was enough time for us to leave, but Bob decided to stay." Terry sank his hand into his pocket, looking down at the ground.

Adrian scowled; he'd raided Bob's mind before, and the price Evelyn offered was very attractive. But he wasn't expecting her to keep urging other gangs to go after Lia instead of doing it herself. It had been a while since he saw her, knowing her, she wouldn't stop gaining power.

Terry squirmed under Adrian's glare before taking in a deep breath. "I can help you fight them. I will tell you everything I know."

Except Bob's little mind is of better use than yours.

Adrian flinched as Lia wrapped her arms around his waist. She whispered into his ear, "C'mon, we could use more help."

He whispered back, "You really think I should believe in a guy that tried to kill you both in the gang's base and in the street just because you think we need extra help with Evelyn? Have you considered that he could be a spy? He could always stab you in the back. You should never believe in your enemy. As I've told you and you tried yourself, kindness to the enemy is cheating yourself."

She rubbed his back, talking to his ear quietly. "Is there something he could hide in his brain from almighty Adrian? Don't you feel bad to see him running away from where he belongs? It is scary to be hunted. Just take him under your wings, would you?"

Adrian's eyes widened, this wasn't what he was expecting, the way Lia put it… sadly hit home for him, he eyed the fire magician again.

William asked that fire magician with a frown. "Are you really going to fight your counterpart with us?" He gestured to Adrian. "If you already tried to fight him, you know what he can do."

"Yes… there's no place I can go. This is not the best reason, I guess, but I just want to stay alive."

"What do you say, Adrian?" William looked at him. Adrian looked between Terry and Lia, still hesitant. *Wouldn't it be easier to kill off the fire magician than risking a betrayal?*

"Adrian…" Lia patted his back.

He stared at the fire magician for another moment before he reluctantly nodded. "You have somewhere to lock him up? I will figure it out soon, whether he should live or not."

William nodded. "I guess there are also things I want to know about magicians not in a clan and under the radar."

Adrian snorted a humorless laugh. "Don't imagine yourself stronger than you really are. There are too many things you little Elements know nothing about." He could sense Lia tensing up next to him. He stroked the back of her hand, giving her a comforting squeeze.

"So you better get on their good side now." Lia smiled

warmly at that fire magician. Adrian wrapped his arm across the back of Lia's waist, pulling her closer.

Adrian said, "William, go find a place for him first. Don't start questioning without me."

William gestured for Terry to follow him, and he obediently did. Helen raised her brows at Adrian, stifling a laugh. As Adrian glared at Helen, she smirked at him, looking between Lia and Terry, as if making sure Adrian knew she was teasing. Adrian rolled his eyes. Fine. He still couldn't say no to Lia. He waved Helen off and she chuckled, following William.

As the three walked off, only Lia was left beside him. She let out a relaxed sigh, beaming at him. "Thank you, Adrian. You're the best."

"Of course I am… Who else is dumb enough to let his enemy live and to leave the murderer of his girl under his wings."

She winced, rubbing his arm. "I'm sorry. Still painful? I really needed to ambush both you and William for my plan to stand a chance. I couldn't let you catch me in the alley."

Adrian stared into her eyes, seeing concern and a bit of guilt in them. His heart was beating a bit too quick to his liking, his throat tight. He wanted to reprimand Lia, to stop her from always risking herself, but he couldn't say a word. She pulled him into a tight hug, clashing her lips on his.

He hugged her back, kissing her with strong passion. His hand was soon lost in her hair, pulling her into a deeper kiss. Her hands reached up to rub his back. He closed his eyes, savoring the touch of her warm lips and feeling her body pressed against him.

What have you done to me, Lia?

Don't blame me. You also hid your plan from me.

Adrian flinched, snapping his eyes open. He pulled

back just enough to stare at her. Lia groaned, puffing her cheek, as if upset from the kiss cutting short. She cupped his chin, "What? Are you surprised? Come on, big boy. You are the one haunting my mind first. Why are you looking surprised at me having a view of yours?"

He gulped, staring at her with wide eyes. "No way… How could you…"

"How do I know? I thought you wanted me to hear you? If you don't, I have no way of hacking into you." Lia tilted her head to the side, clearly confused.

He groaned, shaking his head. "You will be the death of me…"

"Better guard your mind well." Lia smirked, pecking a kiss on his nose.

I really should be more careful, then…

"I don't think I will like what's on your mind now." She rolled her eyes, tracing her fingers along his jaw. He huffed, pulling her into another deep kiss.

They barely pulled away from each other when a passerby muttered something under his breath, staring at the two of them.

"It seems it is time to go." Lia chuckled as she ran her fingers through her hair. He rolled his eyes, tugging her to leave, holding each other's hand. He could use some peace before letting his people know about this. They weren't going to be happy about it.

CHAPTER 42

LIA

As soon as they stepped through the door to his apartment, before Lia could take off her shoes, Adrian pulled her close, pressing his lips on hers. He kissed her with such force, she tightened her grip on his waist to balance herself. Her fingers tangled with his hair, pulling him even closer. She immersed herself in his touch, his scent, feeling his muscular chest pressed against her. She let out a small moan as he rested his forehead on hers. His arm was still on her back, a smirk on his face. "Now that we're back, it was fun catching me off guard out there, huh?"

Lia winked at him playfully, planting a soft and brief kiss on his nose, his breath warm on her lips.

"What if we actually went into a fight? What are you going to do?" He raised his brows.

She caressed his cheek. "Hm, I don't know. Maybe I'll hug you so tight you can't keep fighting and we'll kill William with a pure display of affection?"

He snorted, rolling his eyes. "You will kill me with embarrassment before we get to kill him."

"Did I not tell you how much I love seeing a flustered Adrian?" Lia chuckled, planting another kiss on his lips. He licked them with a wolfish grin. His other arm found its way under her thigh, lifting her up in a swift motion. She let out a small scream, throwing her arms around his neck. He carried her into his room, carefully putting her down on the bed and straddling her. He leaned close to her ear.

"How about I tell you what I love seeing instead?" He cupped her face with a smirk.

Lia laughed, smacking his arm playfully. She pulled him into a kiss, wrapping her arms around his back, deepening the kiss.

"How long will I have to wait this time? Another year?"

He groaned, "I would rather not."

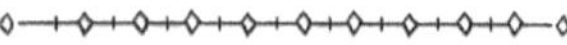

LATER, Lia rested her head on Adrian's shoulder, lying in the comfort of the bed. She traced her fingers along his bare chest, his arm wrapped around her waist. She was so worried that he would hate her for setting him up, but it seemed he was fine with it. It was hard to believe he would go to this length because of her.

She swallowed. She was probably the reason Adrian chose to let William live. Would Adrian still keep William around after they were done with Evelyn? Well, that was a problem further down the road. As his warmth enveloped her, she almost drifted off. Adrian sighed.

Is he regretting leaving William alive?

He might have sensed the tension in her, and he planted a kiss on her forehead. She stroked his cheek with a frown on her face. "Adrian… What's on your mind?"

"You are really so confident the two of us won't fight?"

"Well, I was just hoping for the best. I did gather some pieces here and there. You haven't killed him yet after all these years. Maybe you don't really want him dead. From Helen, William was almost ready to launch an attack at Benjamin's bar. Before you two actually clashed, maybe shaking things up would work. Worst case would be you two still fighting each other, but I'm betting a chance for you not to."

He eyed her with a glint of amusement in his eyes. "That's a big bet you are making."

"Worth the reward. I get to keep people I care about alive." She beamed, kissing him gently.

"And you've picked up a fire magician on the way."

She cuddled closer to him. "I'm sorry, but I can't help wanting to know more about that gang, and I think we can use more help."

His gaze distant, she wasn't sure whether he heard her or not. He pulled her closer, wrapping his arms tight around her. "I… I thought you wanted to get away from me, that you were heading back to the Elements."

Her breath caught. He wasn't wrong; her actions could be read as that. "I didn't mean it. After everything we've gone through, you really think I would run away?"

His eyes narrowed, but a glint of sadness flashed through them. "I hope not."

"Not a 'no'?"

"I'd hate to be too certain of anything."

She traced her fingers along his jaw. He leaned closer into her touch. "Adrian, I'm not going anywhere."

He nodded, but half of his mind seemed to be elsewhere. He shook his head as if pulling himself out of his thoughts. "Maybe I was too pissed to have my plan trashed on. I already planned the most scary and stronger than thunder raid to the clan. Sad I can't get it actualized."

Her breath caught with her heart hammering in her chest until he snorted out a laugh. "If we really fight, who do you think will win?" He pecked a kiss on her cheek, his fingers caressing down to her throat, gently rubbing in circles.

"Is this some kind of trick question?" Lia huffed, squeezing his side. He tilted her chin up, exposing her neck. He nibbled on her gently. The tingle from his teeth on her flesh sent a shiver down her spine. "And is this a threat?"

He pulled away, just enough to meet her eyes, his blue eyes shiny. "I'm trying to be encouraging."

"Fine. I do believe you would win over him. With your dark magic, he doesn't stand a chance."

He smiled, but it soon faded, he turned his gaze away. Lia snuggled closer to him, a light frown forming on her face. "Something wrong?"

"I... I don't know how my people will take this. Not like the Elements. Most of them who fought the war are still alive. I... really don't know what they will think. I would love to believe that they will appreciate the war finally ending, but what if... they are waiting for the revenge I now can't give them?"

Lia relaxed, knowing it had nothing to do with her, to do with them. She laughed at herself. Guilty, she still doubted him. "Talk to them. Maybe you all are on the same page. Don't torture yourself over something you don't know, OK? You are the King. They will do as you say."

"Rookie, you've got it wrong. I am nothing but a dark magician trying to not get himself killed by the Elements and on the way pulling people to my team, also risking their lives. They call me the King out of respect that I don't deserve. I haven't gotten them killed. That's all I've done."

Lia nodded solemnly. "Still, keeping them alive is important enough. I think they will understand. Should I be there with you?"

"You can. You should meet my team anyway, but they can be pretty scary. Think you can handle them?"

Lia swallowed and nodded, her eyes narrowed with determination. Adrian was going through all this for her. Giving him some support was the least she could do.

He grinned and grabbed his phone, walking out of the room to make a call. Her gaze followed his retreating form, traveling down his muscular back and arms. After he closed the door, she flicked her eyes back to the ceiling, pulling the cover over her.

Benjamin was probably on Adrian's team, but there was no telling who else was. He would be supportive of whatever Adrian decided to do. Her breath caught. Hopefully he was fine, and hopefully he wasn't too mad at her. Helen said the potion would only put him into a deep sleep and may lose consciousness for a while, so he should be fine. She shook her head. *Benjamin isn't that dumb; he would understand. Maybe I just have to apologize.*

Lia's mind drifted back to Adrian's people. She pinched the bridge of her nose. Maybe the person in the dungeon when she overheard his plan for the first time was one of them. She spent some time in the bar before things with Adrian got tense, so she was certain she didn't meet that guy before.

With the rules of no one getting to talk about magic, she had no idea who the other dark magicians were. All the people she met in the bar were great, so hopefully the meeting would go smoothly.

CHAPTER 43

LIA

The next day, Lia and Adrian were back in the den. Facing a heavy wooden door, Lia gulped, trailing a few steps behind him. It was still uncomfortable to be there given Adrian had tried to lock her up inside. The place was still old and dimly lit. Was it wrong that it still seemed like a jail? Today, it seemed even creepier.

She held Adrian's hand tightly, flicking her eyes to meet his with a slight frown. He leaned closer, kissing her forehead and squeezing her gently. "Don't worry, I'm here. Whatever you see or hear, don't overreact and don't talk until I tell you," he said with a gentle but commanding voice. Lia nodded.

Adrian released her hand and hugged her briefly. She sighed silently, hoping he would hold her longer. A sign of guilt flashed through his eyes, but he soon focused on the door, pushing in.

Lia lagged a step behind him. Inside the room were four people seated on chairs arranged around a wooden desk, leaving a seat in the middle and another at the end on the left side. Except Benjamin, others were all strangers to her. He was sitting on the right of the empty seat. They all stood as Adrian walked in, bowing their heads. The air around was suffocating, tense.

This looks more formal than I expected...

Adrian cleared his throat. "Thank you all for coming."

"It's our pleasure, my King," Benjamin said. All eyes were soon on Lia. She gulped, fighting the urge to flee from the door. A woman was glaring at her. The other two men gave away nothing. Lia settled to look at Benjamin, who gave her a reassuring warm smile.

At least Benjamin doesn't seem to be angry at me.

"This is Lia. Consider her one of us." Adrian gestured to the empty seat to the left. Lia walked there and stood, like others were. The man on the left of the middle seat was smirking at her. Lia gulped, hoping that was a good sign. Adrian took his seat and the rest followed.

"I intend to keep this short so you all will be dismissed very soon." Adrian looked around, speaking with a flat voice. "I talked to William. We are calling the war to an end, a true end."

The room was silent, the air heavier than before.

Lia's palms sweated. She flicked her eyes around. She could almost hear them thinking. Benjamin was staring at the floor thoughtfully. The others had blank expressions. She kept her hands in her lap, stopping herself from shaking. Her heart was racing as if it was going to jump out of her throat at any time.

"Is this another trap, my Lord?" The man next to Benjamin raised his eyebrows, crossing his arms. He was less muscular than Adrian, but with equally sharp blue eyes. His slicked back dark brown hair perfectly put together, its color matching his leather jacket.

A woman with long light blonde hair glared at Lia. "I agree with Lucas. Why? We're doing great, the best in centuries, and now we are making peace with them? When those two are the last of them? I thought you already put off killing them for long enough. And you calling off a fight is an emergency?"

Lia sheepishly averted her gaze, holding onto her thigh, her heart hammering. The woman looked to be around Lia's age, but it could be the magic misleading her. It was almost impossible to guess the age of a magician by looking at their face. Benjamin cleared his throat. The woman snorted and looked away from Lia, back to Adrian.

"Evelyn is here. That's the emergency I was talking about." Adrian paused, looking around at all the wide eyes. "I don't need the Elements backstabbing us, so I accepted William's request. I got the upper hand, as expected, but there are a few details that still need to be negotiated. As always, I will put you all first and foremost."

The man to the left of Adrian asked, "Although I shouldn't be too surprised, why is Evelyn here? My men reported traces of her a few days ago. I wonder what gives. I thought the pact was still in place?" His eyes flicked to Lia, with a mischievous smirk on his face. He had a large frame and messy square cut hair. Maybe he could best Adrian in a physical fight.

Adrian rubbed his temple. "Yes, Evelyn's coming for Lia, for her life... As we expected... But I am not going to let it happen."

As we expected? So this is not the first time his people have heard about me?

The woman that glared at Lia earlier scowled. "So you are dragging us into a war for your little pet?"

"Parker, mind your words!" Benjamin stared at her, puffing his chest with a clenched fist.

"Although Lia's new here, she has the potential to be

great. She has my type of power, and that's why Evelyn wants her dead." Adrian said with a cold voice.

Parker gritted her teeth, running her hand through her light blonde hair. "Still, we could kill the Elements instead of making peace with them. The dead are more honest. We still have to worry about William betraying us."

"No! He won't—" Lia slapped her hand over her mouth, it was too late. Her eyes widened, looking to Adrian.

Parker turned to Lia, clenching her fist tight. Her hand jerked, seemingly holding back. "How are you so sure, Elements' little pet? You have no idea what your Elders did to us. You have no idea what I want to do to you!"

"Please… Parker! I will make sure they can't stab us in the back. Let me take care of them," Adrian said.

Parker snapped her head to Adrian. She sprung from her seat, the chair slamming onto the floor with a loud thud. "Adrian Kelsey! Are you keeping those two jerks alive because this girl asked? Like how you would rather fight Evelyn than to kill off those little Elements?"

Benjamin shot up from his seat, taking a step forward. "Even if that's the case, you be careful with how you talk to the King."

"So? What does that have to do with you? Grow a backbone."

"What did you—"

"Stop it." Adrian waved them off. Benjamin took a step back, still glaring at Parker. Adrian sighed, staring down. "I know I owe you all for pulling you in a war you want no part of. But I can't let Lia go. So I hope you all will understand. With the Elements going under us, it will only mean more power for us. Better than letting Evelyn get her hands on it."

Parker snorted with narrow eyes, her hand shaking

slightly as she stared back at the ground. She picked up the chair, sitting without another word. Her lips pressed into a thin line.

The man on Adrian's left said, "You are the King. Do we have another choice? Of course, we'll follow your lead. My concern is if she's really worth the fight? I don't even dare challenge your decision. I know the power in her is strong. But will all the time put into her be worth it? Not to mention the possible casualties caused by it. Won't it be easier to just hold the pact?"

Lia shivered at the bitter words. Master of passive aggressive, huh?

"No!" Adrian growled. "Lia is staying with us. She will prove her worth soon. If years ago, at our lowest, Evelyn had to take the pact, at our highest, we aren't backing down."

"But that would be a major violation of the pact, my Lord. I suppose you have a very convincing case for us?" the man asked with a coy smile and a knowing look. Benjamin opened his mouth to speak up, but Adrian waved him off.

Adrian stared into the man's eyes, his Adam's apple moving up and down. After a few awkward and silent seconds, he cleared his throat, averting the man's gaze. "Lia… We're dating… I am not letting Evelyn kill her." He blushed, looking at the ground sheepishly.

Wild energy rushed through the room. The man who asked burst out laughing. Adrian snapped his head to him with a death stare. "Hunter! What's so funny?"

"Sorry, my Lord…" He barely stopped to catch his breath, holding his hand out between them. "I'm just happy to be right all along! The two of you owe me a drink back there." Hunter chuckled, running his hand through his hair, his black eyes shining. Lucas rolled his eyes with a huff. Parker's face was colder than Lia's ice magic.

So they've really known about me for quite a long time. Maybe even before I met Adrian? That is a bit unsettling. Lia gulped, looking to Adrian, who was looking elsewhere.

He blushed even harder than before. "Wait! Are you guys…" He looked around the room at the three of them trying hard to school themselves. "But I never… Benjamin!" Adrian turned and glared at him, he shook his head frantically.

"Not me, my King. I never told anyone."

"My Lord, you aren't that subtle at all. You remember we've talked about this countless times, right? You never agreed to us killing her." Hunter beamed.

Her heart skipped a beat. These people tried to kill her before? Adrian slumped back on his seat, groaning.

Lia shared a gaze with Adrian, he was still blushing bright red. His voice appeared in her mind. *When we first met, it was not the first time we knew about your existence. We had an eye on you when you first joined the Elements.*

You are such a stalker. She blinked, not knowing how to feel about it.

Well, at that time, the Elements were our enemies. After a while, he cleared his throat loudly, and the room fell into silence.

"So… are we on the same page now? Accepting the request from William and getting ready for Evelyn?" Adrian asked.

"I am not ready to kiss my life goodbye. Have some fun with your girl." Hunter laughed, but was soon silenced by Benjamin's glare. Adrian looked at Parker, who was staring at the ground.

"Thank you everyone. I will come back to you all with the arrangement with the Elements and let's look forward to new land to be conquered and new loot to be won." He finished with a wolfish grin, which everyone in the room reciprocated. Lia looked at them, air knocked out of her lungs. Had she brought more fights and wars to the city?

Soon, Adrian walked out of the room and the rest of them followed. He stood by the hallway, leaning on the wall. As Lia stood next to him, he kept looking back inside while the rest of them were leaving. At last, only Parker was in the room. She exchanged a glance with Adrian and he went in, closing the door behind him. Lia slid closer to Benjamin, her mind filled with questions.

Hunter walked past them after discussing something with Lucas. Lia flicked her eyes to him, wanting to greet him. He stared back with a stern look, brushing past her without a word. He was completely different from the one that laughed at Adrian earlier. Lia flinched.

Benjamin smiled wryly, crossing his arms over his chest. "You think Hunter was there to joke around with you? They have no choice but to tolerate you because of Adrian. Like Hunter said, when Adrian insisted on playing the King card, they had no choice. But it doesn't mean they are OK with the decision. You will have to earn their respect if you want their genuine help. If you took notes, you would know Hunter is a beast himself."

If how they sat had any indication, Hunter sure was a scary one. "I… do you have any pointers? I guess I should try to make others like me. At least not sneering at me?"

"Well, I guess you have to show them you can at least pull your own weight in a fight. Or just show some useful abilities. Or you can bribe them with money and power. I mean power other than magic. I suppose you will have plenty of chances, with Evelyn promising a war." Benjamin's face was stern and cold, his arms folded.

A chill ran down Lia's spine. It sounded too scary to be

true. What if they thought Adrian was blocking their wealth by taking her as one of them? Would they do anything to her or to Adrian? As if reading her thoughts, Benjamin patted her shoulder.

"While they will do whatever they need to gain power, and they will go all the way to fight for their position in the den, they won't do a thing to Adrian. One, their positions are determined by him. Two, if somehow Adrian is dead, in theory, they will at least lose all their magic, or worse, they will die with him. We don't do experiments, so we aren't sure what will happen. While we fight for our position, we aren't taking one another's life. The more of us, the stronger we stand. We've been through enough fights and wars to learn that. So you don't have to worry."

Lia nodded, turning back to face the door, releasing a sigh of relief. It was time to plan how she would earn some respect for herself. Probably needing to be saved all the time wasn't going to cut it. She flicked her eyes back to Benjamin. "Ben… about yesterday… I'm sorry. I never wanted to harm you."

He looked at her with a mischievous glint in his eyes and chuckled. "No need to apologize for your win. I wasn't expecting that. It was smart on your part. That's why you asked to go to the tree, right? If only we remembered you had your phone. We didn't even think of it when we used ours."

He let out a sigh, running his hand through his hair. "You are very brave to fight the King's decision. But his patience is limited. Don't try to work behind his back again. While he loves you a lot now, he is still pissed."

"But the two of you are also working behind my back… You know how important William is to me." Lia rubbed her feet together. It would be very unfair if they thought they were the ones that could do that and she couldn't.

"It will take some time for you to understand what the two of them mean to us… In all honesty, I am with Parker when it comes to your two Elders. I don't really approve of it. You better make it a good decision."

Lia's breath caught as Benjamin looked a bit more serious than usual. She averted his gaze, staring at the floor.

Benjamin sighed, shaking his head. "Whatever, we will go with the choice, now that you've convinced Adrian anyway. Just to put it up front, when I don't agree with you down the road, it is nothing personal. While I don't see every one of the others eye-to-eye, we fought alongside each other for too long for me to ignore their feelings. Try to convince them both breaking the pact for you and letting the Elements live are good deals."

"The pact Adrian had with Evelyn that they would kill all origins and not to go to each other's land?"

"Yes." Benjamin's voice was a bit too cold for her liking. She nodded, leaning back on the wall of the corridor as she stared at the heavy wooden door.

After a while, the door squeaked open and Adrian walked out, the frown on his face dissolving as he met Lia's eyes. He laced his fingers with hers with a warm smile on his face, nudging her to go with him. As they turned away, Lia stole a glance over his shoulder. In the room, Parker remained in her seat, hunched over on the desk, burying her face in her hands, shaking. Lia was too far away to hear a sound from her.

CHAPTER 44

LIA

The next morning, Adrian drove with Lia to the clan, pulled over in the parking lot. He turned off the engine. Lia waited for him to get out of the car, but he remained still. He was staring out of the window in front of him, his body tense.

Lia followed his gaze, the outside was perfectly fine. The warm sunlight scattered on the road. The parking lot was undisturbed, silent in the early morning hours. A bird hopped around on the bare branches of trees on the roadside. Things outside probably weren't bothering him.

Now that the music was now off, Lia could hear her own breath. Her hands were glued to her lap; even the rustling of her jacket would disturb the silence. His gaze distant, part of him seemed to be elsewhere. He slumped down into the leather seat. His breath quickened as the minutes went by.

Lia bit the inside of her mouth, she stroked his arm. He flinched. She asked, "Hey, what are you waiting for?"

His eyes flicked to her, a pained look flashed through them. He sighed, resting his head on the steering wheel, burying himself in his arms. The tension in his body was visible.

She asked, "Anxious, aren't we?"

She rubbed his stomach as he flinched in her arms. He turned, their eyes met, his blue eyes stormy. He rested his head onto her shoulder, the tension in him dissipating. He pecked a small kiss on her neck before he sat up in his seat. Lia rested her head in the crook of his shoulder, holding his hand. He held hers as if his life depended on it.

"Adrian's anxious. This is a rare scene. How lucky am I to be able to witness this." Lia kissed his cheek, but he kept staring out the windshield.

"I… wonder why I agreed in the first place."

"Thank you for what you did for me."

"Things you are doing to me…"

"Is the clan making you nervous? I guess you've never been there? It being the heart of the Elements, I can see why." Lia rubbed his side, trying to comfort him.

He cupped her chin, looking into her eyes with a smirk. "You are expecting a 'yes, I've never been there'?" Lia nodded. "In theory, I was never there. But theories don't always work in real life."

"What!" Lia pulled back, her eyes wide. "No way! The day we got the meteorite from the collector, you didn't even want to get close to the block! And you are telling me you've been there? Inside? And the Elders had no idea?"

Seeing how hard Adrian tried to avoid the Elders, and how dangerous he claimed it would be, he'd actually set foot in the clan? The Elders were keeping the place confidential and safely undercover. There was no way he could sneak in without them knowing and there seemed to be no reason for him to do that. Was he simply making it up to impress her?

He shrugged and laughed. "I can't help they didn't find out. I am that good with my craft. I feel bad for them."

So he really went in?

Lia tilted her head to the side, amused. "Still, why did you? You weren't in for a stroll, right?"

"Actually…" He ran his hand through her long brown hair, giving her a sheepish smile. "I went in the night your shoulder was injured." He averted her eyes, blushing hard.

"The monsters? Oh… I wasn't expecting that. I was trying to avoid you, in case you wanted to shut my mouth forever. I stayed there." The memory rushed back to her, it felt like ages ago. She still couldn't believe how the man next to her ended up here with her.

"Not far from my guess. You had me worried. I went to your place, but you weren't there. Then I figured you would be in the clan."

"You simply waltzed in and out as you wish?" she asked with a glint of amusement in her eyes.

"I guess I needed to. Not as easy as that, but I managed. You look cute when you're asleep," Adrian chuckled.

"You are super creepy when you stalk me like crazy." Lia deadpanned him, but soon burst into laughter, shaking her head.

"If you let me check on your wound, I wouldn't have to. So it's your fault I have to sneak around." Adrian gently punched her shoulder.

"Guilty as charged, King Kelsey!" Lia threw her hands up. "I guess you were already head over heels for me then. No wonder I healed up that fast." She searched his eyes for a reaction and got it. Adrian blushed brightly with a coy smile. He pinched the bridge of his nose.

"Right. You are a bit too cute to get injured. And I

don't need you to be in more danger because of the wound."

Lia kissed him, but soon raised her brows. "It seems that's not your prime concern at this moment, then?"

Adrian's smile faltered. He looked back to the window and sighed.

"You think William will ambush you?" Lia frowned. The last time in their war, their meeting probably didn't end well. Lia had no details; Adrian refused to tell her, but seeing his pained look when she asked, she didn't push for an explanation.

"I… I don't know. While I have no problem fighting both of them and getting out unscratched, but it… it still…" He winced, trailing off.

In her hand, his palm sweaty, his breath rapid and shallow. Lia gently guided his chin to her, resting her forehead on his. "Adrian, look at me. Slow your breath… You can do it. I'll always be with you."

Adrian met her eyes, his blue eyes filled with worry. The gaze was charged, and neither were able to pull away. His husky breath on her lips. As the worry in his eyes faded, his eyes darkened with longing. Time seemed to freeze between them. They moved closer to each other until their lips met.

First it was tender, then it turned into a fire, engulfing both of them. She closed her eyes, kissing him like there was no tomorrow, immersing in the sensation, in his scent. Her hand found the back of his head, pulling him closer. He kissed her with equal force. He wrapped his arms across her waist, almost pulling her over the center console.

His eyes remained closed for a few more seconds after the kiss. Lia grinned, running her fingers along his jaw.

He's so cute when he gets soft.

"If they dare put a finger on my man, they can have a

taste of my wrath. You have plenty of experience with that, right?"

Adrian rolled his eyes.

"Let's go, get in, and get out. You are Adrian. There's nothing you can't do. You are a grown man." Lia winked at him, planting a brief kiss on his lips. She nudged him to the car door and got out on her side. He remained seated for another second, but followed her regardless. Outside of the car, he eyed her with a glint of amusement. Lia raised her brows at him. He shrugged, following Lia into the clan, their fingers lacing together.

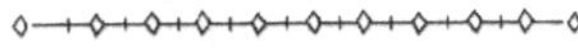

"You really are looking good, *Adrian...*" Eric glared at Adrian as they walked into the meeting room, his eyes flicking briefly to their joined hands.

The meeting room was brightly lit with white light, making everything in the room pale. It was by far the room Lia liked the least. Not to mention the clock always seemed to be louder in there. As if magic, every second would feel like years. Lia shivered as she sensed the heated gaze from Eric on her hand, her grip on Adrian's hand tightened, he squeezed back.

"I'll take that as a compliment, I guess, *Eric...*" Adrian glared back, his body tensing. The two of them took a seat, facing William and Eric across the table. Lia reached to his thigh, stroking him gently. The tension in him eased up.

William nodded to both of them. "Let's get to work. On our part, most of us have no objection to teaming up with you guys. But we want more details on what we are facing."

Adrian smirked humorlessly, seating back and crossing his arms over his chest. "Maybe I didn't make it clear enough last time we met. We are not teaming up. You two are going under my leadership. For your people, you two take care of them. I don't care as long as they don't cause me trouble."

Lia gulped. While she didn't hear what they discussed in the cafe that night, this didn't sound right.

William seemed to be as surprised as she was. His eyes widened, staring at Adrian. "What? This isn't what we talked about."

"You wanted to help and I agreed. This is how you will help." Adrian's eyes narrowed, daring Eric and William to object.

Eric scowled, his body poised, slamming his fist on the table. "You want us to surrender without putting up a fight? Dream on!" Lia flinched, her eyes flicking between Eric and Adrian, then to William. She swallowed dryly.

Please don't fight…

"Do you think I want to settle when I can destroy you two?" Adrian's eyes flicked to Lia for a brief moment, then back to Eric. "I don't think a fight is in your favor. If you weren't sure before, may I further convince you?"

The air around turned denser as his magical power spread through the room, sending the air crackling, intimidating. Lia turned to him with a worried look. He squeezed her hand gently, keeping his gaze straight at Eric. Eric stared back, pushing back with his power. Lia and William exchanged a look, both of them frowning.

The power was running strong in the room. The hair on the back of Lia's neck stood, her stomach twisting. The magical power inside her turned up, rushing, threatening to escape her. She squirmed in her seat, resisting the urge to run out of the room, far away from the suffocating contest of their power. Every hair on her skin stood, she shivered. When she gripped Adrian's hand tight, it was strangely hot. A pain in her head creeped up, she winced, her other hand squeezing her thigh. William's eyes widened, but he too didn't know what to do to interrupt the fight.

The low humming sound of the air conditioner in the room grew numb to her ears and her vision began to blur as her power trickled out from her hands. Feeling light-headed, Lia hunched over on the table, resting her head on her arm, gasping. The world spun in front of her. She closed her eyes, but the void seemed to also be dancing.

Probably a minute later, or shorter, or longer, Lia had no idea. She stirred at a gentle rub on her back, a warm breath on her hair, ticklish. Her eyelids were almost too heavy to lift, but she struggled to open them. Adrian's shiny blue eyes stared back at her, his face filled with concern. She could see her own reflection in them.

Slowly her breath levelled as the discomfort slowly faded, her senses coming back to her. She blinked at him with a relaxed smile. He sighed in relief. The frown on his handsome face disappeared. She was still in the meeting room. Probably she wasn't down for long.

Lia sat up and leaned on Adrian. William was staring at her, his eyes filled with concern. Next to William, Eric was nowhere to be seen.

Her heart skipped a beat. Adrian hadn't killed Eric, right? Probably not, otherwise, William wouldn't be sitting still.

She raised her brows, looking further away. A squeak of the chair turned her head to where Eric was getting up from the floor, gasping for air.

"Eric… any objection?" Adrian glared at him.

He was back on his feet, his shoulders slumped, shaking his head.

"Amazing. My people will be delighted." Adrian's voice was cold. Lia shivered.

The rest of their meeting went well. They didn't fight each other and managed to talk about stuff. Lia was nervous when she knew Evelyn was very keen to get rid of her. With how the Origin could gain power with more acquaintances under their bond, Evelyn didn't want anyone to have the same power as she and Adrian did.

Adrian was very insistent to get William and Eric under his command. William seemed to be fine with it, but Eric absolutely hated it. Despite that, he agreed with the deal. Lia rubbed her temple, pretty certain Eric tolerated all the demands because of William, or maybe herself. With how Adrian could push his agenda, she was proud of herself for making him agree to keep Terry alive.

"It's great meeting you two. Get your people ready. Either they hide safely or get ready for the fight. Don't cause me any problems." Adrian nodded to the two of them and stood. He reached for Lia's hand and they headed towards the door.

"I suppose you beat Eric? I guess you are pretty strong?" Lia whispered as they got further away from the Elders.

"Pretty strong, really? Wait till you see more of me." He winked at her.

She chuckled, pressing her voice low. "Is there anything of you I haven't seen yet?" He blushed, groaning loud enough for her to hear.

They pushed the door of the meeting room open, Patrick was standing next to the door. He jumped out of the way, his eyes wide with shock as a glint of fear flashed through them. Adrian tensed, glaring at him. Lia's held onto Adrian's hand tight, gently pulling him back.

Lia slipped a step forward, half-blocking Adrian from

Patrick. "What are you doing here? I thought you were training with Helen?"

"I… I was walking through the hallway and noticed the power inside. I got curious… and…" He sheepishly glanced down.

"What do you want?" Adrian stared at Patrick, moving to grab him. Lia spread her arms out, stopping him.

"Who… who are you? I suppose William called you here?" Patrick took half a step back.

Adrian glared at him. "William doesn't get to call me here."

Lia shot Adrian a pointed look and told Patrick, "He is with us to deal with whoever is trying to kill me."

Patrick nodded. "I see. I… I know the strong power was from you. Can you teach me?" Patrick's eyes lit up. Adrian pinched the bridge of his nose, shaking his head.

"My magic is not something you can handle. Get lost. Don't eavesdrop anymore. If I see you doing that once more, you are done."

"But I can try, I can do whatever—"

"No! I'll tell you what. You don't get to choose what power you have, go work with what you get. Stop daydreaming." Adrian turned away, tugging Lia along. She followed, stealing a peek at Patrick. He was glaring at Adrian's back, muttering something she couldn't pick up.

Lia made sure they walked far enough from Patrick before she whispered to Adrian, "Hey, were you a bit too harsh on him?"

"Rookie, he's the one stalking you. I don't like that."

"Oh yeah. Only you can follow me around?"

"Of course. You are mine. Any more questions?" He glared at her, his lips curled up. Turning a corner, he pushed Lia up against the wall, kissing her forcefully. Lia hugged him closer, their bodies flush against each other.

Her hand trailed along his chest, stroking his back. His lips were warm and soft, burning with fiery passion, stealing the breath out of her lungs. She closed her eyes, immersing herself in the kiss. As they parted, Lia nibbled his lower lip. He groaned, his blue eyes dangerously dark with lust.

He hissed, "You better stop that. Otherwise we aren't getting out of here."

"You stole my line, big boy. You are the one who started this." Lia smacked his chest gently. Her hand travelled down, stroking his abdomen, feeling the muscle under his shirt. He rolled his eyes, pulling back.

Lia asked, "Can I go to the arena? I think Helen's there."

Adrian nodded. "Wherever you want. You aren't getting away from me."

"Touché." Lia smiled, pulling him to the left turn.

CHAPTER 45

LIA

Lia pushed the door into the arena, waving and calling out to Helen, who was sitting on the floor, panting after her training. Helen jumped up on the shout and ran to Lia, giving her a bone-crushing embrace. "I was worried about you! How did the meeting go?"

"It was fine, I guess. They didn't end up fighting each other in a major way, and they agreed to work together. Although a certain someone insisted on continuing to be the King." Lia laughed, hugging Helen back, winking at her.

Helen looked at Adrian, who was eyeing her, crossing his arms. Helen smirked. "What? King Kelsey, I believe that's something you will do, very you."

He snorted, with a glint of amusement in his eyes, tilting his head. He reached for Lia's arm.

Helen pulled Lia to the side, turning her away from him. "Stop being so possessive, OK? Can't I have your girl for a minute?" Helen hugged Lia closer, looking over Lia's shoulder and sticking her tongue out at him.

Lia chuckled, hugging Helen back. Adrian blushed slightly, clearing his throat.

"I wonder what you've got here." Adrian nodded at the control panel.

"Let's see what you've got instead." Lia pulled him into the field, making him stay there while she and Helen hurried to the machine.

"Great, this is starting to feel like a trap." He rolled his eyes as the glass walls rose around him. The first virtual monster appeared at the corner of the field. At the same time, a few more appeared from all sides. He launched an ice blast at one of them while diving to the back of another. He grabbed its neck, freezing the whole monster into a block of ice within seconds. Lia's eyes widened, estimating the power needed for that, a lot. She kept staring at him, his face solemn, his eyes narrowed as he focused on the targets in front.

He's so attractive when he's in action.

Adrian threw the iced monster to the two others coming at him. He glanced to his side, wielding an ice wall on his right to block a fire ball. He slayed the monster, squinting at Lia and Helen, who were slamming at the buttons, summoning more monsters. With a low growl, his eyes turned red, smirking. "C'mon you two. The buttons are there but you don't have to smash them all."

Lia rolled her eyes, she reached out to push the next button, but her hands couldn't move despite her effort; something was stopping her. She tried turning to Helen, but her neck was also locked up. "Hey, that's cheating. Focus on the monsters!"

"I am!" Adrian jumped at another werewolf, breaking its spine. Clearing the last one, he looked at Lia and Helen behind the machine with a wolfish grin. "How about you two do a better job?"

Lia found her hand moving to the 'End' button. She fought herself, but her hand was still moving as if pulled by an invisible force. "Helen! Some help?"

"I wish I could. This is strong…" Helen was wincing, also trying to fight Adrian's hold, but remained frozen in her spot.

Lia closed her eyes, channelling all her power, trying to fight off Adrian's hold, her hand shook slightly.

"Don't fight me, rookie. I don't want to hurt you." Adrian gritted his teeth, sneering. Lia found herself slowly getting the upper hand. Something inside her snapped, like getting hit by a car. Her hand slammed down on the button. She fell back a few steps. Helen quickly grabbed her before she dropped to the ground. Lia winced in pain, gasping for air, her heart racing.

"Lia, are you OK?" Helen carefully laid her down by the wall. She kneeled beside her, her eyes filled with concern. Lia squirmed around, her eyes closing to keep the pain in her head from chewing on her.

"Lia…" Adrian appeared at the balcony. Helen glared at him. She leaped over Lia, ramming into him as they both fell to the floor. Helen pressed her knee into his abdomen, digging in until he groaned. Her hand wrapped around his throat, squeezing. "What have you done to her? How about you learn to ask nicely?"

"How about you step away and let me check on her?" He rolled his eyes, reaching to Helen's hand around his neck, peeling them off him.

"You better, or else!" Helen pursed her lips, releasing him. As he stood, she kicked him in the butt. He stumbled, glaring back at her, he soon turned to Lia instead.

Finally, they have time for me?

Adrian gathered Lia in his arms. The touch was comforting, but it sent another jolt of pain in Lia. She winced as a moan escaped her. He sighed, rubbing her shoulder. "Hey, rookie, refocus. Channel everything back to your head. Help yourself, OK?"

Lia struggled, picking up bits and parts of her power that had been crushed by him, pulling back her focus. It felt like a truck ran through her mind; it was shattered into pieces. Luckily, it wasn't a tricky puzzle. When she focused, it slowly came back together like she was coming out of a daydream. But it was hard when all she could think of was being in Adrian's arms, feeling his chest pressing onto her. She shook her head slightly, pulling herself out of his spell.

Slowly, she felt better. She wriggled her fingers, her body finally in her control. When she opened her eyes, Adrian was inches from her face. His eyes stormy, filled with concern and some guilt. She planted a kiss on his nose, sitting up straight. Puffing her cheeks, she rubbed her temple.

Adrian gulped and pulled her close, trailing kisses from her ears down to her collar bone. The kisses lit a fire along their path. "I'm sorry, Lia. I did push a bit further. But you did well. I'm so proud of you. I'll consider that a pass." He rested his forehead on hers, caressing her cheek with his thumb.

"You mean that's another part of my training?"

"I didn't plan it beforehand, but I saw it as a chance to push you, to see how you would react. You did well without any hints. If you backed off when I threatened, I would have been disappointed." He smirked, planting another kiss on her lips.

"So, if I get stronger, I will be able to push you off?"

"Don't let it get to your head. You have a long road; that's if I do nothing." He nibbled on her earlobe. She moaned softly.

"Can you two do me a favor?" Helen side-eyed them,

clearing her throat loudly. The two broke away, blushing bright red. "Adrian, I would expect that Lia's perfectly fine?" She raised her brows.

"C'mon, I know what I'm doing. You really think I'm going to hurt my girl?"

"I don't know, normal people won't. But you, I'm worried. Who's to say you won't hurt your own girl?" Helen tilted her head, staring at him with a mischievous glint in her eyes. "And I mean it, Adrian. If anything happens to her, I'll make you regret it."

Adrian's face fell, he tensed. He was almost growling when he spit out the words, "Lia will be great with me. Thank you for your concern." He took a step forward as if launching towards Helen. Lia hurried to wrap her arms around him.

Crap! Why must Helen bring this up?

"C'mon, Helen! I am fine. Adrian would never hurt me." Lia rubbed his back, willing him to let it slide.

Her heart racing as his husky breath weighed on her. Helen was joking, but it could come off as something else to him. She focused her power, willing in her mind to him. *Helen is just making fun of you, all good intention. She doesn't know a thing about Ariel. I swear she is not referring to that. Chill.*

Adrian flicked his eyes to Lia, the fire in them seemed to die down. *Right… She knows nothing. You and your friend will never stop bringing me trouble, I guess.*

Well, you choose to let troubles stay with you. Unconditional return expired long ago. Lia smiled warmly at him, her heart racing. The tension in his body slowly eased. He blinked, patting her hand on his back. She reluctantly pulled away, turning back to Helen.

Helen was frowning deeply, she seemed to smell something wrong. She cleared her throat. "Um… It seems

I said something wrong. I'm sorry. I was just trying to make a joke."

Adrian shrugged. "Whatever. Lia will be very safe with me." Lia's heart skipped a beat; hopefully Adrian was really OK with it.

Lia flicked her eyes between the two. "You two play nice with each other, OK? You'll upset me if you fight since I don't know whose side I should be on."

"Wait, Lia. Are you taking his side against me?" Helen's eyes widened, animatedly putting her hand on her chest.

"I won't let you leave me, rookie. Don't you dare leave me." Adrian stared into Lia's eyes with a pleading look.

"Can the two of you just chill?" Lia rolled her eyes with her arms folded. "If you don't fight, everything will be fine, OK?" Adrian and Helen exchanged a glance, nodding towards each other.

CHAPTER 46

LIA

After having dinner together, Lia and Adrian went back to her place. Entering the apartment, she sighed, looking around. Adrian closed the door behind them. He hugged Lia from behind. "What's on your mind?"

"I... It has been so long since I was here. Do you think my apartment will miss me?" His breath warm on her neck, sending a shiver down her spine. She leaned back into his arms.

"Probably not as much as I missed you," he whispered into her ear, burying his head into her hair, his nose tickling her neck. He gently rubbed her side.

Lia giggled. "Didn't realize you are such a sweet talker, huh? We spent the whole day together."

"One half with the two dummies around, and another half with Helen around." He pulled her closer, pressing her against his body, his hands roaming her.

"C'mon, can I get changed first? How about you keep your hands off me for a minute?"

"I won't mind helping you with that." He sprung her

around to face him, a wolfish grin on his face. Lia playfully shoved him in the chest. He grabbed her wrist. "It seems someone needs to learn some respect."

She leaned in, kissing him tenderly on the lips. "Right back at you. I can do it myself perfectly." She rolled her eyes, walking to her room with Adrian following her.

"You sit there and don't move." She pointed at the bed, pushing Adrian away from her. He sat, crossing his legs as his eyes travelled up and down her curves.

She set aside her phone on the bedside table. She gulped at his intense gaze, making a show as she changed out of her clothes. Adrian growled, hissing, "The things I want to do to you…"

"C'mon, big boy. Have some patience." She slowly removed her clothes piece by piece, revealing her body, enjoying the lustful look from him. His fiery gaze sent a shiver down her spine, making her body burn. After she got done with her clothes, she slowly leaned closer to him, pushing his shoulders until he was lying on the bed. His arms reached up to her back, but she smacked him off.

"I said have some patience." Lia caressed his cheek with her thumb, trailing kisses along his neck. "This is not the appropriate dress code here." Lia tugged on his shirt.

"Oh, yeah. What are you going to do about it?" He grinned, his eyes stormy. With a low growl, he grabbed Lia's shoulder, pushing her to his side, onto the bed. He rolled over, straddling her. "You are paying for it, you dare make me wait?" He kissed her forcefully, sending sparks through her body. She smacked him on the chest, laughing loudly. He kissed her again under her jaw, nibbling lightly on her throat. She tilted her head back, squirming beneath him as her hand fumbled with the buttons on his shirt.

◇—+◇+◇+◇+◇+◇+◇+◇+◇+◇—◇

LATER, Lia cuddled close to Adrian, his arms wrapping around her. They stared into each other's eyes, enjoying each other. Something went through Lia's mind, she tensed. He raised his brows.

She frowned, fighting to slow her breath. "What is out there? After tonight? I'm getting nervous."

Adrian tenderly kissed the wrinkles from her knitted brows on her forehead, rubbing her arm. "I wish I knew. With everything going on, I don't know. We'll have to tackle things step by step. I only know one thing. I am doing everything to keep you safe. I doubt I can live another day without you."

"Hopefully it doesn't include locking me up in the dungeon." Lia's hand trailed down his naked chest, feeling the warmth from his body and his strong heartbeat.

"That's not something I wanted. It didn't yield the desired effect at all." He ran his fingers through her hair, resting his forehead on hers.

Lia smiled warmly, kissing him again, slowly, with passion. They remained wrapped in each other's warmth until they drifted into slumber. Whatever was on the horizon was a problem for the next day.

Thank you for reading, hope you have enjoyed the book.
You can get a bonus story when you join my newsletter.
juneleungbooks.com/prequel
You can also get to know about new releases, updates, and
bonus content there.